MUR

MURDO'S WAR

Alan Temperley

CANONGATE · KELPIES

First published in 1990 by Canongate Kelpies
Reprinted 1994

© text Alan Temperley 1988
© illustrations and map Alan MacGowan 1988
Cover illustration by Alexa Rutherford

The publisher acknowledges subsidy of the
Scottish Arts Council towards the
publication of this volume

ISBN 0 86241 316 8

Printed and bound in Denmark by Nørhaven A/S

CANONGATE PRESS LTD, 14 FREDERICK STREET,
EDINBURGH EH2 2HB

Contents

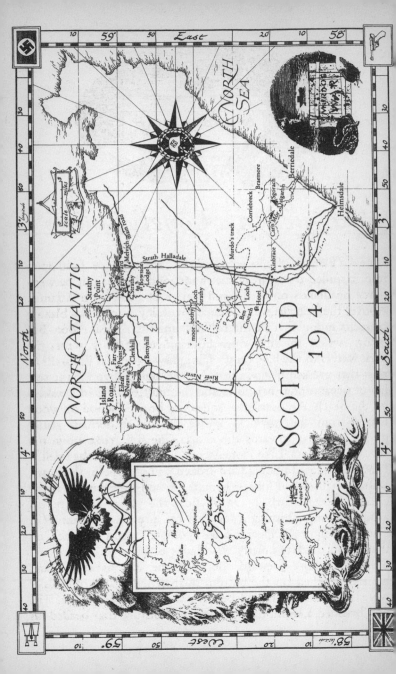

Rogues on a Lonely Shore

A heavy blanket of mist wrapped the bay in silence. Fold upon fold it spilled down from the moors and flowed out between fierce headlands on to the still waters of the North Atlantic. Above, the heavens were spangled with icy stars and a blazing crescent moon that lit the rolling summits of the moor. But below, where the little open boat moved secretly across the dark waters of the bay, only a faint glow lightened the walls of mist that pressed in upon her. All was quiet, save for the soft lap of ocean under her bows and the muffled roar of breakers on the beach. An occasional squeak of bruised wood on wood issued from the rowlocks where the old fisherman gently pulled his boat towards the shore. The fog froze upon her shadowy timbers. Like a lonely cork she bobbed on the swell.

Murdo, seated upon a hard-frozen coil of rope in the bows, shifted slightly and looked behind. His oilskins rustled as the creases were disturbed. On all sides the glassy swell spread around them, vanishing a few feet off into the moonlit mist. The squat figure of Hector was silhouetted, solid as a rock, on the centre thwart; quietly the blades of his oars dipped and pulled the boat forward. Between the old fisherman and himself, stacked on the bottom boards, the crates of whisky were still securely lashed beneath their tarpaulin cover. The boy brushed a warm hand across the moisture that beaded his face, and pushed a hank of wet hair from his eyes. Silently he peered around into the darkness, then settled himself once more on the icy ropes, and resumed his vigil.

For a few minutes more the boat glided forward. The waves began to build up in the shallowing water. The soft roar of their breaking grew louder; they could hear the hiss on the gently shelving sand.

Suddenly, from the beach, a voice rang out, making Murdo jump.

"Is that you, Hector?"

It was the signal they had been waiting for, and came from somewhere to the left.

"Aye."

The old seaman pulled on an oar and the bows swung to port. Heedless of noise now, he rowed parallel to the shore. The sea caught his boat, the *Lobster Boy*, on the beam, so that she rocked and dipped in the waves.

In a few moments there was the loom of a torch ahead, a white patch in the mist. They were almost on top of it before Murdo could make out the dark figure of a tall thin man with a boy beside him, the sea lapping about their ankles. Hector turned the boat in. Her bows glided up the sand, and the *Lobster Boy*, gently lurching to a halt, toppled to one side.

Murdo picked up the frozen end of the painter and sprang over into the shallow water. The stern lifted a little and swung as the next wave came in. The three on shore gathered around the boat's side and heaved as she lifted. She slid a few feet further in and then very firmly scraped to a halt.

"That'll do," the tall man said, flicking the water from his fingers. He turned to Hector, who was sliding the oars out of the way along the starboard side bench. "You're losing your touch," he said smiling. "You were a hundred yards out there." He took the rusty steel pin that Hector handed out to him and flung it to the younger boy up the sand. "Well in, mind, Lachlan," he called. "The tide will soon be turning."

Hector laughed with friendly contempt. "When you've learned to row a boat yourself, I just might listen to you,

8

Donald," he said. "There's two miles of fog out there, and hardly enough swell for a man to hear the rocks. If it wasn't for young Murdo's ears we wouldn't be here for a while yet."

Fifteen yards up the beach the two boys drove the pin deep into the wet sand and Murdo threw a hitch of the stiff rope around it. Then they splashed out to the boat and heaved themselves aboard.

Hector had lit his pipe and was puffing contentedly on the thwart behind the engine casing. A red glow lit his nose and cheek as he drew a mouthful of the strong black twist.

"What's doing here, then?" he said, the old stem clamped in his teeth.

"Not a thing." Donald had a long Highland face. "Quiet as the grave."

"All right to light the lantern?" Murdo said.

"I should say so."

The boy reached into the for'ard locker and produced a storm lantern and a box of matches. In a few moments the lamp burned up, shining cheerily over the ice-sheathed timbers of the boat. A warm paraffinny smell filled the air. As Murdo leaned against the side of the boat the leather sheath of his knife pressed into his waist. He slid it around the belt, remembering afresh that he had left the knife on the jetty in Orkney that morning after a couple of splicing jobs. It annoyed him, for he treasured the knife, not that it was expensive but it had been given to him by his father two years before and he used it all the time. Regretfully he fingered the empty sheath.

Donald was counting the cases of whisky, measuring the tarpaulin with his eye.

"Thirty, is it?" he asked.

Hector nodded. "Thirty-four."

Donald whistled quietly. "That's something like a cargo! What is this stuff — fifteen bob a bottle? Nine pounds a crate." He did the sum in his head. "Over three hundred quid. Yes, that is something like a cargo."

"I daresay the odd half-crown might find its way into your own pocket," said Hector with a smile. "You never know."

9

He reached into the locker beneath him and pulled out a single bottle. The lantern shone on the bright amber liquid; he held it close so that the light shone through, burning and golden.

Donald looked at it, his head on one side. "Aye, it's a bonny colour," he said, pushing his hat back and scratching the top of his bald head. "Do you know, Johnnie had nothing at the bar last night but one pint of beer for every man. One pint of beer. Not a nip between here and the Sahara Desert. It's a terrible thing, the war." Innocently he gazed at the golden bottle, and back to Hector's weather-beaten face. "You know, I was just thinking: well, it's a cold night, and the fog — it gets awful into your bones when you have to stand about for a long time. A — er — wee droppie might just help to keep the cold out, don't you think?"

The slow smile on Hector's face broadened to a mischievous grin. Reaching into the locker again, he produced three glasses. Holding them in one hand, he leaned over the side and swished them in the salt water, then placed them on top of the engine casing beside the lamp. With a squeaking pop the cork came out of the bottle. Carefully, Hector half filled two glasses, and put a drop in the bottom of the third.

"Och, give the boy a proper drink," said Donald, looking at the stocky figure of Murdo. "How old is he now — fifteen?"

"No, fourteen; and that's all he's getting."

Donald raised his eyebrows, then leaned across and picked up his glass.

"Slàinte," he said.

"Slàinte mhath."

Not entirely unaccustomed to whisky, Murdo took a sip. The burning spirit filled his mouth and lungs so that he gasped, but stifled it so that the men should not see. It tasted terrible. Then a warm glow started in his chest and stole down into his belly. It was good in the cold air. He had not realised how chilled he was. Another sip and it was finished.

Lachlan, sandy-haired and twelve, built like a whippet, got none, though he was quite as cold as the men and his older brother. Hector felt inside his oilskins for a packet and passed the boy a strong fisherman's lozenge.

"Made for trawlermen off the North Cape," he said. "Strip your teeth down to stumps. That's better for you than the demon drink."

Donald rolled the whisky round his tongue and smacked his lips appreciatively.

"That's good stuff," he wheezed. "Good stuff."

Hector nodded and added a drop more to their two glasses, then set the bottle aside. "John-George Lyness," he said. "He knows what he's about, that one."

Murdo passed his own glass across.

Deliberately misunderstanding, Hector set it on the engine casing and cupped a hand about the bowl of his pipe. Fragrant smoke drifted across the lantern light. Suddenly he chuckled. "He's a boy, is John-George. When we went there this morning he had it all on the jetty. Broad daylight. Thirty-four crates of whisky for all the world to see, and the police station not half a mile away." He shook his head. "And they're hot, those Orkney bobbies, especially now with the war on."

"Aye, but you can be too clever, as well." Donald pulled a battered tobacco tin from his pocket and carefully rolled a cigarette. "There was something not right up there on the dunes tonight. I left the car beside yours at the graveyard. All the time I had the feeling somebody was watching us. There was another car pulled back off the road at the top end of the wall, a big black one. It wasn't a police car — I don't know whose it was. There was nobody in it, but I'm sure I heard someone in the graveyard. Lachlan heard it too, like footsteps — and it sounded like someone kicked a gravestone. We had a look, but we couldn't see anything."

"Probably just sheep got in," Hector suggested.

Donald shrugged. "The moon wasn't so bright and the fog was pretty thick, sure enough. It didn't sound like a sheep, though."

Hector picked up the three glasses and swished them clean on the dark water. Still dripping, he returned them to the locker, set the whisky bottle in a coil of rope and clipped the door shut.

"Well, police or no police," he said, "it's no good sitting here. Let's get the stuff unloaded."

They pulled back the tarpaulin. Donald and Murdo jumped down into the shallows and Hector passed each a wooden crate. They carried them a few yards up the beach and dumped them on the wet sand.

"Can you carry one safely?" Hector asked Lachlan.

"Aye," said Lachlan.

"Come on, then. Give them a hand."

The boy took the crate of whisky with some effort and splashed ashore as his brother and Donald were returning. It did not take many minutes to unload the boat and soon the stack was complete, thirty-four cases of whisky stranded in the fog, far down the sands of a Highland beach.

"You give me a hand now, Lachlan," Hector called. "We'll take the boat round while they carry some of the cases up."

Murdo pulled out the mooring pin and tossed the painter over the bows. Swiftly Hector coiled it down then moved to the stern as all three threw their weight against the green timbers. The *Lobster Boy* was much lighter; at once she floated free. Lachlan flung himself over the gunwale and clambered aboard as Murdo pushed the boat into deeper water.

"Back in about twenty minutes," Hector called out. "Watch yourself now, Lachlan."

The engine burst into life and the old boat backed out of sight into the thinning mist. Then the note changed and she put-putted away down the shore. The hazy glow from the lantern faded into darkness.

The beach was silent, save for the hissing of the waves at their feet, and a soft roar where they broke over rocks a little way off.

Murdo and Donald turned back to the crates. Each swinging one to his shoulder, they trudged up the long expanse of beach. The sand was flawless, smooth as a carpet right to the high stacks and rock buttress of the cliffs. A moment's searching brought them to the cave, and they dropped their cases in the shadowy mouth. Donald disappeared inside, the light of his torch glimmering into the dark recesses.

The mist was definitely lifting. From time to time the moon appeared overhead and the sands were lightening. Murdo sat on one of the cases and gazed out between the stacks. He was tired and enjoyed the luxury of a huge yawn that stretched his face wide and made his ears crackle. It was followed by another.

Suddenly there was a sound down the beach — a muffled cough! Murdo's heart leaped, his mouth snapped shut. It came from a little to the left, not fifty yards away. Frozen motionless, he stared into the mist, every fibre of his being on the alert. But he could see nothing in the shrouded darkness. There was another sound that could have been soft running footfalls, but equally could have been the wing-beats of a bird or a noise carrying a long way from one of the crofts on the headland beyond the river. Biting his lip, he took a few cautious footsteps down the sands. For a full minute he stood by an outcrop of rocks listening, eyes wide, ears straining. But there was only the noise of the sea. A slight breeze fanned his cheek and stirred his hair, a seagull cried a long way off. Nothing! He waited a moment longer, then walked quietly down to the water's edge. Still — nothing.

Back at the cave a warm light glowed from the shadowy depths, and Donald had lifted the two boxes from the entrance. Murdo followed him inside, squeezing through the narrow neck into the inner chamber. He found the tall seaman clambering awkwardly from a rocky shelf several feet above the tumble of boulders that choked the further end. A lantern shone golden on the lip of the shelf and illuminated the scoured walls of the cave.

"There was somebody on the beach," Murdo said.

"What!" said Donald. "Oh hell! Did he see you?"

Murdo told him about the cough, though he was beginning to wonder whether he had not imagined the whole thing, mistaken the cough of a sheep or a cow on the cliffs above him. He climbed to the shelf, and Donald passed him the second

13

crate. He stacked it at the back, alongside the first one, and climbed down again. Then Donald blew out the lantern, and they made their way out of the cave to the brightening sands.

Fifty yards down the beach they came upon a line of footprints. They were tumbled, very fresh, stretching away into the darkness.

Donald swore softly in alarm.

Murdo's heart thudded and his knees trembled. He was poised for flight. But still there was nothing — no-one. All was still. He knelt to examine the footprints, feeling them lightly with the tips of his fingers.

"They're not big enough for boots," he said, "and there's no tread marks. I think he was wearing shoes, whoever it was."

"Aye," Donald said. "It's not sea boots or tackety boots, anyway."

They followed the footprints down. In a few yards they came to a place where the sand was trampled. Clearly the intruder had been standing there for some time.

"Perhaps he just heard something and stopped for a minute," Murdo suggested. "It might be someone staying at the inn."

"I don't know," replied Donald. "I really don't know." He thought for a moment. "It's not the police, that's sure. They'd have come up and caught us red-handed."

"Unless they've gone down to the stack," Murdo said.

Donald settled his grip on the heavy rubber torch. "You're a real bundle of joy," he said.

Cautiously they made their way to the water's edge. No-one was there. No prints but those of their own barred sea-boots disturbed the sand around the pile of whisky crates. The tide had turned and was now inching back in, spilling into their footprints, drawing ever closer to the stack of whisky.

"Leave well alone," Donald said. "The quicker we get these put away, the better." Bending, he swung a case to his shoulder, tucked a second one awkwardly under his left arm, and started up the beach.

In a few minutes Hector and Lachlan rejoined them. They had moored the *Lobster Boy* beyond a little headland in a rocky pool that Hector sometimes used in settled weather. They lent a hand and soon the pile of crates was well hidden from prying eyes.

Hector rubbed a dew-drop from his nose. "I want to have a look at those footprints," he said.

"Ach, leave them for now," said Donald. "Let's get away out of here."

Hector, scarcely up to the tall man's shoulder, gave Murdo a mischievous wink and picked up the lantern.

The intruder's tracks led down the beach from the direction of the graveyard. They traced them back until they were lost among the coarse grass of the dunes; they followed them down, passing the place where the man had lingered, until they vanished in the rim of the flooding tide. Forty yards on, however, the tracks reappeared, only to be lost for good where the man had climbed from the sands on to the barnacled rocks of the headland.

"Maybe it was somebody out for a walk," said Lachlan, who had so often seen his own line of footprints across the same sands.

"In the fog — on a night like this? No," said Hector. "If anyone was mad enough to go out walking tonight, he'd have stayed on the beach. But why was he hanging about and then running? See how far apart the footprints are, the way the sand's tumbled."

Lachlan stretched his legs in giant steps, but could not nearly compass the length of the intruder's strides.

"No, there was no-one down here by accident tonight. Whoever it was, he was nosing around." Hector scratched the back of his neck thoughtfully, then flexed his shoulders and looked quizzically at the anxious faces beside him. The lantern picked out a glint of laughter, or recklessness, in his shadowy eyes. "Ah well! It's no good hanging around here, anyway. We'd best get on up to the village with some of that whisky. From what you tell me, Donald, there's a lot of desperate men up there."

Donald opened his mouth as if he would speak, then closed it again and shrugged helplessly.

15

Back at the cave, Murdo and the two men each shouldered one of the rattling crates. Lachlan, not yet strong enough to carry one the distance, pushed bottles into his pockets and thrust more beneath his jersey. Hector flashed his torch around the chamber to see that everything was safely out of sight, and led the way out to the moonlit beach.

A few last wreaths of mist shrouded the river, half a mile away across the puddled sands. Little fields on the headland were pale with frost. A line of waves glimmered white along the edge of the sea. Soon the flooding tide would cover the churned-up sand in the cave mouth. By morning it would be as smooth as a carpet once more, flawless, as though no man had trodden the beach for half a year.

Slowly they made their way along the foot of the cliffs and up into the wilderness of dunes. The men held their cases firm, but Murdo's case cut painfully into his shoulder, so that he was continually shifting it to find a more comfortable position. With an effort he kept up, and soon they were wending their way around the wall of the lonely graveyard.

Their two cars were parked in a grassy turning space by the black iron gates where the track ended. Donald, who lived in the little village of Clerkhill ten miles further west, pulled open the rear door of his well-polished Vanguard. Carefully he spread a newspaper over the green upholstery and laid the crate on top. Then he took a couple of bottles from Lachlan and pushed them into a pocket beneath the shining dashboard.

After a brief struggle, Murdo threw up the icy boot of Hector's old Ford. It was half full of odds and ends and there was not room for the two cases of whisky. He pulled out an old pair of waders and a tin of sheep drench and pushed the rest to one side. He was just sliding the first case inside, when beyond the far corner of the graveyard a car engine whirred, then whirred again and burst into life. Startled, he looked up. A big dark car slowly backed out of the grassy siding, then drew away up the rough track towards the main road. He looked at Hector, who stared after it for a moment in silence. Then he bent and handed Murdo the second case of whisky.

Visit by Moonlight

Murdo drove the rattling old Ford. Often Hector let him take the wheel, especially at night. For a boy of his age he drove well. Disapproving, but keeping his opinion to himself, Donald followed at a safe distance behind.

The track from the graveyard to the main road was potholed and twisted, with tussocks of frozen grass between the wheel tracks. It was quite short, however, and in two or three minutes the cars drew up at the first house.

As Hector opened his door Donald wound down the window and called across. "I'll not stop. Better get this lad back to his aunt or we'll all be for it." He looked at the boy beside him who twisted with frustration and made a face. "Now stop that, Lachlan, you know I'm right. We're more than an hour late as it is. And it's an early start in the morning." He turned back to Hector. "The boy's coming down with me tomorrow to see our Jessie in Edinburgh. I promised I'd give them a visit."

"Is that right, Lachlan? Surely you'll be missing your lessons. Would it not be better for you to stay at the school?"

The boy looked down at his knees, unsure how to take Hector's teasing. Then his head came up. "My dad said I could go."

"Aye, so he did," Donald agreed. "Last time he was on leave — if the lad worked hard and kept his nose clean with his

17

auntie. The schoolmaster's given him some books and extra homework — and I tell you, our Jessie will make sure that he does it."

Hector laughed and felt in his pocket for a half-crown. "Here, Lachlan, you take yourself away to the pictures. Never mind all them books."

Somewhat shyly the boy leaned across and took the money.

"And Donald, you take that watery man of Jessie's a bottle or two of this whisky," Hector called. "Do him all the good in the world; better than them religious tracts he's always reading."

"Oh man, shut up. It's more than my life's worth. I daren't even take one for myself. She's terrible down on the drink, and he's just putty in her hands." Donald started the car.

"Aye, well, be good."

Murdo leaned across and called through the open door. "Donald, tell Lachlan I'll be along in about an hour. He's not to go to sleep."

The boy's face appeared in the window. He raised a hand.

With a roar the car pulled away, wheels crunching on the frozen track. Soon it dipped from sight down the steep hill that led to the crossroads. Standing on the verge with the bitter breeze blowing in his face, Murdo heard it slow, then draw away up the road towards the old manse where his aunt and uncle lived.

From within the cottage there was the sound of movement, and a bolt rattled in the front door. It swung open. A young woman stood in the entrance holding an oil lamp.

"Hector, I guessed it was you. I had a feeling it was about time you were up to your nonsense again. Come away in."

"Mary, my linnet! You're looking lovelier than ever. My own Florence Nightingale." The old seaman planted a whiskery kiss on her cheek.

She smiled and pushed him away. "Never mind that, you old goat. Just go on through."

Pulling off his woollen cap, Hector stepped past her into the dark hallway full of coats.

As Murdo followed, she laid a restraining hand against his shoulder. "And you've been with him, all the way this time. Don't tell me, I can see well enough." She laughed, sadness mingling with the affection. "You're going to end up as bad as himself."

After the moonlight and bitter frost, the living room was a jewel of warmth. The walls were of golden pine; a tilly lamp hissed softly on a dresser and a bright fire glowed in the hearth.

"Surely you had a good load of peats this year, Willie, with a blaze like that." Hector's blue eyes were watering from the cold. He wiped them and stretched a hand towards the flames. "It's good to feel the heat when you come in."

"Indeed by the smell of you, Hector, you should be warm enough already," cried the sharp old lady who sat at the fire. "Don't give me your usual old flannel. I suppose you'll be bringing some more of that poison in for Willie now. It seems the only reason you come around here nowadays." She drew her thin lips together and twitched the ends of a woollen shawl closer about her shoulders.

"And how are you, Meggan?" Hector smiled.

"Och, I'm well enough, but I don't like this cold. It gets awful into my bones now. I'm getting old."

The heat made Murdo drowsy after the long crossing from Orkney and he yawned. The radio was on and Vera Lynn was singing her great wartime love song:

> 'We'll meet again,
> Don't know where, don't know when,
> But I know we'll meet again
> Some sunny day . . .'

It was pleasant, and he blinked with comfortable weariness.

"Mary, turn that skirling cailleach off, will you!" cried Meggan sharply. "I'm sick of the sound of her."

Her daughter came from the kitchen and switched off the crackling set.

"Oh, that's better," exclaimed Meggan with a sigh. "That radio — it goes on and on. On and on, until I'm nearly driven off the head with it."

19

Mary smiled at the familiar refrain and went back to the kitchen. With Highland hospitality, she was always on the point of making a pot of tea when friends arrived.

"How's it going then, Willie?" said Hector to Meggan's husband who sat quietly at the opposite side of the fire, seeming very small in the big armchair.

You would never guess, Murdo thought, looking at the wrinkled face, that he had four sons and a grandson away at the war, and two of them dead aboard H.M.S. Hood. It gave the old man an honour somehow. Murdo regarded him with respect, and glanced across at Meggan. In a way they must feel as he did about his father, now a sergeant in the Seaforth Highlanders.

The old man's eyes were bird-bright and alert. Taking the pipe from his teeth, he leaned forward, poking it towards Hector vigorously, as if to wind himself up to the point of speaking. At length the words came.

"Have you got any with you?"

"I might have," Hector replied. "But you're not wanting any of that poison, are you."

Willie nodded excitedly.

"Indeed he does not," said Meggan. "I'm ashamed of you, Hector, coming round like this now."

"Get away with you, Meggan. What harm did one glass of whisky ever do an old man?"

"Hmph!" she snorted in disgust. "A couple of bairns, that's all you are; a couple of bairns."

Murdo smiled. He had a good set of teeth, but his smile showed them to be irregular. For years he had avoided his aunt's scheme to take him to the dentist and have them straightened.

Hector beamed kindly at the old lady, then turned to Willie. "How many is it, then — one?"

Willie shook his head and held up two fingers.

"One," said Meggan.

Willie frowned impatiently and shook the two fingers at him.

Hector looked from one to the other and shrugged. "Well you'll have to make your peace with that woman of yours," he said.

"Och, he's nothing but an old fool," she said. "Hand me that bag, will you." She pointed to a battered old handbag on the dresser. Murdo passed it over and she poked inside. "Here." She thrust a crumpled pound note and a ten shilling note towards Hector. "Go on, I'm just as bad myself. Give it to him." She looked crossly at the old man who had sat opposite her for so many years. He had settled back and was again puffing away contentedly at the pipe. "I suppose he's not such a bad old stick, really," she admitted grudgingly.

Hector took the pound and pushed the ten shilling note away. "A pound's all it is, Meggan," he said. "You're getting forgetful in your old age."

Although he had left his oilskins in the hall, Murdo began to sweat with the heat of the room. He tugged off his khaki battledress jacket and pulled his jersey straight. Stretching his legs across the carpet he yawned again.

Mary brought through the tea, with sandwiches, pancakes and cake, and they all had supper. Murdo knew better than to comment upon the red, fresh-run salmon that packed the sandwiches. They tasted good, he was very hungry.

Hector had other calls to make before his main business of the evening at the Captain Ivy Inn. Murdo left him at the crossroads and turned up the hill towards the house where his aunt and uncle lived.

It was an old manse, no longer attached to the church, tall and dark against the sky. Until a few months previously, when he had moved out to stay with Hector, Murdo had lived there with his brother. Returning now, in the late evening, he hoped to avoid a confrontation with his aunt.

Faint light shone at the edges of the blackout curtains in the sitting room and from the upstairs bedroom now occupied by Lachlan. Very quietly Murdo checked the kitchen door at the back of the house, but it was locked. He returned to the road and let himself into the front garden. Standing by the wall he emptied his trouser pockets, removed his jacket and boots, and hid them in a corner where the moon cast its deepest

21

shadows. The earth struck cold through the gaping holes in his socks.

Briefly he checked up and down the road. All was clear. Swiftly then he climbed on to the garden wall and reached for the bracket on the drainpipe. Hands clutching, feet braced against the wall, he scrambled upwards. Soon he was able to grasp the roof guttering. His fingers were frozen and the edge was sharp. Closing his mind as far as he was able to the hurt, he began to traverse the front of the house, swinging from hand to hand, resting briefly as he reached the upstairs window ledges. A car passed but otherwise the road remained empty.

He had covered threequarters of the distance when from behind the house came the noise of a door opening and closing. He recognised his aunt's footsteps. Milk bottles clinked. Murdo froze, feet hanging in space. Shining over the edge of the roof, the moonlight caught his head and shoulders.

She appeared at the end of the house, descended the track by the wall, and set the bottles in a crate at the roadside. For a moment she stood, arms wrapped about her thin chest, looking down the glen towards the village. She lifted her face to regard the moon.

Murdo felt his fingers cramping. He closed his eyes and gritted his teeth, fighting himself to remain still. The second she was gone, he writhed to ease the cramp and quickly struggled the last six or eight feet.

With relief he set his feet on his brother's window sill and took the weight off his arms. First one and then the other he let them hang at his side and thrust frost-nipped fingers into his trouser pockets.

The window was locked. Softly Murdo tapped on the glass, but there was no response. He tapped again.

Brother Lachlan! Where was he — at the bathroom, or downstairs eating supper? He rapped more sharply — two, three times.

Within the room a door shut. The glow vanished. The blinds were drawn back and his brother stood at the window, clad in rumpled pyjamas. He pressed back the catch and pushed the

22

window down. A breath of warm air brushed Murdo's face and was gone. Carefully he transferred his grasp to the window frame and ducked through into the dark room.

Having for the greater part of his life slept in the same bedroom, Murdo knew the position of every object: it was the sort of house where even in your own room a chair was not moved without consultation. As soon as the curtains had been drawn again, he felt for the box of matches on the end of the mantelpiece and touched a light to the oil lamp. The wick burned up in a smoky flare which settled as he replaced the glass chimney. Carefully he turned it down a fraction, and looked across at his brother.

Lachlan had been sound asleep. Flushed and tousled he stood by the curtains, blinking in the lamplight. The room had turned cold. Half in a daze he passed Murdo, climbed back into bed and pulled the blankets to his chin.

Murdo tucked in his shirt tails and sat on the foot of the bed. He picked up the book his brother had been reading when he fell asleep, and laid it on the suitcase which stood ready packed for the morning.

"Let's have the hot water bottle for a minute," he said.

Lachlan scrabbled with his feet and pushed the heavy stone bottle from the sheets. Murdo took it on his lap and wrapped his calloused fingers about it. The pain of the returning blood was exquisite; he squeezed his fingers and blew on his nails, and soon it passed.

Sitting on the coverlet in that spotlessly clean bedroom he looked dark and unkempt. Small wonder that he distressed his aunt. Fish scales adhered to the old navy serge of his trousers, his jumper was torn and marked with oil. From the constant burning of the sun, wind and salt sea, his face was swarthy as a gipsy.

The radio was on downstairs. The sound of voices drifted up the stairway.

"Are they settled down there?" Murdo asked.

"I think so. What time is it?"

Murdo consulted the lopsided Mickey Mouse alarm clock. "Quarter to ten," he said. "You're a bit early."

"Aye, well, she said I had to have an early night."

Murdo smiled. "No bath?"

"I had that last night." Lachlan was waking up. He rubbed his sandy hair and screwed round in the bed. "Where have you been?"

"We called at Willie and Meggan's."

"Did you have supper?"

"Aye."

"Are you hungry?"

"A bit. Keep your voice down."

"Here." Keeping beneath the bedclothes as much as possible, Lachlan pulled open a drawer in the polished chest which stood beside the bed. In among the shirts and underclothes was a dinner plate, with bread and cheese and butter and a slice of cake. Some spoonfuls of raspberry jam had run around the edge and trickled on to a vest. Carefully Lachlan lifted the food and a dinner knife to the top of the chest, and sucked the vest as clean as possible. "I'll put it on tomorrow," he said. "She'll never know."

For several minutes the brothers ate. Soon the plate was empty. With long experience Lachlan gathered up the crumbs from the plate and bedclothes and ate them, then licked away the last smears of jam.

"You're like a vacuum cleaner," Murdo said.

"Well, you know what she's like." Lachlan hid the plate beneath the pink vest, pulled a shirt on top and pushed the drawer shut.

Murdo stood up. "I'm just going to Dad's room, I need some socks. These ones have had it."

He took up a torch from the side of the bed and blew out the lamp. Softly in the dim beam he passed the foot of the bed that had been his own and pulled open the door. The radio grew louder, but all was still. Swiftly he crossed the long landing and let himself into his father's bedroom.

He knew in which drawer to look. As he pulled it open the familiar scent rose to his nostrils; a clean manly smell, a comfortable smell — his father. He poked about and selected two thick pairs of working socks.

24

Though Murdo wanted nothing else, he pulled open the adjacent drawer. It was half full of oddments; cigarette case, armbands, old brushes, an out of date calendar, a small bowl that Murdo had carved for his father at school. Face down, lay a framed photograph of Lachlan and himself with their sister Maggie. She was four years older and now worked away from home. Briefly Murdo examined it, recognising the sunlit river-bank where the photograph had been taken but forgetting the occasion, for they were all much younger. Before their father went away it had stood on his dressing table. Murdo laid it on top of the chest. He was just about to close the drawer when the torch beam fell on his father's pocket knife, half hidden beneath a tangle of old salmon line. He took it in his hand, a practical knife with a handle of black and white horn. He flipped up the single blade, honed down and concave, very sharp. His father used it all the time. For a moment Murdo was undecided, then he snapped the knife shut and dropped it into his trouser pocket.

A minute later, socks and photograph in hand, he was back in Lachlan's bedroom.

"I've taken Dad's knife as well," he said. "So you don't need to get blamed if they go looking and it's not there. Now I'm off. How long will you be away?"

"Till the end of the week after next — a bit over a fortnight," said Lachlan sleepily.

Murdo switched off the torch and drew back the curtains. The road and hills were bright with moonlight. As he pushed down the window the bitter breeze flowed into the room. He had forgotten how exceedingly cold it was.

"Hey, I'm not going out there." He shivered. "You can let me out the back door."

Softly in the darkness the two boys tiptoed downstairs and flitted into the kitchen. The top bolt of the door was stiff and resisted Murdo's tugging. Suddenly it gave and shot back with a loud bang.

"Oh blast!" In a moment he had turned the key in the lock and was outside. "Have a good time in Edinburgh."

There was no time to say more. A door opened in the hallway and there was the sound of voices. Murdo took to his heels, stubbing his protruding toes against a hidden boulder.

Light flooded the back of the house. He heard his aunt's voice. "What on earth are you doing out here at this time of night, child? And in your pyjamas. You'll catch your death of cold."

"I just wanted to see what kind of night it was," Lachlan replied. "The moon and that."

"The moon and that! I should have thought you would have seen enough of the moon and that, being out till all hours with Donald Sutherland." There was a pause. When she spoke again her voice was a little softer. "But it's a nice night, sure enough."

"Yes, it was foggy before. I wanted to see if it would be all right for going down to Edinburgh tomorrow."

"Lachlan, I don't believe a word of it. You only had too look out of your bedroom window. I wouldn't be surprised but you were down for more food. Where you put it all I'll never know, The amount you ate at supper, all that bread and cheese. And you're still as thin as a rake. I'm sure the neighbours must think I starve you. Perhaps you've got worms."

Again there was silence. Then Murdo, crouched behind the shed nursing his damaged toes, heard a sharp intake of breath.

"I know what you were doing, That brother of yours has been round, hasn't he? That's what you were doing, wasn't it, giving him food?"

"No, Aunt Winifred." Lachlan's voice rang with innocence and injured righteousness.

But again she did not believe him and Murdo saw the lamplight wavering down the grass towards him. Soft as a wraith he flitted away down the side of the house, sprang over the wall into the front garden, collected his boots and jacket, and vanished into the shadows at the far side of the old manse.

Stranger at the Captain Ivy

Hector's car was parked in its usual corner outside the Captain Ivy Inn. Due to black-out restrictions the building looked deserted. Murdo found the car doors unlocked and searched among the jumbled oddments on the floor behind the front seats for his tackety boots. Sitting on the edge of the horse trough, he pulled off his sea-boots and stripped off the damp, not over-fresh remains of his socks. The breeze from the bay blew bitterly cold about his feet, Though a little on the large side, his father's socks were thick and comfortable. He reached for his nailed boots. The leather laces, short through having repeatedly been broken, were hard and difficult to knot.

When he had finished, his feet felt luxuriously warm. Briefly he stamped on the frozen yard, then looked for a place to dump the discarded socks. There were no dustbins. He tried to roll back a stone on the moor, but it was frozen into the peat and immovable. Finally he opened the car again and dropped them, already stiffening, among the rubbish in the back.

Murdo was about to close the car door when it occurred to him that although the crates of whisky had been delivered, Hector would certainly have held on to at least one bottle to share with friends. He felt in the pocket beneath the dashboard and at once his fingers lighted on the smooth, cold glass of a lemonade bottle: the distillers used whatever bottles came to hand. He drew it out and pressed back the spring clip with his thumbs. Carefully he sniffed and grimaced. Then throwing caution to the winds he took a good swig. The whisky tasted even worse than before and the boy shuddered to his very toes. A chill flush passed across his face. On the instant he knew it had been a mistake and wished he had left the spirit alone.

Hector could hardly fail to notice that the neck of the bottle was a couple of inches down. Spitting and guilty, Murdo hurried to the tap at the corner of the inn yard. It was frozen solid; an icicle reached halfway to the ground. Quietly he let himself into the inn and topped up the bottle at the wash basin in the toilet. Drops clung to the glass and smeared as he rubbed it against the sleeve of his jacket. He looked for a towel or cloth, but there was none. At length he wiped it dry on the tail of his shirt, and returned the bottle to the car.

As Murdo pushed open the door of the bar-room the light and warmth and beery smell washed over him. Though it was nearly an hour after official closing time a dozen men were still present, for no-one bothered very much in that remote part of the country.

Murdo closed the door behind him and crossed to Hector at the bar. A few of the men smiled and nodded abstractedly, but their minds were elsewhere. From the crackling and fading bar radio the gravelly voice of Winston Churchill rolled out, a recording of his broadcast earlier in the evening. Again, it seemed, as well as hardships to be endured, he could tell of some success — Montgomery in Tunisia, the Russian resistance at Stalingrad. But still, perhaps more than ever, there was need for resolution and courage, the greatest danger might yet be to come. The might of the German army in Europe was moving west; already there was news of a considerable build-up near the Channel ports of France. The conclusion was not to be avoided that Herr Hitler was planning a bold and desperate strike against Britain itself, the very heart of the powers that rose against him. As the Nazi lion's teeth were drawn it grew more savage. In the bar-room the men were still, no-one spoke.

Murdo listened with them. A man he had not seen before came through the door that led to the guests' accommodation. He leaned easily on the end of the bar and jingled the coins in his pocket. The landlord motioned him to be patient and listened on.

To Murdo it all meant very little. The war, in this January of 1943, was vague and remote. They had explained it all at school, of course, and he heard the daily news. But though he knew the names of the various battles and theatres of war — El Alamein, Leningrad, Guadalcanal, the Battle of Britain — he was not very sure where they were or what had happened; and the Allied generals and politicians, he knew their names but not exactly who they were or what they did. Hitler was the main enemy, of course, with Mussolini, and Goering, Goebbles and Himmler, like the rude soldiers' rhyme that one of his pals had brought back from the army camp.

Whoever they were, however, or whatever they had done, none of their actions really concerned him. In the wild and remote Highlands it was hard for a boy like Murdo to understand. He had seen the occasional gangs of prisoners working on the farms and roads of Caithness. But his life was affected more by a northerly wind that kept him from the lobster creels than it was by the fall of Paris, or the capture of Tobruk and Singapore. Sometimes he stood on the headland with Hector's binoculars and watched the British fleet moving along the horizon, cruisers and destroyers, frigates and little corvettes, a magic lantern show. The noise of their gunfire on manoeuvres off Cape Wrath echoed across the moors. He knew some of the men who sailed in these ships, and this touched him more, especially with his deep love of the sea: also Hector had told him something of his own years as a coxwain in the Royal Navy during the First World War.

But for Murdo the single great tragedy of the war was that it took his father away from the village and left him homeless — homeless and rootless — that at least was how it had felt, despite their aunt's care. Apart from that, and the absence of nearly all the youger men from the district, the war meant simply the stopping of comics and ice cream and sweets, and the curtains that had to be kept tightly closed at night.

But the men in the bar listened raptly. Murdo looked at their faces, the serious faces of men too old to do the fighting, who had done their bit twenty-five years earlier, and whose sons and grandsons now fought in their place. Among them was a young soldier, Billy, home on convalescent leave. His tank had been blown up in the desert, and he was newly out of hospital, burned and suffering from shell-shock. Heedless of the regulations he lounged at the bar in an old sheep-stained jacket. At the end of the bar the stranger, less intent on the radio than the local men, stood waiting for his drink. He looked like a business man, plump, with a middle-aged baby face and gold-rimmed glasses. Idly Murdo regarded him.

The broadcast ended and life began again in the bar-room. The landlord pulled some half-pints of beer, a whisky bottle appeared and the men talked. It was all about the war — bombings in Glasgow, letters from their sons in the forces, the possibility of invasion.

"For God's sake give it a break, will you! Talk about something else."

Billy's voice cut through the bar-room talk like a knife. For a moment there was an embarrassed silence.

"I'm sorry." He was trembling, the scar tissue was livid against his brown skin.

"That's all right, boy," said old Danny.

Slowly the talk began again and turned to cars and work and local aquaintances, all the daily things men talk about when they are together.

Murdo sipped a glass of shandy, which was all Hector would allow him. He tipped the damp bag of salt into a packet of crisps, an unaccustomed treat.

Hector was on the point of leaving. He waited for Murdo to finish his drink and tossed back the last inch of beer in his own glass, then began buttoning his jacket against the night air. Murdo buckled the battledress across his stomach. Bidding goodnight to the company, they made their way to the door.

They had hardly reached it, however, when the stranger crossed the room and addressed himself to Hector.

"Mr Gunn?"

Hector nodded.

"I wonder if I could have a few words with you."

Hector looked at him for a long moment, his old weather-beaten face expressing nothing.

"What about?" he said.

The stranger looked towards a table in the far corner of the room. "Perhaps we could sit down," he suggested.

"All right."

Somewhat diffidently the stranger led the way to a plain varnished table. Hector seated himself with his back to the wall and Murdo sat beside him, the unfinished bag of crisps in his hand. The stranger pulled in a rickety chair opposite.

"I suppose I should introduce myself," he said hesitantly. "My name's Smith, Henry Smith." The English accent and rather high-pitched voice sounded strange and forced after the low, soft speech of the Highlanders.

Hector said nothing, but sat waiting for him to continue.

"I've been up in Sutherland for a day or two now, staying at the inn here." He paused for a moment. "It's a lovely spot."

"Aye."

"Well, it's partly a holiday, but I'm mixing business with pleasure, and I've been trying to find a man who can help me with a bit of — well, business."

Murdo belched and made a face. The whisky and shandy were playing havoc with his insides. Hector regarded him keenly for a moment and repressed a smile.

Mr Smith took a packet of cigarettes from his pocket and lit one up. The backs of his hands were covered in a mat of golden hairs. He looked quizzically across the table at Hector and drew a deep breath.

"I suppose I've got to come to the point sometime. I want a few things bringing across from Island Roan, and I hoped you and I might come to some arrangement. I need a boat."

31

"Island Roan!" Hector exclaimed. "I'm afraid someone's been misleading you, mister. The last people came away from Island Roan the year the war started. There's nothing there now but empty houses and a few sheep."

"I know that."

Hector regarded the man opposite him afresh. "You mean you'll be taking something there first?"

Henry Smith shrugged. "Maybe. It depends what things are like over here. And if I can get a boat."

"Mm." Hector's distaste was obvious. "What is it, black-market goods — clothes, tinned meat, chocolate — stuff like that?"

"No, it's not stuff like that. I'm not a profiteer, if that's what you're thinking. It's . . . machinery, as a matter of fact." A look of shrewd intelligence flickered across his pale eyes and then was gone. "I don't exactly want it spread across the front pages, but I'll tell you something about it anyway. Then you can see if you're interested."

Hector settled back a little and laid one leg across the other. "Well, if you want the *Lobster Boy* I'll need to know more. Hearing does no harm — not with me, anyway."

"As I said, I don't exactly want everyone to know about it. I can rely on you to — er . . ."

The muscles stirred along Hector's bristly jaw, his nostrils widened a fraction. Murdo felt a shiver up the back of his neck.

"I've got a factory down in Oxford," said Mr Smith, "and we're doing some work on a new type of engine. Runs on paraffin. I don't need to tell you how important that could be with the war as it is right now. Ten years I've been working on it. Anyway, the only other people doing the same work was a Norwegian firm, Thörsen's of Stavanger. When the Germans over-ran Norway in 1940, old Edvard Thörsen hid his records and data, and took all the prototype machinery to a secret place down the fjord. The Germans aren't always too nice in their methods — the Gestapo, anyway — and they caught hold of a couple of Thörsen's managers and . . . well, they talked. Thörsen himself was hiding, but word got to him and they shifted the stuff to a new spot out in the Lofoten Islands. A real underground job.

"Things quietened down a bit after that, but the Germans never forgot and a month back, quite by accident, they got a new lead. They weren't slow in following it up either; not with an engine like that at the end of it. Edvard Thörsen had to run for it. They moved the engines to another part of the islands, and he got a message out to me on one of those Shetland fishing boats. I didn't know him very well, although I'd met him at conferences, of course, and he knew I was working along the same lines. He said that he believed it was only a matter of time before the Germans found the machines, and wanted to get them out of the country. He asked me to take the work over and develop it as a joint effort in my factory."

"Why bring the machine parts across?" Hector said. "Why not just the drawings? They could drop the machinery in the fjord."

"It would take months to cut new moulds and set up the plant. A year at least. He was a great engineer. I haven't seen the figures yet, but I understand it's a magnificent engine, and from what he wrote the experimental work was finished. I'm nowhere near that stage."

"He *was* a great engineer?" said Hector.

"Yes. A fortnight ago the Gestapo caught up with his wife and himself. First he shot her, then he shot himself. They'd agreed about it beforehand. He was a leader in the Norwegian underground."

Hector nodded slowly.

"An engine like that, why don't you tell the government? They'd bring it over for you if it's that important."

"I've had dealings with the government before! Two years ago they were going to take me over, lock, stock and barrel. Never so much as a 'by your leave'. Then some boffin told them it could never work because of the jet/power ratio, and they forgot all about it. I've spent ten years of my life on this, Mr Gunn — ten years! And now, with Edvard Thörsen's help it's coming to fruition. This engine is the only really important thing I will ever do. My life's work." His eyes glittered intensely behind the gold-rimmed spectacles. "Don't expect me to throw that away and let some milk-sop office boy take all the credit. That's happened too often: it's not going to happen to me!"

He lit another cigarette and drew several deep lungfuls of smoke. When he continued his voice was calmer.

"It's important. They can't bring everything over, of course, just those parts small enough to crate and handle. The rest we'll have to produce ourselves."

He sat back, the pale blue eyes once more blinking nervously, pink fingers tapping the ash off his cigarette into a big ashtray beside the discarded pipe.

"So, there you are. If you're not interested, just say so and forget all about it."

There was a long silence. This time it was Hector who broke it.

"How did you come to ask me?"

"I've been asking around — oh, generally of course — and Johnny here," he indicated the barman, "said I should perhaps have a word with you."

"Oh, did he?"

Henry Smith leaned forward. "Can I buy you a drink?"

Hector shook his head. "Not just now, thank you." He looked across at his old friend the barman and smiled slightly. "I don't think you'd get it, anyway. One pint a night these days." He shifted in his chair and clasped the fingers of his big gnarled hands together, shrewdly regarding the man who sat opposite him.

Murdo looked from one to the other, and an odd pair they made; the weather-beaten fisherman in his old sweater and seaboots, the smooth-cheeked businessman in a country tweed suit.

This time the silence remained unbroken. Murdo felt the tension mounting.

"Well, it's up to you," Henry Smith said at length. "I've told you all I can for the present. You'll be well paid, I can promise you that."

34

For a long moment Hector did not reply, then, "How much stuff is there?" he asked.

"About eight or ten loads, I should say — if your boat is the size I think."

"How is it packed?"

"Boxes and crates, I suppose. Nothing very big, anyway."

"And where do you want them taking?"

"Well, I thought if you brought them here we could stack them away somewhere until I get a lorry to pick them up."

"What, here?" Hector indicated the inn.

"Hardly."

"What do you mean by 'here', then?"

"Somewhere near the beach, I thought."

Murdo sat up and looked towards the bar to hide his growing excitement.

Hector shook his head patiently. "It might be a quiet place, this, but you can hardly leave a great stack of cases on the beach in the middle of a war and expect nobody to see them."

"Naturally not." A trace of impatience showed on Henry Smith's face. "I'm not entirely stupid. We'd find a place to put them."

"Where?"

"I don't know. But there must be some fairly deep caves around here, some place they would be safe for a few days."

Murdo's eyes widened. Quickly he glanced at Hector.

"I don't suppose you were anywhere near the beach tonight?" Hector said.

"No, I was away at Thurso until I came in here. Why?"

"I was just wondering." Hector put yet another match to his pipe. He spoke through the smoke. "You've got a car, then?"

"Yes, of course." The Englishman leaned forward again, not to be deterred. "Is there a cave," he said, "or an old croft house, or somewhere like that?"

Hector shrugged. "I suppose you could find some place, right enough."

Casually Murdo looked down at the man's shoes, but they were neat and well-polished and bore no trace of sand.

"One thing I should say," Mr Smith continued. "Some men will be coming over with the crates. They used to work in the Stavanger factory and I want them to join me in Oxford. One of them could come across and keep an eye on things if you thought it was necessary."

"Mm." Hector drew himself up and took a deep breath. "Well, I'll let you know."

"Tomorrow?"

"No; say Wednesday."

"What time?"

"Oh, around six-thirty." Hector turned to Murdo. "Come on, boy. It's time we were home."

Murdo stood up and pulled his jacket comfortably around him.

"Goodnight," Henry Smith said.

"Goodnight," and the two, old man and boy, made their way across the smoky bar-room.

As they stepped out of the door, Murdo felt the night air grip his face like a giant, icy hand.

In a moment his eyes accustomed themselves to the moonlight. He looked down the hillside to the bay from which the soft, ceaseless roar of the waves rose on the breeze. Suddenly he touched Hector's arm and pointed. Almost invisible among the shadows of the inn yard was a big black car. It had not been there an hour earlier, of that he was certain.

The old Ford was hard to start and needed a few cranks to get it going, but in a few minutes they were home. The tilly lamp was lit, a fire roared up the chimney, and Hector busied himself over the stove. Soon they were seated at a small table tucking into black-pudding, bacon and eggs while a big teapot steamed gently on the hob of the fire.

Hector was first to finish. He pushed his plate back with a sigh and rubbed the back of a hand across his lips. Taking a couple of biscuits from the tin, he carried his mug of tea to the fire and topped it up from the big teapot. A minute later Murdo joined him, and at either side of the fire they stretched back in the old armchairs and gave themselves up to the heat flung out by the blazing peats.

Murdo propped his thick-stockinged feet on the hearth and gazed into the heart of the fire. He was a dark boy with shaggy black hair that tumbled down his forehead, not particularly tall, but thickset for his years. He was growing up quickly, already his upper lip was shadowy with down. Although no relation, he had been living with Hector more or less since the previous summer when he had left school. The two of them got along very well. The old fisherman was glad of the boy's company in a house which had seemed empty since his daughter went down to England to be married; and Murdo liked living with Hector, whose rough and ready ways were so warm and homely, especially after his aunt's spick and span house.

How he had hated that shining place they had to call home. They had lived there almost since Murdo could remember, for his mother had died when Lachlan was born, leaving his father, still in his early twenties, with three children to look after. At length circumstances had compelled him to accept the generous offer of his sister Winifred, ten years older than himself, to move into the old manse. She had done her best, but a joyless sort of place it had been. As he stared into the fire Murdo remembered — the complaints, the smacks, the punishments.

"Murdo, don't play on the stairs, I've just brushed them; and put that china dog down, you'll break it. Goodness sake, child, watch the wallpaper. Let me see your hands — go and wash them! I don't know how you get in such a mess. Why can't you be content, like Geoffrey, and read a book?"

Geoffrey was the son of the local minister, a blond boy with white knees and soft hands. Murdo's hands, in contrast, were broad and usually stained or cut. The top joint of the third finger on his right hand was missing as the result of an accident with a wire rope when he was ten.

Sandy, their father had been the one bright spark in all those years: his father, strong and sandy-haired as his name, who would take him out in the boat to the lobsters, or fishing up the river; who bought him the second-hand bicycle and fishing rod; who would swing him up before him on one of the horses and gallop wildly about the fields. And then he had gone, volunteered for the army in the early days of the war — and Maggie, Lachlan and himself were left to the dreary round of existence with their Aunt Winifred and Uncle George. A few months later Maggie had left school and went to work at a hotel in Thurso, twenty miles away.

By then Murdo was eleven and old enough to keep out of his aunt's hair. Increasingly as he grew older, however, they seemed to come into conflict. He and Lachlan, towards whom he felt a growing responsibility, were in the house as little as they could manage. Certainly they were unjust to her, for she gave them good meals and warm beds, and their clothes were always well cared for. After all these years, however, she still thought that boys should not have mud on their trousers, should not get dirty hands, or tear through the house, or shout or get into trouble. She wanted them as still and cool and well-ordered as her own shining rooms, and life was one long battle.

A few days after his fourteenth birthday, Murdo had left school. It was his ambition to join the merchant navy and work his way towards bosun — or possibly to become a trawlerman — and when he was older to work a croft and run a boat of his own, like his father and Hector. For a year or two in his spare time he had helped Hector with the creels, and begun to set a few that he made himself. Now, since the merchant fleet was cut back by enemy action and there was no work locally, he began to go fishing and help about the croft more regularly. Despite the old fisherman's reputation as a rogue, Murdo's father was pleased at the unlikely friendship.

So Murdo worked alongside Hector on the *Lobster Boy*, and with little success tried to prompt him into doing something about his neglected croft, where the shed roofs leaked, the tools grew rusty, and rank grass and weeds were only kept at bay by marauding sheep. Soon they were together so much that Murdo started taking his meals there, and gradually settled in until at length he had his own room and kept most of his belongings at the house.

Not surprisingly, his aunt disapproved of the situation, but her remonstrations went unheeded, and after she had written to tell his father about it she said no more. Now Murdo saw her only occasionally.

But Hector's activities, were not confined to lobster fishing and tending his sheep on the hills. Periodically the two would sally out in the dark hours with a twenty yard length of salmon net in the boot of the car; or perhaps, if the time of year and the weather were right, with a couple of sharp knives and a pony, and a rifle slung in the crook of an arm. The following Sunday a dozen cottages in Strathy would be filled with the savour of roast venison. This, however, was the first time Hector had let the boy cross the dangerous Pentland Firth with him to Orkney, to bring back a load of the moonshine whisky.

Murdo stirred, then stood, warming his legs at the glowing peats. His hand found a crumpled, much-read forces letter in his back pocket. He smoothed it, looking at his father's handwriting, and set it behind a tin on the mantlepiece, then changed his mind and decided to take it upstairs. He yawned, without putting a hand up.

"I think I'll go to bed."

"Aye, it's high time," said Hector, glancing at the old chiming wag-at-the-wa'. "No hurry in the morning, though." He mused for a moment. "What did you make of yon chap — Smith?"

Murdo shrugged. "I don't know. It all seemed a bit fishy to me — the caves and that. And that big black car outside the Captain Ivy — it must have been his." He poked a corner of peat into the flames with the toe of his stocking. "He seemed all right, though. The money should be good."

Hector nodded, looking across at the youth who already meant so much to him. For a moment he felt a disturbing twinge of uncertainty, but with careless optimism he quickly cast it aside. Murdo was looking down into the flames, his dark face glowing in the firelight.

"What do you say if we give him a go?" Hector said. "A bit of excitement, eh? Give him a run for his money."

Murdo looked over, smiling. The old seaman's blue eyes twinkled like a mischievous boy's in the lamplight.

"Good," he said.

The Men in Hiding

It was a funny business. The previous evening Hector and Murdo had kept their appointment with Henry Smith at the Captain Ivy, and the deal was confirmed. To their surprise, they learned that the machinery, along with nine men, had already been sitting out on Island Roan for the best part of a week. Now Mr Smith was waiting for them up at the graveyard, and in two and a half hours they would be out on the island themselves. What would they find?

Still, twenty pounds a trip with a bonus at the end was not to be turned down. Not if you were in Hector's position. In his mind Murdo had half of it spent already; a better tractor, new roof for the barn, a couple of loads of hay. Perhaps they would be able to get the croft going again, properly this time. Though Hector was promising nothing, his hopes were high. Eight or ten trips, Mr Smith thought. Well, better hope the weather held.

Hector came downstairs, struggling with a safety-pin to hold his braces. As they drove through the deserted scattering of houses and forked left on the track to the graveyard, Murdo pulled off his nailed boots, tucked the thick blue trousers into his socks, and reached for his seaboots.

Henry Smith was waiting for them, his big car parked on the green opposite the graveyard gates. The earth was hard as stone

41

as they walked around the end of the old graveyard wall. Then they were descending the dunes. The world was black and silver: the dry-stane dykes on the headland were sharp-etched above impenetrable cliffs; the beach below shone white as a cornfield. Though all three carried torches, they had no need of them as they dropped to the shore, and passed beneath the high stacks on the smooth carpet of sand.

Murdo led the way, happy in the face of such an adventure. The bitter breeze, slight as it was, froze his face and clouded his breath, but within the layers of clothes he glowed with warmth.

"Go straight in and when we get there," called Hector. "Light the lamp."

Murdo turned from the moonlight into the shadow of the cliffs and switched on his torch. The cave mouth loomed up before him. Six tides had washed the sand since he had sat there on the crate of whisky and heard the cough in the fog; and four since the following evening when four men and two boys had removed the whisky to a safer spot in the shed behind Hector's cottage.

He paused for a moment and looked back towards the beach. His footprints scarred the sand, sharp-etched with shadow. An idea struck him. He stepped aside to a rock and pretended to pull up one of his socks.

The men passed into the cave ahead of him. As soon as they were gone he stepped back and turned his torch on the two sets of footprints. They were very distinct in the damp sand. Hector's, like his own, showed the barred imprint of a sea-boot. But Henry Smith's! Murdo's heart thudded. He crouched to examine one more closely. It looked exactly the same as those they had followed below the dunes, where the intruder had been walking; the shape of the toe, the curve of the heel, the little drag where it had been put down and lifted. If only he could be sure.

"Murdo!" Hector's voice echoed in the depths of the cave.

"Coming." He rose and scuffed his own tell-tale prints, then shone his torch back along the winding tracks, resolving to tell Hector as soon as he had a chance.

As he pushed through the narrow neck into the inner chamber, Hector was putting a match to the lantern. He settled the mantle and adjusted the flame to a fish-tail of brilliant white.

Murdo knew the cave, the whole beach, like the back of his hand. He clambered to the broad ledge, sat in his usual place and shone the torch about. The shelf was about nine feet above the sand, high enough to ensure that only a northerly storm or a big spring tide with the wind on-shore could reach it. The waves broke their force on the narrow entrance, spurting and heaving impotently through the main body of the cave.

Since the war started, children had been kept away from the beaches, for what looked like a box or a mooring buoy might not be so innocent. More than once a mine had exploded on the rocks with a force that blew in the windows quarter of a mile away; and several times the navy had towed a stranded mine out to sea for detonation. After all, the naval base of Scapa Flow was only thirty miles away across the Pentland Firth.

Murdo was recalled from his day-dream by a light flashing in his face. Hector and Mr Smith were peering over the edge of the shelf.

The Englishman nodded. "Yes, it will do very well." With surprising agility for a man whose appearance was so sedentary and urban, he climbed up and shone his torch around the shelf. Then from this vantage point he surveyed the whole cave, turning slowly, his torch winkling into corners that the lantern light did not reach. "Yes, very good." He nodded again and climbed down. "And you say no-one will come nosing around."

Hector was sitting on a boulder. He looked up at Murdo and back to Henry Smith.

"None of the men in the village," he said. "Not at this time of year. It's just the old fogies left, all the young ones are away. And the children don't come down here much nowadays."

"Excellent," he said. "It will do very well. Now for the island."

A few minutes' walk along shelving rocks brought them to the *Lobster Boy*, bobbing at her mooring in the black water of the inlet. Their creels, which they had lifted in the morning, formed a dark mound against the crag, well above the reach of any winter storms. The moon cut a glittering track across the wet sand at the edge of the sea, and silvered the boards of the old boat. Hector pulled her over with a rope and they clambered down.

Murdo sat on the side bench and the thick hoar frost crunched beneath his oilskins.

"She's going to be cold tonight," he said.

"You're right there, boy." Hector turned to his passenger. "You've got plenty of clothes on?" he said.

The Englishman pulled up the fur collar of his splendid coat in reply and showed the thickness of the material. "This should keep the cold out well enough," he said.

"Mm." Hector was unconvinced and reached into the locker for his ancient oilskins. With long familiarity he stepped into a ragged pair of trousers and tied an equally shabby coat around himself with a length of cord.

"Well, all ready?" he said.

A moment's careful adjustment and the motor shuddered into life, freezing though the night was. For a moment it faltered, another tiny adjustment, and it settled to a fast throb. Clouds of white vapour puttered from the exhaust. "Good old girl." Hector replaced the engine cowling and patted it. "Just give her a minute or two to warm up."

Hand over hand Murdo pulled the heavy boat through the water until he reached the little buoy to which she was moored. At a word from Hector he cast off and hauled the dripping line aboard, his fingers aching with the cold. As the end flicked in, scattering a shower of drops across his face, Hector slipped the engine into gear and moved the throttle forward. The motor throbbed into low power. Moving from the anchorage they slid slowly through the rocky channel and out into the swelling waters of the bay.

Thirty minutes later they were heading west on the twelve mile haul from Strathy Point to the island. The waves blew on to the starboard beam and they rolled a little in the troughs. The swell was slight, but now the *Lobster Boy* rose and fell as well, a pitching, yawing movement, perfect for making the landsman clutch his stomach and hang his head over the water.

They rarely spoke. Sitting a companionable arm's length from Murdo, Hector placidly puffed his pipe and occasional wafts of rich smoke came to the boy's nostrils, mixed with fumes from the exhaust. At the other side of the engine, Mr Smith pulled his collar close and pressed his feet against the metal casing to try to find a little warmth.

As they crossed the western bays the land sank into the sea. The coast was dark, lit only by the stars and the moon on the port bow. Every now and again a pinpoint of light shone out where someone had failed to observe the blackout restrictions.

"Keep her head out a bit," Hector said. "You're heading for Eilean Neave. See that big crag there, on the right?" Murdo nodded. "Craig Dubh — nasty wave-bounce if there's a sea running. Coming in this way you want it about half a mile to port. Island Roan's always further out than you think."

Murdo swung the boat's head a point to starboard and lined it up against a star. The dark bulk of Island Roan loomed beneath, a night monster heaving itself infinitely slowly from the sea. He glanced down and checked the compass heading.

"West by north?" Hector said.

"Magnetic?" Murdo watched the compass card for a few moments. "Threequarters north," he said with a smile.

Craig Dubh and Eilean Neave drew abeam and fell astern. Murdo re-aligned the boat's head on the middle of the dark island that slowly climbed up the wall of sky ahead.

As they drew close Hector pointed to what seemed a nick in the battery of sheer cliffs that faced the sea, and a few minutes later they were heading in. Murdo passed the tiller to Hector and leaned forward, throttling back the engine to half revs.

Hector glanced critically at the height of the tide on the barnacled rocks and swung his boat neatly around a patch of tangle and surge at the entrance to the channel. The cliffs drew ever closer, towering above them so that as they reached the gap Murdo had to crane back his neck to see the sky above them. The moon was blotted out and it was dark. The water swelled against the crags with an oily menace. Then they were through and chugging across the moonlit levels of Candle Bay.

It was a small bay, ringed by steep rocky slopes. A little shingle beach lay at the head. Murdo throttled back still further until the boat was barely under way. Small ripples spread from the bow. Hector swung the *Lobster Boy* in a tight circle to starboard and headed straight towards the base of a precipitous spur a little to the left of the bay entrance. When it seemed they must surely strike the crag and damage the boat, a pale glimmer of starlight appeared ahead through a hole in the rock face.

"Stop the engine," Hector said.

Murdo pushed the throttle right back, threw the engine out of gear, and switched off. The sudden silence clapped about their ears: then they heard the musical lap of waves under the bow, the murmur of the sea on the rocks, the complaints of a disturbed sea-bird on the cliffs high above them.

Slowly the boat drifted into a long dark fissure. Using their finger tips, all three guided her through. A minute later they slid out of the other side into a big rock pool protected from the sea by a wilderness of shore rocks. As they reached the middle, Hector dropped the anchor over the side.

"Fender, Murdo," he said.

Murdo slung the two half motor-bike tyres over the side on their ropes, and took up the end of the painter. Gently they bumped. He sprang out on to a surprising concrete jetty built along the rocks.

Hector held the boat alongside while Mr Smith climbed out, then stepped ashore himself.

"There's a ring over there." He pointed.

Murdo pulled the boat to the anchor and secured the painter to the heavy iron ring set in a corner of the jetty. The tide was coming in so he left a little slack.

46

Hector pulled a watch from his inside pocket. "Two hours," he said. "Not bad going. I thought it would take all of that."

He led the way to a small platform-jetty built on the seaward side of the rocks, at the precipitous entrance to the bay. From it a long flight of steps climbed steeply up the crest of a ridge to the top of the cliffs.

"I'll go first," Hector said. "I know the path. Don't use your torches. And don't rely on the handrail." He looked past Henry Smith to the boy. "You hear, Murdo?"

A hundred times more sure-footed, Murdo smiled in the darkness. "Aye," he said.

Soon they were high above the sea. Murdo, who brought up the rear, paused to look back. The crag fell sheer away on either hand. He kicked a loose stone over the edge from one of the crumbling steps. Several seconds later it hit the water with a loud splash, too close to the boat for comfort.

At length, blowing noisily, they came to the top of the cliffs and rested for a moment. The view from the open sea to the shadowy mainland was breathtaking. But the cold air chilled their brows and soon they set off again. As they walked across the rolling pasture and patches of heather, the frozen stems rustled beneath their feet.

The houses were widely scattered, and from a distance seemed in good repair. When they came close, however, it was apparent that already the northern gales were beginning their work of destruction. Windows had fallen, frosty roofs showed black gaps where slates were missing, a door hung lopsided on one hinge.

"You can tell it's deserted," Murdo said. "You can feel it."

"Aye, it's a sad sort of place now," Hector agreed.

A few minutes' walk brought them to the door of the old school, with the schoolhouse adjoining, a simple stone building surrounded by grass and a tumbling wall. For a moment they paused on the threshold. There was a noise of men's voices from within, then voices raised in anger, and a crash as if something had been knocked over.

47

Impetuously Henry Smith knocked three times on the door, and called in a loud authoritative voice.

There was silence. Murdo shifted uneasily and looked at Hector, then across the island to a rocky outcrop beyond the empty crofts. Nothing moved. He turned back to the dark door. Suddenly the silence was threatening: the deserted school was not what Mr Smith had led them to believe. He pushed his hands through the side slits of his oilskins into warm trouser pockets and drew a deep breath.

Henry Smith stamped his frozen feet and coughed. He called a second time, his voice modulated and more like that which Murdo recognised.

A moment later there was the sound of footsteps on bare boards, and a lantern glimmered briefly through a window in the hallway. A bolt rattled, and the door opened a fraction. The fair head of a young man appeared in the gap, but his eyes were not accustomed to the dark and he could not see who stood outside.

"Who is it?" he said softly.

"It's me — Henry." The Englishman pushed against the door, but it opened no further. "Come on, Peter. Let us in."

"I can't see you. Shine a light on your face."

Henry Smith did as he was told and the door opened a little wider.

"Who's that with you?"

"Friends, Peter, friends! They've come to help. Let us in."

The door closed again. There was a murmur of voices in the passage, and hurrying footsteps. Then the door was flung wide. A blond giant of a man stood on the threshold, his face beaming with pleasure.

"Henry!" he cried. "Hello! It's damn nice to see you. Come in." He sniffed harshly and touched the back of a hand to his lip.

"Hello, Bjorn," Henry Smith said with a smile. "How are you all doing?"

"Fine, fine," the big man said. "Sick of the damn bully beef."

They filed past him into the small school porch. The children's pegs were hung with an assortment of men's winter clothing. He closed the outer door and turned to the door into the school room which stood ajar.

Henry Smith laid a restraining hand on his sleeve. "Before we go in; everything *is* all right?"

"You see. I say nothing. You see for yourself."

He seemed a nice fellow, Murdo thought. He was quite young, in his early twenties. Beneath his checked shirt you could see the shoulders on him like an ox. Half turning away from them he put a hand to his trouser pocket and produced a handkerchief, pretending to blow his nose, but wiping his mouth. As he took the handkerchief away Murdo saw a red smear of blood upon it. In the light that came from the doorway, Murdo saw a dark split down the middle of his lower lip.

The room they entered had once been the old schoolroom. It was the full size of the outer building and brightly lit with oil lamps. It seemed to be full of men, though when Murdo came to count them there were, in fact, only nine. Most were fair and they were young, probably none over the age of thirty-five. At the far side of the room a splendid fire roared up the metal chimney of the old pot-bellied stove with a huge pile of sawn-up fence posts and driftwood beside it. A number of bed-rolls lay around the walls, and beside each a large rucksack and a few personal belongings gathered tidily together. Two school tables stood in the middle of the room, set round with an assortment of half-broken chairs and fish-box stools. A few ancient desks, deeply carved and inky, were scattered about like occasional tables, and strewn with an assortment of mugs and books and garments casually thrown down. Someone had found a handful of coloured chalks and the mouldy blackboard glowed with a beautifully executed yacht race. The large schoolroom windows were thickly blanketed with sheets of cardboard and heavy blackout curtains.

Murdo looked round for some sign of what had been overturned, but whatever it was it had been straightened again.

49

All he noticed was a large wet patch on the floorboards against one wall where it looked as though a mug of tea had been knocked over and hastily mopped up. A few brown drops still trickled down the green paintwork. Although the men were all smiling and talking at once, an atmosphere of tension lingered in the air.

They clustered about Mr Smith, asking a hundred questions.

"Give me a minute," he cried after a while, raising his pink but now slightly oil-streaked hands in the air. "Give me a minute. It's been a long, cold journey, and I want a cup of something hot." He looked over at Hector and Murdo. "And I'm sure they do as well."

"Sure," big Bjorn said. "What you want? Soup? Real coffee? English tea?"

Hector's sharp eyes spotted a tin of condensed milk in the middle of the table. Some of his old naval habits remained.

"Cocoa?" he asked.

"Of course." Bjorn turned to Murdo.

"Cocoa," he said, though in fact he did not like it and would have preferred tea or soup. The peculiar situation and the presence of so many strangers were a bit over-whelming.

"Cocoas all round, then," Henry Smith said.

Bjorn nodded and crossed the floor to one of the broad schoolroom window-sills where a couple of primus stoves stood amidst a confusion of saucepans. He busied himself with a bottle of methylated spirits.

"Well, that's Bjorn, Bjorn Larvik," Henry Smith said, perching himself on the corner of an old school desk and taking charge. "Now, let me introduce you all. This is Mr Gunn and Murdo Mackay. He's got a fine boat, the *Lobster Boy*. I think we might all be working together."

Hector stood near the door and gazed pleasantly around the group. Murdo, at his side, was very aware of the eyes upon him and unsure how to react. He brushed the troublesome hanks of hair from his face and looked back at them without smiling, his eyes very black.

Mr Smith continued the introductions. "Now, our friends from the Thörsen works in Stavanger: Dag ... Sigurd ... Gunner ..." He nodded towards each man as he was named. "Arne ... Peter — you met him already at the door ... Knut ... and Haakon."

They seemed a good-natured crowd of men. Though some were watchful, they were obviously pleased to meet the two Highlanders.

One man stood apart from the others, leaning against the wall and gazing morosely and half contemptuously at the back of Henry Smith's head. He was dark, thick-set, with a heavy brooding face, and made no effort to conceal his apparent dislike of the two Scots — indeed everyone in the room. One side of his face was flushed and there was a dark swollen mark on his cheek-bone, as though he had recently been struck.

Henry Smith was counting. "Eight," he said. "We seem to have lost someone." Then he turned and confronted the black-browed face behind him. "Oh, yes." His voice took on a dry edge. "Carl Voss."

The solitary man's shoulders stirred and his head moved a fraction in a cold acknowledgement of the introduction.

Bjorn crossed the room with three mugs of black cocoa. He wedged a book under the lid of a desk to make it level and set them on top, with the sticky tin of condensed milk and a jam-jar of sugar, stained with drips. They helped themselves.

Murdo found himself a seat on a bench against the wall beside the big stove. He wrapped his hands about the scalding mug. Following Hector's example he had taken a good pour of the condensed milk and plenty of sugar. To his surprise the cocoa was delicious, thick and creamy and sweet, very different from the thin brown liquid prepared by his aunt. Bjorn passed him a big biscuit tin and pressed him to take a handful. He accepted two.

Most of the men gathered about Henry Smith and Hector. Murdo sat back and watched them. For a while the conversation ebbed and flowed, and Murdo found himself trying to discover just what it was that made the Norwegians different from other men he knew of the same age. It was not the way they spoke or behaved, there was something about their faces that was different. They seemed fresher, more open and alert.

As he listened and watched, two things struck him which he was unable to explain. The first was how disinclined to talk about the war they seemed to be. Every man he knew talked about the war; but here, whenever the subject was mentioned, they began to talk about something else. It seemed a bit odd, when they had just left their homes and country because of the German occupation. Evidently they kept up with the news, however, for a grey steel radio stood on one of the broad window-sills.

The second thing that puzzled him was the excellent English they spoke. Indeed they all, with the possible exception of Bjorn, spoke with hardly the trace of an accent. As he listened, it occurred to him that in a strange way they spoke rather like Mr Smith himself, though of course his English public school voice was very distinctive.

It seemed a bit rude to ask about it, but finally he turned to Haakon, a heavy and prematurely balding man, who sat close beside him on a tiny infant's chair, gazing into the open stove.

"How is it everybody speaks such good English?" He had not intended the question to be quite so direct.

Haakon shrugged and thought for a moment. "I suppose it's the work," he said. "We meet a lot of people, and most us have stayed in Britain for a while, I was at your university in Cambridge for three years."

Murdo sipped his cocoa. "Everyone seems to know Mr Smith very well," he said. "I thought he just arranged for you all to come over."

"No. He crossed to Norway himself with the Resistance to make the arrangements. He won't say very much about it. The family he was staying with were taken away by the Gestapo."

"He never even mentioned it," Murdo said.

Again Haakon shrugged. Shortly he joined a group chatting to Henry Smith at the far side of the room. Murdo watched them for a while and saw two pairs of eyes turn in his direction.

He leaned forward and scorched his legs and face in the heat of the stove.

Henry Smith heaved himself to his feet and stretched his legs. "Right. Which way do we go?"

The man named Gunner lifted a lantern from a hook and handed it to him. "Through the house," he said, "and upstairs."

Murdo saw that a small smile hovered about Gunner's mouth, as at some private joke. He did not like it and it made him uneasy.

The door into the schoolhouse was at the far end of the room. Murdo followed Mr Smith and Hector out of the light and warmth and into the chill hallway. As they paused at a peeling door, two Norwegians following behind bumped into Murdo and they all jostled forward.

The room they entered was stacked to the ceiling with wooden crates and boxes. There seemed to be tons of them. Murdo whistled to himself at the thought of carrying some of the larger crates down the cliff steps.

The second door opened into a cupboard, but the next revealed a room like the first, only larger, stacked to the roof. Henry Smith gazed from the cases to Hector's face, to see what he thought.

"The rest are upstairs," Gunner said.

Henry Smith led the way up the steep stairs. A dozen cases stood on the landing, and fifteen or twenty were stacked against the back wall of what must have been the main bedroom of the schoolhouse.

"And that's the lot," Gunner said.

Hector took a deep breath and wrinkled his brow. "Mm," he said thoughtfully.

"What do you think?" Henry Smith said.

"Hard to say," Hector replied. "Ten loads perhaps?" He took the end of a case and lifted it a few inches to test the weight. "If they're all as light as this there should be no trouble."

Henry Smith smiled. "I'm afraid they're not. Some of them are rather heavy." He crossed to a small box only about eighteen inches square, which stood on a long crate near the window. He put his arms about it, settled his legs, and lifted. His muscles strained, and then the box was in the air, but clearly it was very heavy.

He put it down again and dusted his hands to remove some clinging dirt. Then he reached into the side pocket of his tweed trousers and pulled out a small metal lever.

"Better let you see what's in them," he said. "If I was in your place I'd be wanting some kind of reassurance." He shifted the lantern to give himself better light, and began to prise the boards from the top of a case that stood conveniently at hand.

While he was busy, Murdo went over to the small box near the window and tried to lift it for himself. To his surprise, as he took the box in his strong hands, it hardly moved at all. He set himself more firmly, grasped the rough edges, and heaved upwards. Slowly the box came up until he clutched it against his chest. It was very heavy indeed. Carefully he set it down again. At the far side of the lantern, big Bjorn saw him and smiled. Murdo, who knew that he was quite strong for his age, looked across at the busy figure of Henry Smith. There was more power in those pink hands and that tweed-clad body than he had thought.

Once the binding wire was removed, the boards came off surprisingly easy. Carefully Henry Smith laid the silver nails and wooden planks to one side. Then he was tumbling wood shavings to the floor as he lifted out a long object, wrapped in brown wax-paper. Moving the men backwards to get better light, he carefully folded back the paper to reveal a gleaming, steel-blue metal arm. Three long diagonal whorls of bronze teeth were set near the head, and at the foot a complex series of cams and two white metal inlays for ball-bearing races. It was beautifully finished and polished to a satin smoothness. A film of fine oil glistened down the shaft as he turned it in his hands.

"Well, it doesn't mean a thing to me," said Hector, passing a rough finger down it. "I know a bit about engines, but I've seen nothing like this before."

"It's a new design," Henry Smith said, gently laying the arm back in its crate of shavings. "The principles are entirely different." He pulled the lever from his pocket again and turned to one of the smaller cases. "I think this will be a cooling block, or valves."

"It's all right," Hector said, shaking his head as the first board splintered slightly, and a nail tinkled to the floor. "Don't bother. I've seen all I want."

"You're sure?" Henry Smith looked up, his gold-rimmed spectacles flashing in the lamplight. "It'll only take a minute."

Hector looked around the room and through the door to the head of the stairs. The murmur of the men's voices drifted from below and there was a short, sharp burst of laughter. Someone was playing a happy little tune on a tin flute.

Henry Smith stood back from the case, "It will do, then? You're satisfied?"

"I think so," Hector replied.

"It's a deal?"

Hector glanced at Murdo and raised his eyebrows. He smiled ruefully. "I suppose so."

Delighted, Henry Smith clapped him on the arm and his face lit up with pleasure. Leaving the cases as they were he raised the lantern high to give them light, and they filed out on to the bare landing.

After the icy chill of the house, the schoolroom was aglow with warmth and light and friendliness. The Norwegians' eyes turned expectantly towards them as they walked in the door. The smile on Henry Smith's face told them all they needed to know.

"It is fixed," he said jubilantly. "We move on. We have our crossing to the mainland."

Their eyes turned to the stocky old seaman and the boy who stood behind him.

"I think this calls for a drink." Henry Smith reached into his jacket pocket and produced a half bottle of whisky, roughly corked, with the label half picked away. "Here, Bjorn, pass over a few mugs."

Bjorn and the man named Dag, a small, red-haired, happy fellow, with a silver flute sticking out of his shirt pocket, carried two clusters of mugs across to a basin and came back with them dripping clear drops on to the bare boards of the schoolroom. They laid them on top of the levelled desk and Henry Smith poured a generous tot into each, emptying the bottle. He tossed it into an old fish box full of rubbish, and the men gathered round, reaching for the wet mugs. Only Carl Voss did not join the throng, but crossed to a chair beside his bed roll and took out a knife, trimming his nails and watching them sardonically. Henry Smith regarded him for a moment, and imperceptibly the expression on his face changed. His lips narrowed, his nostrils flared, a shadow passed across his pale eyes. He decided, for the moment at least, to ignore the man. Turning back to the crowd around him, he raised a chipped mug.

"A toast! Calm seas and may our good luck continue." The men drank, gasping as the fiery Orkney spirit reached their throats.

Hector opened his jacket and consulted an ancient pocket watch on which the silver casing had long since faded to brass. "It's — quarter to one. If you want a load taking over tonight, that's fine with me. We might as well, since we're here. But I want to get *Lobster Boy* out of the pool soon. If we don't we'll be here for the night."

"I don't see why we shouldn't," said Henry Smith.

He looked questioningly at the tall, thin man named Knut. He was a striking figure with very fair hair and a dark curly beard. His nose was a mere button in the pale Nordic face.

"You can be ready?"

"Any time," Knut said. "Five minutes to change, that's all."

"Knut will be coming with us as guard," Henry Smith explained.

Hector nodded.

"Good. Well, then; if you'll all get ready, we can start taking some of the cases down to the shore." The Englishman smiled wryly. "At least it will be easier than carrying them up." He began buttoning his heavy coat and turned up the fur collar.

Those Norwegians who had not finished their drinks tossed them back and crossed to their bed-rolls and rucksacks. In a couple of minutes they were ready. At the far end of the room Knut had pulled off his sweater and was carefully unfolding a set of neat black clothes. Murdo saw the glint of gold. It looked to him like a uniform.

Ten minutes later they were on their way. Murdo shifted the heavy box on his shoulder so that the sharp edge did not come against the bone. Before and behind him a line of men, shouldering and clasping similar boxes, stumbled across the rough heathery ground towards the cliff top. Murdo was not at all sure he would be able to manage his case down the steps when they came to them. He imagined clutching the wobbly rail for balance; felt it lurch out under his weight. He thought of the sickening drop to the rocks — at the very least his priceless case falling to destruction in an avalanche of stone, box-wood and twisted metal; or landing in the sea with a splash, and sinking.

In the outcome, no-one suffered any mishap, and a few minutes later they all stood safely on the little concrete jetty by the pool. Dag was the last man down. He laid his case on top of the others and wiped a trembling hand across his forehead.

"Dear God," he said, and sat on one of the boxes with his head in his hand. Then he shrugged his shoulders to loosen the shirt that was sticking to him with sweat.

Murdo did the same, and ran a dry tongue around his lips. There were not enough boxes yet to make a load, they would have to go back for more. He closed his eyes for a moment at the thought, but said nothing.

A hand fell on his shoulder and he looked up to see Bjorn smiling down at him. He raised his eyebrows and smiled back.

"Right." Hector took charge. "Let's not waste too much time. You leave the cases there. Murdo and I will load them into the boat."

Raggedly the Norwegians crossed the rocks and began to climb the shadowy path once more. Henry Smith looked briefly and pointedly at the man called Arne, then turned away towards the steps with the others. Murdo was surprised, he would not have expected him to negotiate the steep path a second time when it was unnecessary. Already many things were puzzling him about Mr Smith.

They passed from sight. Arne alone remained by the pool. He was slightly built and so fair as to be almost an albino, with cropped hair and red rims to his eyes.

Hector addressed him. "It's all right," he said. "Murdo and I can manage. You give the others a hand."

"No, I'll stay and help you," Arne said. He slid one of the crates nearer to the edge of the jetty.

"As you like," Hector said.

Murdo pulled the boat from her mooring and tied her up alongside. It was the work of only a few minutes to pass the cases across and stack them neatly on the bottom boards.

Arne was not disposed to talk. When they had finished he sat on a corner of the jetty and smoked a cigarette, sheltered from the wind by a projecting rock and looking over the moonlit sea.

The men were soon back, and after four of the Norwegians had made a third trip the boat was full. Murdo spread a tarpaulin over the boxes and lashed it in place.

Hector checked his boat's level in the water. "She'll do fine at that today. Not much freeboard, but the sea's calm enough." He looked up at Henry Smith. "Murdo and I will take her through the passage and pick you up at the other jetty. It's going to be a bit of a squeeze."

"I'll come with you, if it's all the same," Henry Smith said.

Hector shrugged. "Come if you want," he said. "Do you expect us to go off and leave you?"

"You could." Henry Smith stepped neatly aboard and seated himself amidships. He looked up at the men on the jetty.

"Knut," he said.

The Norwegian who was going to act as guard at the cave stepped forward. He had removed a long parka, and now it was revealed that he had changed into the uniform of a British naval sub-lieutenant. A white scarf hung about his neck and he carried a navy-blue duffle coat over one arm. With his dark

58

beard and erect, easy bearing, he looked every inch the young officer.

"We'll pick you up at the far jetty," Henry Smith said.

Hector looked coldly at the uniform. Distaste welled up in him.

"Does he have to wear that?" he said.

"I think it's a good idea," Henry Smith answered. "Just in case someone strays down to the cave."

"I told you, nobody will."

"You can't be that sure."

"What if it's the police?"

"He has documents," Henry Smith replied smoothly.

"Where did you get that uniform?" Hector said to the young Norwegian.

Knut shook his head.

"What does it matter where he got it?" Henry Smith broke in impatiently. "He stole it! The captain who brought them over had a spare one! It doesn't matter! I told you, everything's arranged — it's all been worked out."

Again there was silence. Two of the men on the jetty shifted their feet against the cold.

"Well, I don't like it," Hector said.

Murdo pulled a hard end of rope straight. "What boat was it," he asked, "you came over on?" The question had been in his mind all evening.

Henry Smith smiled and shook his head. "Sorry," he said.

Murdo looked down again and toyed with the end of rope.

"Well, if he's coming anyway, he might as well get in now," Hector said at last. "Four's the same as three. Maybe keep us a bit lower in the water when we go through."

Knut, who had listened in silence, swung his rucksack and bed-roll to Murdo and climbed into the boat.

"Move for'ard a bit," Hector said. "We'll have to use the oars."

The two passengers shifted towards Murdo in the bows.

"All right, then," Hector said. "Let's away. Throw down the ropes will you."

In a moment they were gliding through the channel, crouching as the ragged roof slipped past their heads. A little way along the bow struck a particularly low fang of rock and the boat jarred to a halt with a little splintering crack, which swung them sideways so that the stern struck as well.

Hector handed Knut a box of matches. "Here, give us a bit of light."

It was eerie in the dim orange light of the match; the black water slurping on the barnacled rocks, the jutting roof so close above the gunwale of the boat.

Two minutes later they were chugging beneath the towering crags that curved like pincers about the narrow entrance of the bay. The shadowy group of men on the rocks waved as they drew past. Then Hector pushed the throttle wide and the engine note picked up. The little boat surged forward, heading once more for the open sea.

The journey back seemed shorter than the trip out. Soon Island Roan had sunk to a dark shadow against the glittering sea behind them. They seemed perpetually to be heading into the darkness. The wind had shifted slightly and now blew straight into their faces from the north-east, from the snowfields of northern Europe. It was witheringly cold. With the added weight of cargo the boat swung less. Unaccustomed to such a load, Murdo felt her driving through the waves rather than riding lightly above them, as she had done on the way out. But the *Lobster Boy* made good speed, and almost before he was ready for it Strathy Point was looming up ahead, the blinded lighthouse squat above the cliffs. Well clear of the sucking rocks he rounded it to starboard. Twenty minutes later the thin white line of the beach was rising to meet them.

The flooding tide was nearly to the stacks. They landed the boxes on the upper beach, and while Hector took his boat round to the anchorage, Murdo and the two men carried them up to the cave. The sand was very trampled, a broad path from the sea's edge to the cliff, but already in the backwash of the waves their tracks were obliterated. Long before morning the night tide would have washed the beach smooth again. It occurred to Murdo that even when they were making two trips a night and arriving home shortly before dawn, this would still be the case. He remarked on it to Mr Smith.

"Yes, we are very lucky with the tides," he said. "I confess that was something we —" he bit the word back "— that I did not take properly into account. We have the guard — but still, it could have been important."

Within half an hour of landing, the boxes were neatly stacked away on the ledge. Knut spread a sheet of heavy waterproof canvas by the tumble of boulders at the inner end of the chamber, and laid out his bed-roll.

"Seven o'clock tomorrow, then," Henry Smith said to him.

Knut pulled on his cigarette and nodded, accompanying them to the mouth of the cave.

The cars were thick with frost. With the palms of his hands Murdo melted a small patch on Hector's windscreen and rubbed it dry with a rag. Henry Smith watched him, resting an arm on the roof of the car.

"Well, that's the first load," he said cheerfully to Hector. "I thought it went off very well."

"Aye, it went all right," Hector said.

Henry Smith reached into his inside pocket and pulled out a wallet. He counted out some notes and passed them across. Hector counted them for himself and pushed them into his back pocket.

"Thank you very much."

"And the same to come again when the job's finished."

"Aye." Hector climbed into the driving seat.

"I'll see you tomorrow, then. At the cave — seven o'clock."

The car was hard to start. After eight or ten shots with the button, Hector reached back for the starting handle on the back seat. A few vigorous cranks and the engine sprang into life, shuddering violently.

Stormy Seas

The fine weather continued. The following night — it was Friday — they made two trips, and the night after they made two more. The Norwegians had the cases ready by the jetty at the entrance to the bay. As they were loaded the *Lobster Boy* rose and fell beneath the cliffs, sheltered from the Atlantic swell. They kept to schedule, four and a half hours for the round trip, with a break of thirty minutes between midnight and one for a mug of hot soup prepared by Knut. The moon set shortly before they arrived home. It was six o'clock in the morning.

On the fourth night, however, Hector had refused to go out. There was heated argument. As they prepared to cast off for the last run home in the early hours of Sunday morning, the old man resolutely shook his head. Henry Smith's face was dark, he was unused to being thwarted. The men on the jetty leaned forward, but Hector was quite impervious to their pleas.

"No, it's no good going on. We've been out three nights running, and it's the Sabbath. That's it till Monday. I never went to sea on the Sabbath all my life —" he sniffed "— well, not very often; and the sea's been good to me. I'm not starting now. No — no! It can blow a hurricane on Monday if it likes, but I'm still not coming out. Besides —" even in the lamplight he could see the tiredness on Murdo's face "— the boy needs a night in his bed. We all do."

There was unconscious prophecy in his words, for on Monday the weather, which had been so fair, changed. The barometer fell. The wind moved around into the east and soft grey clouds began to roll up out of that quarter. All day the frost did not yield. Dry, icy reeds clattered as the wind swept, strengthening, over the moorland bogs. The ice-fringed lochs, which had rippled and glinted in the winter sunshine, now turned steel-grey, ruffled and blown into small waves like minature seas. The hills, where the dead bracken had glowed russet in the sunshine, turned their fires off and hunched forbidding shoulders against the clouds. Shepherds ranged the hills with dogs, bringing in stragglers to join their flocks in the fields, where they could be watched and fed when the snow came. The sheep huddled for warmth in the lee of stone dykes and under peat banks. Men and women came indoors gladly, rubbing their hands and shivering, to the fires.

But the sea held its legacy of fine weather, and on Monday night Hector, Murdo and Henry Smith were able to make the two trips. The sea was beginning to rise, however, and the boat sheered and fell in the troughs of the waves as she chugged across the miles of open water between Strathy Point and the island.

It was on the last run home that the snow began to fall, blind flakes that struck softly on their faces like a hundred tiny paws, pattering over cheeks and lips and eyes, icy and tickling. The shore disappeared. Hector made his way to the for'ard locker and produced the lantern. When it was lit he set it in a bracket by the compass, adjusted a rough shade, and took the tiller from Murdo. Murdo, in Hector's place on the side bench, shook his arm and the settling snow fell in a flurry to the bottom boards. It was not lying there yet because of the dried salt spray. But by and by the salt was washed clear and the snow began to settle and gather in corners and crevices. On top of the boxes it lay from the start, and soon a half inch layer covered the tarpaulin.

By the time Hector swung to starboard around Strathy Point, the whole boat, with its occupants, was mantled in white.

Knut had set a guiding lantern on the beach, hidden from the village by a wall of damp sand. As the boat ran in they saw the spark of light in the swirling darkness. It was dead ahead.

It was a relief when the last case was carried up the beach and stacked away on the shelf. Leaving Henry Smith and Knut talking in the cave, beneath what now was an impressive pile of crates, Murdo and Hector trudged wearily up the dunes and home.

Murdo was too tired to wait for tea and took a rough jam sandwich up to bed with him. But within ten minutes of entering the house he was sound asleep, the bread half-eaten on the chair beside his bed.

Twenty minutes later, on his own way to bed, Hector knocked softly and pushed open the door. Murdo had fallen asleep with the candle still burning. He was dead to the world and looked very young. With troubled eyes Hector regarded him and thought of the strange life the boy was presently leading. An arm lay outside the bedclothes, the blankets had fallen from his shoulder. Hector hesitated, then left him as he lay and blew out the candle.

While Murdo slept the snow swept on, settling, always settling over the wild landscape. For a while before dawn, the wind rose fiercely, a precursor of what was to come, rushing under eaves, singing its wild arctic tune in the wires and fences. A pale gloom displaced the darkness of night. Straggling herds of deer made their way down from the hills. Daylight came, struggling through the clouds and thick air, revealing dykes plastered on one face and capped with six inches of snow. Roads were white plains between flawless embankments, blocked on the exposed heights and at field gates by slanting snow wreaths. Black lochs appeared bottomless, rivers wound their inky paths from somewhere beyond. In the glens and along the coast the jumbled fields resolved into simple patterns, outlined in the contours of walls and black splinters of fence posts.

By eleven o'clock the snow had stopped and the skies cleared, but the sun brought no warmth. The landscape glittered and the snow did not melt. The hills cast blue shadows in the low winter sunlight, and beneath the pale sky the sea was a dark misty blue.

When Hector woke at midday the first thing he noticed was the unaccustomed brightness of his room. A strip of diffused light spread across the ceiling. He grunted, remembering the snow, peered at his ancient watch on a nail at the head of his bed, and turned to the window. Like Murdo, he rarely closed the curtains and it was dazzling. There had been a good fall, the snow was weighing heavy on the heather. Beyond the headland he could see white horses, suggesting a blow of force six or seven. He listened to the sigh of the wind around the house and caught the faint keening in the landing skylight — force seven most like. He reached for a packet of Woodbines: it was the only time of the day he liked a cigarette, first thing in the morning before he got up.

The snow was beautiful. With a romantic eye Hector appreciated it; as a countryman it disgusted him. He gazed at the wintry scene and wondered how long it would last. Gradually as the new day swam more fully into focus, he became aware of an occasional swishing, scraping sound from outside. He could not place it. Intrigued, he swung his feet to the bedside mat and reached for an old coat which served as a dressing gown. Tying the cord at his waist he crossed to the window.

Murdo was nearing the top of a rough knoll at the side of the house with an old tin tray in his hand. He dropped it on the snow, settled the toorie on his wild hair, sat on the tray and launched himself at the steepest part of the slope. Legs and arms flying he shot down, slewing wildly out of control bucking over boulders and little cliffs, finally tumbling and careering head over heels to the bottom. He sat up smothered in snow, brushed himself down and rescued the tray from wilderness of whin bushes. Earlier tracks showed where he had started on more gentle slopes.

Hector was pleased to see him enjoying himself. He pushed open the window. A ledge of snow whirled in and sifted to the bedroom floor.

66

"Have you had breakfast?"

Murdo looked up, his face glowing, and nodded vigorously.

"Well I'll make dinner for two o'clock. All right? Don't be late."

"Right. What time is it now?"

"Just on twelve."

Murdo raised a hand and returned to the top of the knoll.

Because of the bad early conditions and the fact that many children had a good distance to travel, school had been cancelled for the day. Murdo saw boys sledging on the main hill at the far side of the village. Tucking the tray beneath his arm he went off to join them.

From his seat at the fire after lunch, Murdo could see the white waves racing up the bay. A long, low swell was beginning to surge across the rocks of the headland, sliding in from the north-east. Throughout the afternoon it worsened. Ominous clouds began to rear above the horizon.

"I doubt that's it for tonight, boy," Hector said, turning once more from the window. "It's not the sort of weather I like out there."

Murdo looked up from sharpening his father's pocket knife, seeing the dark thrusting clouds beyond Hector's silhouette. They were hostile and forbidding, and spoke of storm. The coming night was not one in which to be abroad — on the land, let alone upon the water. He had been carving a small mallard from a piece of drift-wood. Brushing the chips from his lap, he picked the matches off the dresser and put a light to the lamp.

As he did so the clock whirred into life and chimed once: half past three. Hector gazed at its fine yellow face, then down at Murdo, and once more out of the window. He was restless.

"Well," he said. "I think I'd better go down and have a word with Mr Smith. See how he feels about it."

Murdo tested the blade of the knife with the tip of a finger, and snapped it shut.

"I'll come with you," he said.

The snow had not thawed at all. As the sun declined over the snowfields they walked in blue shadow. The few cars and lorries had compressed the crystals into shining ribbons. Murdo ran along the road in his rubber boots and slid in the tracks. When he bent to make a snowball to throw at a neighbour's chimney the snow was too powdery to stick, and crumbled as he threw it. His fingers ached with the cold and he thrust his fists into the pockets of his battledress.

When they reached the inn they found that Henry Smith had been drinking. He was sitting by himself in a corner of the hotel lounge and did not see them for a moment as they came through the door. The lamp was lit and a peat fire glowed in the hearth. A small side-table stood at the arm of his chair, with a part-empty bottle of the Orkney whisky and the remains of a plate of sandwiches upon it. His hands rested in his lap, curled loosely around a glass. An inch of the golden spirit rocked slightly in the bottom as he breathed.

When he saw them he jumped to his feet. Half of the whisky splashed down his cardigan.

"Oh damn!" He brushed away the drops with his fingers and mopped it with a clean handkerchief. "Come in, come in. Do sit down." He set the glass on the table and pulled a couple of armchairs towards the fire.

They sat as they were bidden, but he remained standing. He leaned towards Hector. His face was flushed and his eyes a little clouded.

"You'll have a drink," he said. "Whisky?"

Hector shook his head. "No thanks," he said. "Not right now. I'm just after my dinner."

"Beer, then." The Englishman smiled a little tipsily. "Anything you want, so long as it's beer."

Amused to see him so, Hector smiled, but shook his head.

"Nothing at all?"

Hector gave way with a good grace. "Oh well, then. A whisky. Thank you very much. A small one."

Henry Smith went to the door and called to a lady in the private part of the inn. A minute or two later she came through

68

with a tray of coffee and an empty whisky glass. Hector and she were old friends. Unseen by the Englishman he gave her a conspiratorial wink. Briefly her eyes twinkled, though the days were long gone when the comings and goings of the incorrigible old man caused her any surprise. When she had gone, Mr Smith poured a heavy measure for Hector, and a drop into the bottom of his own glass.

"Good health," he said.

"Slàinte mhath."

Hector drank, and the Englishman tossed the last of his own whisky down his throat. His face twisted with revulsion. He pushed the glass far from him and rubbed a hand over his face.

"Where's the coffee?" he said. "I'm not used to that stuff, it's devilish."

Hector felt it burning in his stomach along with his dinner, and burped behind his fist.

"Well," he said. "What about tonight?"

Anxiously Henry Smith looked up from pouring his coffee, and glanced at the door, but it was shut.

"I don't like the look of the weather at all," Hector said. "It's fairly rough now, and it's blowing up nasty. It will be bad out there. I think it might be wise to leave it for tonight."

Henry Smith had been expecting it. He too had watched the weather deteriorating throughout the afternoon. 'If only the old fool had gone on Sunday', time and again the thought had recurred. Now he suppressed it.

"We've got two more crossings," he pleaded. "Just two small loads, and the men. If a real storm blows up it might be days before you can get over again." He removed his spectacles and rubbed his eyes, then shook his head slightly to try to clear the alcohol from his brain. "I know I'm a little drunk, but is there no chance?"

He was so anxious that Hector sighed and scratched the back of his neck. He looked at Murdo and raised his eyebrows.

"Well, I've been out in worse," he said. "If we went now we might get one load in. But I must say I don't like it."

Henry Smith nodded. "That's fair enough; we can but try. Thank you, Mr Gunn."

Hector chuckled. "Wait until we're out there. You can thank me then."

The afternoon was wearing out as they put to sea. The edge of the clouds that had been rolling westward obliterated the low-burning sun, wiping the last vestiges of colour from the landscape. All turned grey and black and white. *Lobster Boy* was very small amid the ocean of waves that poured in from the north-east. Her bows rose and fell, leaped and splashed, as she chugged steadily northwards up the bay towards the point. Icy spray whipped into their faces, and Murdo tasted the familiar salt tang on his lips.

A violent smack lurched the boat sideways and Henry Smith slithered awkwardly to the bottom boards. Dripping, he pulled himself back to his seat.

"It's not so good!" he cried.

Hector pushed the tiller across, bringing his boat back on course. "Och, she's not so bad at all here," he called above the noise of the wind and waves. "We'll do fine. We've got the sea on the bows now. It'll be a bit bouncy when we get round the point and have to turn beam-on, though."

He shrugged his head comfortable in the clumsy merchant navy life-jacket he kept at the cottage for such seas. On the side bench by the engine, Murdo also was wearing one. Hector only had the two. An old motor-bike inner tube, fastened to a lanyard, lay on the boards for Henry Smith, who had insisted on coming.

As they rounded Strathy Point it was just as Hector had said. Head-on the *Lobster Boy* might pitch, but beam-on, as she exposed her starboard flank to the waves and wind, she rolled and swung, yawed, pitched and flung her head in every direction.

Braced against the engine casing, Murdo loved every moment of it, feeling the boat leaping beneath him. His dark eyes shone as the spray lashed up and struck him with hard rattling smacks. Beneath his oilskins he remained dry and warm, save at the neck where a heavy scarf absorbed the salt water that trickled from his face.

"How do you think she'll do?" he shouted to Hector, turning his sou'wester into a heavy veil of sea-water that whipped across the boat.

"All right. She'll do all right if it gets no worse than this." Hector turned to Henry Smith. "We'll get you there, anyhow," he said cheerfully.

But there was no answer. Henry Smith had turned ashen pale. With hollow eyes he stared wretchedly at Hector, then hung his head and gave an enormous yawn.

"Not feeling too good, are you?"

He shook his head abjectly, and looked up at the water. A huge wave swept in from the near-darkness, towering above them. The little boat heaved, lurched up sideways, and slid down the far side. For an instant Mr Smith paused, then suddenly he twisted round, grabbed at the gunwale, and hung his head far out over the water. There was an ugly, coughing sound.

Murdo looked across at Hector and grinned.

With the wind behind them it took little longer than usual to reach the island. By the time they arrived Henry Smith had collapsed into a sodden bundle of misery at the lee gunwale. The tide was not yet half way in, and despite the surge of the sea it was calm enough in that sheltered corner of the bay for Hector to nurse his boat through the tunnel into the mooring pool. Murdo climbed to the jetty and Hector passed him the shaded lantern.

"Well, we're here, at least," he said a minute later, as he stood with Henry Smith watching Murdo pull the *Lobster Boy* out of her mooring in the middle of the pool. "Let's hope we get back as easily."

The Englishman stood shakily in the circle of lamplight. He wiped his lips with a handkerchief and mopped the cold sweat and sea-water from his face. A thick skein of spray rattled on the concrete at their feet.

"Get back?" he said weakly. "Through that? Heading into it?"

"Well I'm going back, anyway," Hector said positively. "I'm not sitting out a storm on this island. You're the one that wanted to come: and now we're here. So where are the cases?"

Henry Smith turned and surveyed the white water that roared across the rocks at his back, then picked up the lantern and made his way to the higher rocks at the foot of the cliff steps. The last of the crates were stacked in a sheltered cranny where even the highest waves would be unable to reach them. They were covered with a heavy tarpaulin. The top of the tarpaulin and all the rocky ledges were thick with snow.

"That's the last of them," he said.

Hector surveyed the stack briefly and sniffed. "Too much for one load in a sea like this," he said. "We might have managed a few days ago, when it was calm, but not now." He turned to Henry Smith. "So — what's it to be? Take as many as we can now, and come back for the rest later? Or do you want to take some of the men? They haven't got life-jackets, mind."

Henry Smith thought for a moment. "A mile or two off shore in a sea as cold and rough as this, I can't see a life-jacket makes all that much difference," he said. "I think we'll take some of the men. Half the cases and some of the men."

"Fair enough," said Hector. "You go up and tell them to get ready. Murdo and I will take the boxes down to the boat."

Henry Smith did not reply, but from his silence it was clear that he did not like the arrangement. He tapped Murdo on the shoulder. The boy turned back from looking at the sea.

"You go on up to the house and tell them, will you? You're more sure-footed than I am. I'll give Mr Gunn a hand with the cases."

Murdo looked to Hector for confirmation, then back to the bespectacled Englishman. He nodded.

"Remember the names," Henry Smith said. "We'll take Peter, Sigurd, Arne, and —" he paused for a moment, thinking; "— and Carl Voss. Got it?"

"Peter, Sigurd, Arne and Carl Voss," Murdo said.

"Yes. They're to put their stuff together and get themselves down here as quickly as possible."

"Right." Murdo turned to the gale-swept cliff steps.

"Watch how you go," Hector called across to him.

He nodded and started climbing. The gale was wild, rattling the oilskins about his body as he went higher. The crumbling ascent was treacherous beneath the snow and he had to feel carefully at every step, kicking his boot to the back of the tread. Once his feet skidded from under him and he fell forward, knees and toes digging in for dear life, hands grabbing at the steps to prevent himself sliding backwards. A foot went over the edge. When he began climbing again he was shaking. But he reached the top safely, and within five minutes of leaving the boat, was being blown across the crown of the island with the gale at his back.

It took only a minute to deliver Henry Smith's message, and he waited in the warmth while the men got ready. They were quick, and in less than ten minutes they were all making their way back across the island to the cliff steps and the jetty.

Hector and Henry Smith had finished their job and were sheltering behind a big rock having a smoke. They had double-lashed the tarpaulins and anchored the boxes securely to the bottom-boards and deck cleats. Tight lines ran to a for'ard thwart and the engine mounting so that they could not possibly shift.

Hector stood up as he heard them approaching. A moment later they appeared through the rocks.

"Let's get straight away, then," he said. "The sooner the better." He pushed the pipe into his jacket pocket and untied the painter.

Soon they were all sitting in the boat, the shaded lantern on the bottom boards at their feet. Its light caught Mr Smith's face, grim as he prepared for his personal ordeal of sea-sickness. He looked up at the Norwegians who were not leaving that trip, and had accompanied the others to the shore with two boxes of provisions.

"We'll be back when we can," he said. "I hoped it would be tonight, but . . ." he shrugged and held his hands out.

Little Dag, red hair blown back from his good-natured face, raised an arm in acknowledgement.

Hand over hand Murdo pulled them out to the anchor and heaved it up. Three minutes later they were heading out between the cliffs into the very teeth of the gale.

The waves broke against the crags with explosions that flung sheets of white water fifty feet into the air. In torrents it roared across the rocks. The wind had torn the lower clouds into tatters and stars danced between the dark masses of snow clouds. Ahead, where the sky was clear to the horizon, a sick orange moon heaved itself out of the sea. The ragged waves leaped up as if to pluck it down again.

Dauntlessly Hector headed his little boat straight out from the rocks into the open sea. She swung violently as the waves thudded against her planking, and the spray whipped across the faces of the passengers. The men looked anxiously from one to the other and at the old man at the tiller, sou'wester flattened over his forehead by the wind. His wrinkled eyes flicked down to the lamplit compass and back to the waste of waters ahead, never flinching in their concentration.

Murdo made his way from the bows, clinging to one of the tarpaulin lashings as they shot dizzily up and dropped like a stone down the back of a roller.

"It's too rough," he cried above the noise of the storm, his mouth close to Hector's ear. "We'll never make it around Strathy Point in this."

"You're right. But I'm not going to sit out a storm on that island for anybody." Hector ducked as a huge slice of icy water slapped over the boat, then looked up again, his oilskins streaming. "We'll put in to Farr Port."

"What are they going to say about it?"

"By the time we get to Torrisdale Bay they'll be glad to put into any port at all," Hector cried, his voice whipped astern by the wind. "We can sit the storm out well enough in Clerkhill."

Murdo settled himself securely on the lee side bench near Hector, and turned his shoulder and sou'wester into the main force of the wind. From beneath his brows he regarded the Norwegians. They looked scared and miserable, all except Carl Voss. His face hard set, he stared out over the water as though daring it to try to do him any harm. It was a dangerous face. Henry Smith was being sick, and as Murdo watched, Arne too, with the albino face, suddenly jerked convulsively and vomited into the bottom of the boat. Murdo looked away, it made him sick to see it.

"They're the ones who wanted to come," Hector said. "They'll be glad enough to put ashore in half an hour or so."

Eilean Neave crawled past, a dark shape to starboard. The cliffs dropped away, and as the moon vanished into the clouds they were completely out of sight of the land. Suddenly Murdo became aware that the atmosphere had changed. It was no longer fun. The *Lobster Boy* seemed infinitely small and frail, a nut-shell on a big and dangerous ocean. The circle of lamplight illuminated the timbers and huddled fligures like a painting. The light was comforting, yet made them more vulnerable, as if beyond its gleam, where they were, blind, dark forces were watching. Looking across, Murdo found the eyes of Carl Voss fixed like a hawk's on his own. He stared straight back for a moment, his own black eyes shining in the lamplight, then looked away over the water.

Suddenly, without any warning, a huge wave rushed in from the darkness, towering above them, with another foaming on its tail. *Lobster Boy* had no time to turn head-on and slithered sidways up the massive wall of water. For a moment she poised on the crest, then slewed down the back into the black trough. The second wave was right above them. Two men cried aloud, then all was confusion and water. Great gouts of breaking sea surged over the gunwale. The lamp was extinguished. Suddenly the boat was very heavy, wallowing.

Murdo was flung to the deck. Struggling to get up he sprawled on his back as the water they had shipped surged from side to side and end to end of the boat. For a moment he thought they were going down. A man cannoned into him. Then out of the confusion he heard Hector calling for light. He fought his way to the for'ard locker and dragged out the spare lantern. Hector was still at the tiller, struggling to keep his boat's head into the wind at half throttle. He thrust his matches into Murdo's hands. But Murdo was sodden and awkward and could hardly handle them. As he opened the box, half the matches tipped out and fell into the water. Then he managed to light one, but as he opened the lamp the match fell from his fingers and was extinguished.

"Come on, Murdo!" Hector called sharply. "Pull yourself together."

Forcing himself to be calm then, the boy turned his back into the wind and knelt in the water, holding the lantern against his stomach. Very carefully he extracted a match, closed the box, struck it, and quickly held the sputtering light to the wick. It flared. He snapped the lamp shut and adjusted the flame.

The light, casting its warm yellow rays over the boat and enabling them to see, made things much better. It was not so bad as it had seemed, they had got off lightly. Though *Lobster Boy* had shipped nearly a foot of water, they were by no means swamped. The boat was very heavy, though, and floundered up and down in the waves, making no headway. If another giant wave came they would not ride it so well; indeed, they might not ride it at all. The sooner the water was out of her and they put into harbour the better.

"Come on, Murdo," Hector called again. "The bucket. Find them something to bale with."

Soon they were all baling as hard as they were able. Murdo used the bucket, Sigurd had a tin, and Henry Smith a wooden box that poured from the seams as soon as he lifted it from the water. Carl Voss sliced himself a square of canvass from the end of the tarpaulin, and holding it by the corners was scooping up the water and tipping it over the side very efficiently. Though a good deal fell back inboard, and occasionally they shipped a little more, the level steadily fell and soon the boat was rising to the waves less sluggishly.

"Hey!" Hector beckoned to Henry Smith. "Come down here a minute."

The Englishman handed his leaking box to Peter — he seemed little more than a boy in the lamplight, with the fair hair stuck across his face — and lurched awkwardly down to Hector in the stern.

"There's a little harbour over there." Hector shouted above the noise of the engine and the gale. "As soon as we've got the water out of her I'm putting in."

Henry Smith nodded, agreeing. Fearing they might become storm-bound on the island, he had taken the precaution of telling the innkeeper's wife that he might be away for a day or two. Salt spray ran down his face.

"It's a quiet sort of place," Hector cried. "We can put up at Donald's house in Clerkhill. He's a friend of mine — away just now. The neighbours know me, there'll be no-one bothering us. Stay there for a day or so till the storm dies down a bit."

"Will the cases be safe so near to a jetty?"

"It's not that sort of harbour. Just a beach. Have to pull the boat up on the winch. It's safe enough, though. No-one goes round there much this time of year." Spray caught him across the side of the face. "Anyway, I don't see we've got much choice."

Again Henry Smith nodded his agreement.

Hector leaned back and once more gave all his concentration to the wind and waves.

Soon they were riding light, little more than a swill of water rushing about in the bottom of the boat. Hector watched the sea like a hawk. At length the long, strong roller for which he was waiting bore down upon them, towering against the sky. In one movement he flung the throttle wide and thrust the tiller hard across. The *Lobster Boy* leaped up the wave, sheered round as she fell away, and almost before the others knew it they were racing for the shore.

The waves now roared from astern with what seemed the speed of an express train, sweeping past them and rolling on ahead into the darkness. *Lobster Boy* rode them like the wonderful sea boat she was. Suddenly it was exciting again. And ten minutes later they were in calmer waters behind the sheltering rocks of Farr Point.

Henry Smith and the Norwegians, all except Carl Voss, glanced at each other with relief. Murdo had rigged the hand-pump and was ridding the boat of the last of the sea water as it drained into the bilge. He looked up at Hector, but the wrinkled face showed no more emotion than it had when the waves were leaping about them on the open sea. He knew this trick of countenance of old, and that inside Hector was as glad as he was himself to be out of the storm. He reached over with one foot and kicked him lightly on the boot. Hector looked humorously at the boy from beneath his brows, and winked conspiratorially.

In another five minutes they were turning into the small cove known as Farr Port. Sheltered by a series of high headlands from the easterly gale, the sea here was little more than moderate, a low, rolling swell that rimmed the rocks with foam. They slipped past a little concrete jetty into the inner haven of the cove itself. Huge sea cliffs rose on either hand. Ahead, in the cleft beyond the shingle beach, a narrow fishermen's path zig-zagged to the cliff tops. Glancing up at the night sky, Murdo saw that the stars had disappeared.

Hector cut the engine. For forty yards the little boat glided forward. With a gentle crunch her bows drove up the smooth pebbles of the shore and she lurched softly to a halt.

Murdo leaped out with the painter and led it up the beach. The Norwegians stood, uncertain what to do.

"Come on, everyone lend a hand," Henry Smith called, climbing down to the stones rather shakily. A wave broke roughly, swilling around his legs and making the boat rock.

They jumped ashore and gathered along the sides of the boat. As a succession of waves came in, they heaved her as far as they were able up the shore.

"There's a winch up by the path," Hector called out. "We'll be able to haul her up, but we'll need to take the boxes out first."

Peter was frozen. He clapped his arms about himself and stamped his feet to try to get the circulation going. Sigurd did the same.

Carl Voss climbed back into the boat and removed the ropes and tarpaulin from the boxes. Splashing to and fro in the shallow water, the rest carried them up the beach and made a stack a few yards from the overhanging cliff, well above high tide. When it was complete they flung the canvas over the top once more and lashed it down firmly.

While they did so, Murdo went up to the old hand winch at the foot of the path. It was covered with snow, and he had to brush it clear with a frozen hand to find the end of the wire. Having done so, and stabbed his finger painfully on a broken strand, he put the machine out of gear and walked back down the beach, heaving the wire behind him. He led a rope strop through a ring-bolt in the boat's stem-post and shackled it to the wire, then walked back to the winch.

"Give him a hand," Henry Smith called.

Peter went up to join Murdo on the winch handles, while the others gathered along the boat's gunwale. It was hard work on the handles, and soon the cold was gone from their bodies as they forced them round and the boat slowly ploughed a turtle-like track through the stones of the shelving beach. At length she was lying in the snow of the upper shore, well above the bare pebbles of the last high tide.

"That'll do," Hector called.

Panting, and smiling to each other, Murdo and Peter left off winding and joined the others by the boat. Murdo examined the bruised palms of his hands, and pushed them into the sodden pockets of his trousers, then pulled them out again.

While they were winding, the snow had started once more. Soon the air was thick with whirling flakes. The inlet closed about them. It was a bleak and a lonely place.

"I think we could all do with a warm and a cup of tea," Hector said. "It's a wee bit on the nippy side tonight." He nodded towards the steep track up the rocky cleft and started forward.

Henry Smith turned to Peter. "You stay with the cases," he said. "We'll give you a relief in a couple of hours."

Peter was shivering. Already the glow of the exercise had faded and the cold was eating into his body. He clasped icy arms about his chest and nodded.

Hector had stopped. He turned to face Henry Smith. "For heaven's sake!" he cried, exasperated. "I don't know why the boy listens to you. What on earth do you want him to stay here for? Who do you think is going to walk all the way down here in the middle of the night, in a blizzard, on the off-chance of finding thirty cases of whatever it is — machine parts." He held the lantern high so that the light fell on their wretched, bedraggled figures, the clothes clinging about them. "Good God! Look at him. He's frozen and soaked to the skin. We all are. If he stays down here for two hours he'll catch pneumonia. The lad needs a hot drink and a set of dry clothes. If it matters that much, why don't you stay yourself? They're your cases."

Henry Smith drew in the corners of his mouth and stared at the ground, then looked again at the men about him. He nodded. "All right."

Once more Hector set his face towards the fishermen's track and started forward. Obviously relieved, Peter fell in with the rest behind him.

For a moment Murdo lingered, looking back at the boat and the pile of cases, already shrouded with snow. Then he, too, set off up the steep path. Carl Voss stepped out of the shadows behind him and brought up the rear.

The Boy in the Night

The lantern swinging in Hector's hand, threw dizzy patches of light on the flanking crags, ledged with snow. Slowly the shivering chain of men plodded up behind. Though it was commonly used throughout the summer, the snow and ice made the winding patch treacherous. Murdo rested his hand against the rocky wall and waited for Sigurd, who was carrying a box of provisions, to negotiate an awkward corner.

They had climbed into the gale, buffeting and roaring above the cliffs. Murdo thrust his hands inside his oilskins and came up to Hector. A heavy lock of hair fell from under his sou'wester and flapped in his eyes. He was shivering, and cramping in his stomach with the cold.

"Watch you keep above the cliff," Hector shouted back above the noise of the wind. "The gullies cut a long way in. Keep high up."

He set off walking diagonally up the side of the hill. Murdo hunched forward and kept pace at his side. The snow whipped horizontally through the swinging circle of lamplight and plastered their sides and backs.

Ten minutes later, having climbed two stone walls and a wire fence, they arrived at the tiny cluster of houses that made up the village of Clerkhill.

81

"I'll just let the neighbours know it's me," Hector said. "They'll wonder what's happening, otherwise."

He left them sheltering in the lee of a little croft house and vanished around the corner of the barn. They were a wretched group, but thankful to be out of the wildness of the storm. Peter beat his arms against his sides and swore softly under his breath. Arne pulled the soaking, snow-covered collar of his jacket up his cropped neck, and hugged his elbows against his body for warmth. A little apart from the others, Carl Voss stood motionless, then crossed to the end of the barn and looked across the thirty yards of snow to where Hector was standing at the door of the nearest house. Murdo also went to look, standing a few feet back. The door opened and a shaft of light spread across the snow. "Hello, Chrissie," he heard Hector say, but the rest of the conversation was drowned by the wind.

A couple of minutes later the old man was back. He lifted the iron door key from a nail in the barn and led the way into the house.

"Try not to make a mess of the place," Hector said, stamping the snow from his boots and brushing it off his oilskins in the tiny passage. "You can leave your coats here. I'll get some blankets for you."

Like most seamen of the old school, Donald was very tidy. The fires were laid in the two downstairs rooms and Hector put a match to both, piling the peats high as soon as they had caught properly. In quarter of an hour they were roaring up the chimneys and starting to throw out the heat. Murdo, stripped of most his clothes and wrapped in a blanket, padded barefoot into the kitchen to make cocoa. Soon they were all roasting themselves in front of the blaze in the sitting room, scalding their tongues and throats with the thick, sweet drink. In the other room next to the kitchen, the fire was masked by a circle of sweaters and trousers, hanging from a pulley and draped over the backs of chairs. The air was thick with steam and the smell of wet wool.

To one side of the fire, half in the shadows of the tilly lamp, sat Murdo. The heat scorched his legs pleasantly as he gazed about the room. His eyes lingered on a calendar of a girl in a red swimming costume which hung beside him. Over the months he had found himself in some odd company with Hector, very odd company for a boy, but nothing remotely as strange as this. For a long time as he sat there, half-listening to the desultory conversation, his mind ran back and forth over the events of the past week. It was a real adventure. So much had happened: so much was still a mystery. If they did not contain machine parts, what *was* in the cases down there on the beach? Holding his mug in both hands he lowered his head and took a good mouthful.

Suddenly, with a shock of realisation that made him slop the cocoa on the blanket, it came to him that now, for the first time, the cases were unguarded. Piled up down there in the gully, and no-one within half a mile. How reluctant Mr Smith had been to leave them so. If only, Murdo thought, he was able to get out of the house for an hour, he could return to the shore and examine them for himself. Then he thought of the blizzard and almost dismissed the idea. He had been out in blizzards before; indeed he was just in from one, and glad to escape the wildness and cold. The audacity of the scheme appalled him, but even as he shivered with sudden nerves by the side of the fire, he knew that he would go.

Hector had seen him tremble. "Are you still cold, boy? Here, I'll make another cup of cocoa for you. Have a drop of whisky in it to warm you up."

Murdo shook his head. "I'm O.K. I'll have another cup when I've finished this."

"There's a couple of beds upstairs," Hector said. "Away up there and get yourself some sleep." He smiled. "He likes his comforts, Donald; there'll be a hot water bottle about somewhere."

Murdo nodded. "Aye. In a while."

"Not too long, then," Hector said. "Don't want you catching pneumonia."

Murdo took another drink. Forcing himself to appear casual he glanced around the circle of Norwegians. Clad in blankets, their clothes in the other room drying — surely he would be safe. Sigurd, fresh-faced, with hard blue eyes and a mop of curls growing low on his forehead, said something to Arne and laughed loudly. They were too busy talking to be bothered with a boy.

Half an hour later, when his second mug of cocoa was finished, Murdo rose to his feet and stood for a moment, yawning heavily. Hector looked up. For a fleeting second an odd, penetrating expression flickered across his weather-beaten face, but it was gone so quickly that Murdo thought it must have been his imagination.

"Donald won't mind, will he?" he said. "Me using his bed?"

"What do you think?" Hector replied. "He'd be annoyed if you didn't. Go on, get yourself away. Got a hot water bottle, have you?"

"Aye; the kettle's boiling," Murdo said.

"You know which room it is, do you?" Hector asked. "The one on the right at the top of the stairs. Along at the end of the landing."

Murdo nodded.

"Go along with you, then. There's no point you staying up half the night. Take a candle with you, we'll need the lamps here."

"Goodnight, then." Murdo blinked sleepily in the firelight, hoping he was not over-doing it.

"Sleep well."

A scatter of voices came from the Norwegians.

"He's a good boy, that." Peter's words followed him into the cold hall. Hector's reply was lost as he closed the door and padded barefoot through the living room into the kitchen. He turned off the Calor gas, and hitching the blanket securely about his waist, poured the water, still boiling, into a blue rubber hot water bottle. He would need light on the beach. He tipped a dozen matches into the palm of his hand and left the box on the table.

84

Two minutes later he had the bottle in Donald's bed and was trailing the heels of a pair of slippers, several sizes too large for him, across the lino and rugs of the cold bedroom. He set the candle on top of the chest of drawers and sat on the bed, bouncing so that they would hear it creaking in the room below. For a while he waited, feeling vaguely dissatisfied with his plan. What if they should come up and find him gone? He thought for a moment, then pulled off his vest, which had survived the worst of his soaking but was still a bit damp on the back. It could be a sign of his innocence. He carried it downstairs to the crowded sitting room.

The men had glasses now and Murdo could smell whisky in the air as he opened the door. The bottle, already threequarters empty, stood on the carpet at the side of Hector's chair. There was plenty more where that came from. If they were going to be drinking heavily, as it seemed, all the better for him.

"It's still damp." Murdo hung his vest over the back of a chair. "I'll just leave it here, the other room's full up."

A minute later he was back upstairs. Very quietly he pulled open the door of Donald's wardrobe. The scent of old tobacco wafted out at him. Other people's clothes always seemed so strange. He hunted through the hangers until he found what he wanted, a pair of really old trousers and a jacket and coat. Then he went to the chest of drawers and searched for a shirt and sweaters and socks. The drawers were stiff and it was hard to open them without making a noise. The last of the things he wanted were in the very bottom drawer. Gently he eased it shut. As he worked he could hear the voices drifting up from downstairs.

It was the work of only a couple of minutes to dress himself in the unfamiliar garments. Donald's thick shirt reached to his knees. The trousers were much too big, and he was unable to find braces or a belt. He pulled the laces from Donald's Sunday shoes and knotted them about his waist. The trousers were still too long, so he tucked the bottoms into the ankles of his socks. Then he was ready, clad like a tramp. He dropped the matches into his pocket, thought for a moment, and once more lay on the bed, shifting his weight until the frame creaked, so that they must hear him below. Then very quietly he climbed down and stuffed the blanket he had been wearing and a pillow beneath the covers to make it look as though he was sleeping.

Five minutes later, having checked that everything was as he wanted it, Murdo drew a deep breath to steady his nerves, and blew out the candle. Then, his heart still pounding, he crossed to the door and eased it open. It was very dark. A chink of light shone through the crack of the sitting room door below. The next moment he had tiptoed on to the landing and pulled the bedroom door shut behind him.

Their voices came very distinctly to him now, drifting up the black well of the staircase. They were louder, the whisky was having its effect. He paused, leaning over the bannisters. Already his eyes were becoming accustomed to the darkness and he could distinguish the outline of the front door, the staircase leading down. He crossed the landing, then breathlessly — pressing against the wall and holding hard to the bannisters to lessen his weight, stepping at the edges of the treads lest they should creak — as cautiously as a cat he crept downstairs. Near the bottom a board cracked and he froze, but no-one came. A moment later he had reached the hall. Now they were just on the other side of the door beside him. A button of his coat clicked against the bottom of the bannisters. Like a shadow he flitted through into the fire-lit living room, picked up his sea-boots from the side of the hearth, and carried them into the kitchen.

So far so good. But this was the most dangerous part. Did Donald keep his windows in good repair? Murdo pushed the kitchen door wide to give him what light there was. For a moment he listened, then quietly climbed up and knelt on the draining board beside the sink. Biting his lip, he carefully forced the catch back, took hold of the heavy little sash window, and pulled up. It did not move. He pulled again, harder. Still it stuck. He shifted slightly to get a better grip and pulled with some force. Suddenly the window shot up and jammed his fingers. The wind burst in, whirling snowflakes across the kitchen and billowing the curtains wildly. He smothered them in his arms and grabbed at a packet of washing powder that was toppling towards the floor. Alarmed, he listened, straining his ears and nursing his fingers, waiting for the noise of doors and running feet. But no sounds came from the further room save a sudden burst of laughter, hard to hear above the roaring of the gale outside.

The faster he was gone the better. Carefully Murdo replaced the washing powder on the shelf where the wind would not blow it down again, and pushed the curtains wide. Then he tossed his boots out into the night, ducked his head, and scrambled through the window after them, head-first like an eel, taking the weight on his hands then tumbling into the snow, head and shoulders buried in a drift. In a moment he was on his feet, reaching back inside to mop up the snowflakes on the draining board and pull the curtains straight. Then swiftly and quietly he pulled the window down behind him.

He could not find his boots for a moment, for they were buried in the snowdrift. But he unearthed them, tipped the snow out, brushed what snow he could from his socks and pushed his feet in. It was bitterly cold. Too late he realised that he had not brought a hat or gloves with him. Already his fingers were aching. Fumbling, he fastened the button of Donald's coat at his neck and pulled the collar up. Then plunging his hands deeply into the coat pockets and screwing up his eyes against the stinging snowflakes, he set his back to the village and trudged out on to the open hillside.

The wind buffeted Murdo in the darkness. His face ached and the driving blizzard caked his front with snow. Coming to a great black gap in the hillside, he thought he had reached the inlet already, but a few more steps revealed nothing but space, wind and darkness. He scrambled back and traversed a huge buttress of rock. His foot struck a boulder and he fell full length. Cursing under his breath, Murdo picked himself up and fought on.

Two minutes later the ground fell away again and the roar of the sea mingled with the wind from the black emptiness below.

This was the right gully. Soon Murdo was feeling his way down the treacherous path a step at a time, steadying himself against the rock face as he descended. It was a relief to be out of the force of the wind. The tide had retreated, but the sea sounded far more violent that it had been two and a half hours earlier. The huge, rolling waves poured into the neck of the sheltered cove and broke with a thunder that filled the air.

Murdo crossed the snowy shore to the stack of cases, feeling for the knot where Carl Voss had tied the rope around the canvas. It was tight and covered with snow. He brushed the flakes from his hands and blew on his fingers, then walked down to the *Lobster Boy*. Clambering aboard, he pulled open the stern locker and felt for the lantern that had been doused by the sea. He shook it — there was still plenty of oil. Pulling it open he crouched in the stern and fumbled for a match in his coat pocket. It was not easy to find anything to strike it on, for the tool-box was oily and most things were wet. There was a file, however, and after rubbing it dry against the leg of Donald's trousers, his third match ignited. Huddled in the locker doorway he held it to the lantern. The wick spluttered, but it caught, and after giving off a deal of smoke that half blackened the glass, settled down to a steady flame.

He shut the stern locker and scrambled for'ard. The boat was a mess. He kicked aside a tangle of ropes and pulled open the bows locker. Clumsy with freezing fingers, he laid his hands upon everything but what he wanted: bits of canvas, lengths of rope, bottles, tins, a Stillson wrench, the sea-anchor. But at length his hand fell on the long, smooth shaft of marline spike, and lying beside it a hammer. He pulled them out.

Walking back to the cases he wished the lantern was not so bright. He sheltered his eyes from it and stared up the winding track, listening.

Before he untied the knot Murdo examined it: he would have to re-tie it the same way. Fortunately it was a simple reef knot with a couple of half hitches. He shrouded the lantern behind a fold of the tarpaulin and got busy. It was easy, once he had seen it, despite the frozen ropes, for as Hector often told him, 'the

88

right knot never jams'. The lashings fell slack. He pulled back the stiff, snow-covered canvas and trampled it into a corner where it would not blow around.

Which case should he open? Murdo picked up the lantern and looked at them. One of the longish ones, perhaps. Again he hid the lantern as well as he was able and dragged one of the cases into the snow at his feet. For a moment he hesitated, looking fearfully through the blizzard in the direction of the track. Then his mind was made up. He had come so far, he would finish the job! He reached to the top of a flat rock for the marline spike and hammer.

The spike lifted the staples easily, and once the staples were out the wire bands slipped over the ends of the case. Then he was hammering the flattened tip of the spike under the end of one of the boards, being careful not to split the wood. It was simple. The silvery nails slipped out. He laid them carefully beside the staples and lifted a board clear. He removed the board next to it. Despite the blizzard and the cold, a hot shiver of apprehension passed through him.

He set the marline spike and hammer on top of the planks in the snow and pulled out the lantern.

The contents of the crate were covered, wrapped in brown wax-paper. Gingerly he pulled some of the wrappings open. The paper fluttered in the wind. The light glimmered on metal. He picked the lantern up and held it high so that its beam fell full into the open crate.

"Oh no! Oh God!" The appalled cry burst from his lips and he sprang to his feet. "Guns!"

The dark, sleek shapes gleamed below him in the lamplight. He stood the lantern in the snow and carefully lifted one from the box. It was a beautiful weapon, a ·303, lovely to hold. He turned the rifle on its side and ran a hand over the oiled metal and glossy stock. He saw a name stamped into the blue steel beneath the breech and felt it with a finger. Then he crouched and held it to the light.

"M-a-u-s-e-r." He spelled the letters out under his breath. "Mauser. Mauser! . . . German!"

Heedless now, he dropped the rifle on top of the open crate. Already the inside was white with snow. Turning again to the pile, he dragged down one of the small heavy boxes. It was much more difficult to open, but he was reckless. A few rough blows and wrenches snapped the steel band. Hammering the marline spike under one of the boards he forced it up. From end to end it split down the grain of the wood. He pulled the pieces apart and flung them to the ground, then tore back the waxed paper. Row upon row of glinting brass and steel cartridges shone from the dark recess.

"Ammunition!" Murdo's heart leaped and he recoiled before it. His shoulders bumped into something soft and he spun round wildly. A hand of steel shot out and clamped like a vice on the throat of his coat, half throttling him.

"That's right — bullets!" The voice was harsh.

A powerful light suddenly sprang out of the darkness, dazzling him. Murdo screwed his eyes up against it, twisting and struggling against the hand that held him so tightly. The light flashed towards him and something struck him violently across the side of the head.

"Keep still!"

His head ringing, Murdo could dimly make out a black figure before him. The light shifted and he found himself looking straight into the face of Carl Voss.

"So now you know," he said roughly. "Bullets! And explosives! And guns!"

'Operation Flood-Tide'

The hand that held Murdo by the throat thrust him back violently, so that he stumbled and fell against the sharp corner of the pile of crates. In an instant he was on his feet, but Carl Voss already had a heavy service revolver levelled at his chest. The torchlight gleamed along its wicked barrel.

"So now you know," Voss repeated, his voice quieter. "You young fool, what good do you suppose your meddling is going to do you now? Who do you think you are to set yourself up against us — against the might of the German Reich? An ignorant Scotch boy and his whisky-smuggling friend!"

Murdo remained silent, hypnotised by the revolver.

"I should shoot you now," Voss mused, his voice cutting through the roar of the storm. "It would save a lot of trouble." His lips came together and his nostrils flared as he considered the idea for a moment. Almost with reluctance he shook his head. "No. We might need you yet." He sighed, then gestured with the revolver towards the pile of crates. "Come on! Get them put away. Then we'll see what 'Henry' wants to do with you."

Murdo bent, horribly aware of the gun at his back, and began repacking the shavings and brown paper into the box of ammunition. He laid the splintered boards across the top and hammered them down as well as he was able. The broken steel band nodded in the wind. Glancing up at Carl Voss, Murdo saw that the revolver had fallen to his side.

He lifted the heavy cartridge box into place and turned to the case of rifles. Carefully he wrapped the waxed paper around the Mauser ·303 and set it back in its slot. He laid the boards on top and hammered them home. From the corner of his eye he saw Carl Voss shrug his shoulders against the snow; he was cold. The revolver still hung at his side. Shaking with fear, Murdo reached across casually for the heavy steel marline spike as if to lever the bands back into place. Then suddenly, acting before he had time to think about it, he whipped round, flung the metal spike with all his strength into the shins of the man behind, and dived to one side.

There was a loud cry of pain and a deafening bang. A bullet ripped past his shoulder and thudded into the boxes. Like a cat Murdo leaped at the lantern. A violent kick smashed the glass and extinguished it. He flung himself headlong into the snow. There was another shot. In a split second he had regained his feet and was scrambling behind the stack. Keeping it between himself and Carl Voss's torch, he raced behind the boat and disappeared into the darkness.

Gasping with the pain in his shinbone, Voss struggled to regain possession of himself. It took a few moments. Then he limped around the corner of the pile of boxes. The light from his torch flooded through the falling snow. He turned it on the cliff face, illuminating every cranny where Murdo might be hiding or attempting to climb. The boy had not made a break across the open shore, of that he was certain. He was somewhere down that black tail of crag at the edge of the beach, hidden at the moment from his torchlight.

Murdo reached the rocks by the sea. There was no shelter, no way up. Without pausing, he plunged into the turbulent waves and waded out along the foot of the crag, seeking a way over the rocky spur to the hidden shore beyond. It was a sheer buttress, yet the ragged crest rose no more than twenty or thirty feet above him. The water swirled about his thighs, then a wave surged in more than head-high, lifting him from his feet.

It sank, and he was standing waist-deep. He scarcely noticed the clutching chill of the water. Still there was no way up. He panted and held against the crag for support. Another wave surged past, throwing him backwards. In the following trough he found bottom again and looked up. In the dark and stormy confusion a black streak four or five yards ahead looked like a cranny. Pressing his hands against the rock and barnacles, feeling no pain as his fingertips tore against the sharp white shells, Murdo fought his way through the sea.

He reached the spot. His groping fingers caught a good hold above head height, his scrabbling sea-boot found a support. A heave, and he was half out of the water. Another crevice, another foot-hold. Spreadeagled against the rock face, the leaping waves now reached only to his knees. Twisting his head to look, he saw the light of the torch slowly moving down to the water's edge. It flashed up as Voss searched the darkness above him. Murdo turned his face away and reached for another hold.

He was fifteen feet above the water when the ledges ran out. Desperately he cast about, scrabbling now with his left hand, now with his right, scraping his rubber boots along the rock, but there was no cleft, no protruberance, no hold at all. Below, the light of Carl Voss swept across the sea as though he suspected Murdo might be trying to creep past him in the waves. Slowly it moved back and along the seething foot of the crag, then up.

He did not see Murdo at first, dark and wet as a seal, pressed into the spray-swept buttress. Murdo hid his face against the rock wall, so that the whiteness should not give him away. Twice the light passed over him, but the third time it moved more slowly, and returned, and stayed.

Voss was taking no chances. He waded into the sea himself, keeping back from the crag so he had a clear view.

"All right!" he shouted, his voice harsh and loud above the storm. "Come down!"

Murdo looked at the leaping waves below him and wondered for an instant, about jumping, but Carl Voss was too close, and in those clinging clothes he would never have made it in such a sea.

"I will count. If you are not down by the time I reach five, I will shoot you dead. Now! One . . ."

Murdo reached down with his foot and began climbing. Two minutes later, wide-eyed and shivering with fear and the beating he had taken in the sea, he stood once more on the beach. Carl Voss stepped up to him, and Murdo reeled full length as a savage blow struck him above the ear. Suddenly he was frightened no longer. He pulled himself to his knees and looked up, eyes blazing in the torchlight.

"That's more like it, my little Scotch boy!" the man taunted. "Now we're seeing what you're really made of."

He lifted a boot as if he would kick Murdo to the ground, but Murdo raised a guarding hand and the boot fell.

When Voss spoke again his voice was cold and full of menace. "Get those boxes packed up. And don't even think of another trick like that. Get up!"

In ten minutes the job was finished and Murdo was tying the rope around the awkward tarpaulin. By this time he was so cold that he could hardly grasp the ends of the rope. Carl Voss watched from a distance of two or three yards, the heavy revolver in his hand, his powerful torch illuminating every move Murdo made.

"There's no need to put your precious tools back in the boat," Voss said, as he made a step in that direction. "Push them under the edge of the canvas. That will do for the present."

Murdo did as he was told.

"Now." Carl Voss motioned towards the track with his revolver. "You first. Don't go too fast." He smiled thinly. "If you want to try any more of your clever tricks — remember, I'll be right behind you."

It was Peter who let them in. Pushed from behind by Carl Voss, Murdo lurched into the room where the cosy atmosphere had been replaced by an ugly tension.

Carl Voss came in behind him. He was smothered in snow. He flung his black revolver with a clatter on the polished dresser, and put a foot on the edge of Sigurd's armchair. Carefully he pulled up a trouser leg to examine his damaged shin. A dark, painful-looking split was still oozing blood down the front of his leg.

Shocked, Hector looked from the shin to Murdo. A lump of snow fell from the boy's black hair and slithered down the side of his face. One of his eyes was blood-shot. A dark bruise spread across the cheekbone. There was a wild look in his face, a fierceness, that Hector had glimpsed before but never seen so nakedly revealed.

"Get over there beside your friend." Carl Voss said contemptuously. "We'll decide what to do with you later." Then he turned to Henry Smith. No longer did he bother to use English, but spoke in his native German. Arne butted in and suddenly Voss was angry. He burst into a torrent of words, his eyes burning, finger pointing at the two Scots and then away in the direction of the cliffs.

His own voice icy and authoritative, Henry Smith cut him off abruptly. Speaking in German himself he asked a question. Carl Voss calmed down with an effort and replied. Soon they were talking among themselves.

Unable to follow a word, Hector and Murdo listened for several minutes. In the heat of the room the snow melted on Murdo's coat and fell to the floor, making puddles on the linoleum and soaking into the rug. After the cold of the night wind and blizzard his face flushed scarlet.

Quietly he told his old friend what had happened. Hector listened until he had finished, saying nothing. His face was set, no more than a slight shadow of anxiety about his blue eyes. It expressed nothing of the turmoil of distress that was raging within him at the danger and violence into which he had led Murdo. He raised his eyes to the purple bruise across the boy's face, saw the cut fingers and torn nails where he had dragged himself out of the waves. There was no need to say how he felt.

At first Murdo did not notice that the Germans had fallen silent. Then he was aware of their eyes upon him, and he stopped talking. For a while no-one spoke. Sigurd reached across to the bucket at the side of the hearth and put a couple of peats on the fire, thrusting them into the glowing heart with the sole of his thick sock. Carl Voss went through to the other room and took off his soaking trousers and hung them in front of the fire. He came back in his shirt tails, wrapping a blanket around his waist. The trail of blood was drying into a thick, dark streak down his shin.

It was Henry Smith who spoke first. "Well, Mr Gunn, while you try to make us all drunk, your young friend goes exploring. He has — er — put the cat among the canaries, as they say." He glanced, not without a certain reluctant admiration, at the sodden, steaming figure of Murdo. "He is a resourceful boy. But it would have been better if he had stayed in his bed. We would have completed the shipment, you would have been well paid. Everybody would have been happy. Now . . ." He shrugged. "It makes no difference. We will still finish the operation. You will not be paid. All we have to do is keep an eye on you, and then, when the last of the cargo is in the cave . . . well, we will decide what to do with you when the times comes."

Hector smiled ironically. "Do you imagine I am going to run German guns for you? In the *Lobster Boy*? He shook his head.

"I don't think there is much doubt about it," Henry Smith said calmly. "As you said yourself a few minutes ago, there is a war on. You don't want to run the guns for us — we want you to. If it came to the point, we could run the boat ourselves. It is unlikely that anyone would interfere with us. Sigurd there is about your build; near enough to pass for you, at a distance anyway, wearing your oilskins and hat. Everyone knows the boat well enough. But it would be better if you took us yourself."

"Never," Hector said. "I would run the boat on the rocks first."

"With the boy in it?" Henry Smith said. "It's not hard to tell how much he means to you. It would be a pity to end a life so young, especially as it really makes so little difference. We would bring the guns across anyhow."

"You wouldn't touch him," Hector said. "You're not the type. Kill a young boy!"

"You don't know much about me, do you Mr Gunn? Would you take the chance? And even if you are right — well, what about Mr Voss, there? We are at war. Desperate times require desperate measures. It would be a pity, but what is one boy when so much is at stake? No Mr Gunn. You will run your boat for us."

Murdo looked across at the ruthless face of Carl Voss. The brooding eyes met his own. For a few moments he held them, then looked away.

Henry Smith waited for Hector to speak, but the old fisherman said nothing.

"Well, so that is settled," he said cheerfully. "We will wait here for a day or two until the storm dies down, then we will bring the rest of the guns and explosives across to the mainland in your boat. . . . I take it you do realise by now that that is what you have been carrying: guns, dynamite, grenades, ammunition." He smiled. "Good! Now I really do suggest that the young man changes out of his wet clothes. He will be catching that pneumonia you keep talking about, and that wouldn't do at all."

Hector looked up. "Aye, go and change, Murdo. Get another blanket off the bed for yourself. I'll put the kettle on." Suddenly seeming very old, he heaved himself out of his chair and started across the room towards the door. He had gone no more than a couple of paces when Carl Voss pushed him back roughly. He caught Hector off balance; he staggered, tripped, and fell half in and half out of the armchair.

The blood rushed into Murdo's face and he started forward. Hector flung out an arm to keep him back.

"Peter will do it," Carl Voss said harshly. "Peter, put the kettle on; make us a hot drink."

Peter picked up a torch and went out of the room, slamming the door behind him.

Sigurd tapped Murdo on the shoulder and nodded towards the room where their clothes were drying.

"Come," he said quietly.

Murdo made a space for himself by the fire and stripped off Donald's sodden clothes. Briefly he rubbed himself dry on the towel they had all been using, then crouched by the flames with a blanket over his back, getting warmed through.

When the worst of the chill had gone, he removed Carl Voss's trousers from the back of a chair and dropped them in a wet heap in the coldest part of the room, then arranged his own clothes in the full heat of the fire. Peter came from the kitchen and handed him a mug of steaming tea. Murdo sniffed at a run in his nose and nodded thanks. Holding it in both hands, he took a drink. It was nearly boiling but good and sweet. A thick trail of condensed milk ran down the side of the mug.

He stayed where he was, soaking up the heat, until his chest was scorched red and he had to pull the ends of the blanket over his legs because they were burning. Then he wrapped the blanket around himself and went back to the other room accompanied by Sigurd.

Henry Smith lit a cigarette and lay back in his armchair musing for a moment.

"You see, they know me at the hotel now. So I shall simply stay on for a few days until the lorries come. If you and young Mr Mackay there, decided not to co-operate, I might even pass a little of the time attending your funerals. 'So sad,' I shall say, 'Yes, I went out fishing with him a couple of times. He was a great character ... And the boy — a tragedy! He was so young!' And we will have a few of those terrible whiskies to speed you on your way. Then, when the lorries come, we load them up and your 'Norwegians' will vanish. I shall pay my bill and depart. Two days later — 'Operation Flood-Tide'."

Murdo looked at Hector. His weatherbeaten face was shadowed by wretched thoughts. The pipe had gone out and had scattered grey ash over his lap. Murdo pulled the blanket closely about his legs and sat by his armchair at the edge of the hearth.

"Yes, 'Operation Flood-Tide'," Henry Smith continued. "You see, these are not the only guns, these are not the only explosives that are being landed on your British shores. You think your coasts are well protected. Well, so they are — against an armoured landing. But everywhere, from the north of Scotland to Land's End, there are places, like here, where people who know the area can find a corner to slip in quietly, and no-one any the wiser: silly old men, like yourself, who can be bought with a story and a handful of pound notes. So, we are not the only people smuggling arms ashore in a quiet corner of the British coast. There are more than a dozen groups like ourselves."

Hector nodded. "And how do you plan to bring in the men to use them? You've got enough guns there to equip a small army. Parachute drop? The Spitfires would have your planes out of the sky before you reached the coast."

Carl Voss chuckled, saying nothing.

"You're not going to try to smuggle that number of men in?" Hector said. "You'd never get away with it."

"We could have had ten thousand men on Island Roan, for all you knew," Henry Smith said. "But no, we're not going to smuggle them in."

Hector looked from one man to the other. They were both smiling. Even Sigurd could not prevent a little grin from lightening his frown of disapproval.

"That's the whole beauty of it," Henry Smith said at length. "We don't need to bring in any men at all. They are here already."

Hector's complete bewilderment made Carl Voss chuckle aloud.

"Heinrich!" Sigurd touched their leader on the arm and leaned across. He spoke earnestly, shaking his head. Henry Smith ignored him.

"Sigurd, here, thinks we should tell you no more," he said to Hector. "But I want to tell you. I want you to know who you are dealing with. I want you to *know*, as you ferry our Mauser rifles across to the mainland, exactly what you are doing." He pulled himself up in his chair and leaned forward.

"You see, when we Germans take prisoners of war we are sensible. We lock them up in prisoner of war camps and put guards on the fences. But you British! No, you are incredible. You send them out to work with a lot of old farm labourers and roadmen. German soldiers! You drive them about on tractors and carts. You say: 'You are a prisoner of war, Fritz. We could lock you up, but it would not be very nice. Now wouldn't you prefer to work on a farm in the good fresh air? A farmer's wife will give you your lunch — she might even have a pretty daughter. Or would you rather dig an old lady's allotment? But you must promise to come back at night for your tea. You won't run away, will you? Scout's honour? You madmen, do you think we are school children? It is war, not kindergarten." He paused.

"You begin to understand? We already have our army. The men are here. Tens of thousands of German soldiers, sworn to the service of the Fatherland — spread all across Britain, every day working on your farms and roads. Italian prisoners too; they are our allies. And we have the plans to mobilize them. We have the leaders: we have the guns! 'Operation Flood-Tide', that is what we call it. 'Es flutet, es flutet, es flutet' — the tide is flooding!

"On that day when the call comes from Berlin, we will mobilize our soldiers, supply them with arms, lead them against your key installations; your radio stations, telephone networks, power stations. We will storm your armouries, blow up your bridges and railway lines. And who have you to deal with them when the army is on the south coast awaiting the invasion? The Home Guard, a lot of old men." He laughed and reached for another cigarette. "So, your government has a choice. They leave us alone, and we bring the country to a standstill: or they withdraw your troops and aircraft from the Channel ports to fight us — and we invade from France. You have heard the news, the build-up of forces along the French and Belgian coasts. Not just men, you realise: aircraft, warships, tanks, artillery. It is as simple as that — the troops of the Reich come flooding in. Where will your fat Winston Churchill and your stuttering king be then?"

Hector was silent.

"So you see," Henry Smith went on, "we are not playing. We have too much to lose. If you give us any trouble, we will shoot you: the boy first, just in case you feel in a self-sacrificing mood." He looked at Murdo, wrapped in his blanket, black hair dishevelled and face flushed with the heat of the fire. "One more young life — it does not matter."

Carl Voss reached for the revolver he had tossed on the dresser and broke it open, ejecting the two spent cartridge cases to the floor. He replaced them from a box in his rucksack, and snapped the weapon shut again.

"It really is a pity you did not leave them well alone," Henry Smith observed almost sadly to Murdo. "It was all going so well. I was getting what I wanted: your friend was being well paid. A satisfactory arrangement on both sides."

"A pity for you," Murdo said.

The German shrugged. "A pity," he said.

Carl Voss wiped a few drops of water from his revolver and polished it with the oil from his fingers, fondling it and smoothing the metal until it gleamed. Henry Smith sat somewhat apart, withdrawn into his own thoughts, staring into the fading heart of the fire. Murdo stretched a hand to the bucket and threw on the last scraps of black peat before it got too low. Hector reached down for a nearly full whisky bottle and poured himself a big tot.

The old grandfather clock ticked loudly in the corner. It was nearly midnight.

Murdo shivered suddenly and drew in closer to the fire. The movement disturbed Henry Smith. He glanced at his watch and rose from the armchair. He looked tired, and there were deep, hard lines around his mouth that Murdo had never noticed before.

"Well, I am going to bed," he said, turning to the boy, "since you, apparently, do not want it. Much better if you had stayed there. Still . . ." he stretched. "The storm sounds as though it will continue for a long time yet, so I suggest we all get some sleep. You two stay at the side of the fire. Carl will keep an eye on you, I have no doubt." He turned to the others. "Everyone takes a turn — an hour about. And watch them well!"

The noise of the storm reached a crescendo, tearing and roaring around the windows. A big blue puff of peat smoke belched out into the room.

The door closed behind him and they heard his footsteps climbing the stairs.

Sigurd took up the whisky bottle and poured drinks for the four Germans. Soon they were once more engaged in quiet conversation.

For a while Hector watched them, then he sighed and reached down the side of the chair for his tobacco tin.

"How did they know I'd gone?" Murdo asked, as Hector leaned forward and knocked out his dottle on the edge of the hearth.

"Yon fellow." Hector indicated Carl Voss with a glance. "When you went out the window the curtain got snagged on a corner of the shelf, and the ledge was wet where the snow had blown in. We heard him running upstairs — and that was that."

"I didn't make a very good job of it," Murdo said.

"You did fine," Hector reassured him, squeezing his arm and looking at the bruise on his cheek-bone. It had darkened and spread; the skin around his blood-shot eye was turning black. "You're going to have a shiner." Briefly he smiled, then dropped his voice. "But I'll tell you what." He looked across at the Germans, who were still talking among themselves. "You've got to try and get away. Any chance you get. Forget about me, I can't run the way you can. I'll hold them back if it's possible. But get to a telephone and let the police know. Dial 999, tell them everything. If you pass any houses on the way, let the people know; spread the word. So far as . . ."

Carl Voss had seen them whispering and was watching closely. The others fell silent.

For a while they sat. Murdo yawned and rubbed his eyes with the back of his hand. He winced as his knuckles struck the bruise. Gently he explored it with his finger-tips.

Hector regarded the boy's brown, work-roughened hand, and the rounded end of his finger where the joint was missing. Murdo's face was pale. "Why not try to get some sleep," he said. "Find yourself another blanket and settle down there by the fire. Here!" He reached behind his back and pulled out a cushion.

Peter, the young pilot, was watching them and overheard Hector's words. He was only five or six years older than Murdo himself. His brother, back in Aachen, was just about the same age. He left the room and came back with another blanket which he tossed down, masking the gesture with gruffness.

"Thanks," Murdo said.

Then, while Hector poured himself yet another tot of whisky and lay back in his armchair, he curled up on the floor beside the fire with his head on the cushion. For a long time he lay awake thinking and listening. He was no wide-eyed innocent, but the extent of the German scheme had caught him unprepared. Hitherto untouched by the reality of the war, it was a cruel awakening. The Germans were real and all around him, no longer mere words on the radio and photographs in the *Picture Post*. Enemy soldiers, whom his father and friends were fighting, were among them in Clerkhill and Strathy. All that he knew was being threatened. The thought made him angry and his eyes glittered in the firelight. As he lay there he determined to do anything in his power to stop them.

The Last Trip

When Murdo woke up it was coming daylight and the Germans were passing to and fro through the hall with mugs of coffee and bowls of porridge. Their clothes had dried and once more they were warmly clad. Carl Voss was without his trousers, which to his fury he had found chill and sodden in the corner where Murdo had dropped them the evening before. With bare legs he mounted the stairs to seek a pair of Donald's in the bedroom.

It was a wild cold dawn. Murdo clutched a blanket about himself and went to the window. He rubbed the melting ice from a pane and peered out. The snow had ceased during the night and the wind had abated, though still it rattled the windows from time to time and moaned in the chimney. Across the hillside white swathes, caught in gusts, swept up and vanished into the air. Closer at hand the flakes swirled in mad fragmentary dances, then fell softly into the pattern of ridges. At the bottom of the walls the drifts lay deep, the fence posts and the side of the stone barn were plastered white. It was freezing hard. A gull swooped low, its wings juddering, then caught the wind and whirled away out of sight.

The blanket was warm, and wrapping it tightly about himself, Murdo went outside to the toilet at the end of the house, for there was no bathroom. The snow was icy on his feet, and the wind bitter. Behind him, right at his heels, Carl Voss strolled casually with his hand inside his jacket holding the revolver. Only one neighbour's cottage was to be seen from this position, and the curtains were still closed. Murdo was glad when they got back into the house.

A large saucepan of porridge, still a quarter full, stood on the Calor gas ring in Donald's kitchen. The man who had made it was not very experienced, for the grey mess was lumpy and thick. Murdo lit the gas beneath it, so that the porridge was at least hot, and squashed out some lumps against the side of the pan. With a good sprinkling of salt and a cup of tea it made a fair breakfast.

The day passed slowly and uneventfully. It was still much too stormy to consider launching the boat. Back at the cave, Knut would assume they were sitting out the gale on Island Roan: on the island the last of the guns and the four remaining Germans could only wait.

Henry Smith made a courtesy call upon the lady whose house Hector had visited the night before. He told her that Hector had a touch of cold, and was taking the chance to spend most of the day in bed. There was no need to call, they were fine and had all they needed. She was charmed by her polite, gentlemanly visitor.

The Germans took it in turn to keep watch over the boat lest a crofter, searching for strayed sheep, should see the pile of crates from the cliff top and go down to investigate.

Steadily the wind abated, and by mid-afternoon the skies were clearing. The thermometer fell. Ice formed thickly on the inside of the windows in every room, save the very warm sitting room they were occupying, and even there, by the time they came to draw the curtains, it was eating its way towards the middle of the panes.

They prepared to spend a second night in the house at Clerkhill.

The following morning broke clear and bright. The wind was light and the sea had fallen sufficiently for them to think of taking the boat on to Strathy before evening. The waves continued to abate throughout the day, and late on that Thursday afternoon, as purple shadows were rising in the east beyond the snowfields, and the frosty sunset glimmered pink and green above the bay, they tidied Donald's house, gathered their few belongings together, and set off for the little cove.

The snow was tracked with footprints where the German guards had made their way to the boat during the two days of their stay. Soon they were all on the beach, and while the others removed the frozen canvas from the stack of boxes and carried them down to the water's edge, Murdo, under the surveillance of Carl Voss, began to clear the boat of snow with a flat piece of driftwood, It was cold work. Soon his hands were red and aching as he scooped the snow up and flung it over the gunwale.

Twenty minutes later *Lobster Boy* was in the water and the cases were securely lashed into place. Murdo shoved off, the waves foaming about his sea-boots and making the boat leap so that he could hardly hold her bows-on. Quickly he clambered aboard, keeping his legs dry. Carl Voss watched him carefully from the stern. Sigurd pulled them clear of the shore with the oars, and held the boat steady while Hector tinkered with his engine. At the second push of the starter it coughed into life: a cloud of blue smoke rose into the fading light and drifted over the water. Soon they were away, heading out into the sea from which, not two days before, they had been so glad to escape.

The *Lobster Boy* pitched and yawed, sometimes even violently, but no water came aboard, and steadily she ploughed her way out into the open sea. Darkness fell and the brilliant icy stars came out, spangling every last black corner of the night.

An hour and a half later Strathy Point was looming up on the starboard bow. Then they were heading down towards the beach.

The cases were soon stacked, and everyone was more than ready for the hot soup which Knut, the bearded guard, had prepared while they worked. As they ate, Hector and Murdo were positioned on the boulders at the inner end of the cave. There was no chance of making a break for it. There never had been.

Then they were heading back into the ocean, on their way to the island for the last time. Hector and Murdo were in the stern, Henry Smith and Carl Voss, wearing the two life-jackets, sat amidships. The revolver rested in Voss's lap.

Hector was unusually preoccupied. Sitting with his arm along the tiller he steered the boat unconsciously. Once or twice he raised his eyes to Murdo, but said nothing, and soon looked away again.

Only at last, as Island Roan rose up ahead, did he reach over and touch Murdo lightly on the arm. The two Germans, lit by the rising moon astern, were gazing forward at the snow-capped island.

"How good a swimmer are you — really?" Hector breathed, as Murdo leaned towards him.

Surprised by the question Murdo shrugged fractionally. "Quite good — about average."

"Could you swim in a sea like this?"

Murdo's eyes widened, He nodded. "Yes, a bit, I should think. Where?"

"Near Strathy Point."

Concentrating on Murdo and the Germans for'ard, Hector had let the *Lobster Boy* wander a few degrees off course. He corrected it with a short movement of the tiller.

Henry Smith glanced back, heavy with sea-sickness, saw that everything was all right and turned once more towards the island.

"There's a place where I can put the boat on the rocks. You should be able to swim ashore safely. It may be the last chance we'll get." Hector laid a hand on Murdo's leg. "You're sure — about the swimming?"

Murdo swallowed and nodded, though his stomach turned over and a wave of blackness passed behind his eyes. He had known, since he was a child, that one day something would happen to him on those rocks near the point. He had always

108

feared them. In his mind's eye he saw the swell and suck of the wicked currents. He took a deep breath to steady his voice.

"Aye, I'll be fine," he said.

Carl Voss was peering in their direction. He saw their silhouettes together, whispering, but could hear nothing, for their soft voices were well covered by the roar of the engine.

"You know the Geo Borbh?" Hector said. "Across the hill from Andy Mackenzie's?"

"Aye."

"Just off there. Get yourself ashore and make your way up to the phone box. . . . We've got to try, but take care, boy. Look after yourself." Hector's voice broke a little and he cleared his throat, hiding it behind a bout of coughing, "After all, I'm wanting you to paint the barn when we get a dry day."

Murdo smiled slightly, not for a moment taken in by Hector's joking. Touched and embarrassed he nodded, then looked away.

They moored *Lobster Boy* in the pool and Henry Smith left Carl Voss covering the two prisoners while he went up the cliff steps to bring his men down from the house.

They were half expecting him and it was not long before he was back at the jetty, accompanied by big Bjorn, Gunner the seaman, balding Haakon, and happy red-haired Dag. Behind them the deserted house was left as they had found it: every last trace of their presence had, so far as possible, been removed. Henry Smith had informed them of the changed circumstances, and now they gazed with different eyes, almost warily, at Hector and Murdo, and the gun in Voss's hands. Bjorn saw the boy's black eye and bruised face, and his normally good-natured expression tightened as he looked across at his violent comrade.

With bold hostility, Voss stared back at him for a moment. Then he turned away, unbuttoning his coat, and pushed the revolver back into its holster.

The antagonism between Bjorn Larvik and Carl Voss was well known to everyone. Henry Smith regarded them for a moment, then ignored it and addressed himself to Hector.

"I'm sure I don't need to remind you what I said two nights ago, in your friend's cottage," he said pleasantly. "I think we can trust you to load the cases and tie them down without any 'accidents'. The pool appears very deep. I imagine there is plenty of room down there for more than a case or two of guns, if the need arises. But why the pool — there is a lot of water and a good fast current anywhere off the island. Carl, by the way, has views about that: he was telling me on the way across. But I'm inclined to give you a chance, So, it's up to you."

Hector climbed down into the boat and took the case that Murdo very carefully handed to him. Soon the last of the arms and the remainder of the Germans' provisions were neatly stowed, covered with the tarpaulin, and securely lashed to the bottom boards.

A few minutes later they were heading out between the towering cliffs of the bay for the last time. Ahead lay the twelve mile haul to Strathy Point. The slight but withering east wind blew straight in their faces.

"Well, that's that!" Henry Smith rubbed his hands together gladly. "The end of that wretched island." He smiled mockingly at Hector.

The old fisherman raised his grey eyebrows non-committally and looked ahead, holding his boat carefully into the bow sea so that he got the maximum pitch and swing for the benefit of the unaccustomed Germans.

He was successful, and soon Henry Smith and Haakon were being sick, and to Murdo's delight Carl Voss too began to look unwell, yawning and belching, always a sure sign.

"Are you not feeling too good?" he called sympathetically above the noise of the engine. "What you need is a dish of nice fat pork with plenty of dripping, and a couple of greasy eggs and some fried bread to settle your stomach."

Though unfortunately his words did not have the desired effect upon Voss they were not wasted, for Henry Smith suddenly moaned afresh, clutched his middle, and hung wretchedly over the side.

110

Otherwise the trip was uneventful. But as the miles passed, Murdo felt his fear mounting. In his mind's eye he visualised the crags, the sudden plunge into that icy water, the struggle through crashing waves and rocks to the shore. At the same time he could hardly believe it, for Hector and the *Lobster Boy* were one of his earliest memories; indeed, they had been sailing out of Strathy since his father was a boy. Somehow the boat seemed invincible. Beneath his feet the weather-beaten timbers flung the seas aside with familiar ease; the sturdy prow lifted above the waves, a glinting silhouette against the moonlit sky, then plunged down into the trough; the old engine throbbed powerfully, never faltering.

A mile or so short of Strathy Point, Hector leaned forward and eased back the throttle. The engine note fell.

"What are you doing?" Henry Smith fought back his sickness and called out warningly.

Hector indicated Haakon. "We won't jump about so much if I cut the revs a bit," he said.

Relieved, but still watchful, Henry Smith nodded.

Fifteen minutes later Hector swung to starboard around the ragged rocks of the point, three miles out into the open sea. The lighthouse, unlit for the duration of the war, gleamed white, high above them on top of the cliffs. He kept well out, but once clear of the point pulled close in towards the shore, then straightened out on the long run home.

Suddenly Murdo found himself on the verge of panic, his lips were trembling and his heart thudded. Hector's words kept running in his mind: ' . . . you're sure? . . . you *should* be able to swim ashore . . . look after yourself.' He watched the sea foaming over the rocks, saw it breaking up the face of the cliff. The old fear of his childhood. His stomach cramped, making his shoulders fetch forward.

"You are very close to the rocks." Henry Smith's voice rang out from near the bow.

"Get a bit of side shelter," Hector called back. "Make the most of it."

"Pull out a bit," Henry Smith shouted.

"It'll be worse further out," Hector said, taking no notice.

As if to make his point more clear, at that moment Haakon leaned over the gunwale once more, and retched.

Not satisfied, Henry Smith moved closer.

Hector laughed. "Do you think I'm going to put her on the rocks?" he called. "Some chance while you and bully boy, there, are wearing the life-jackets."

Henry Smith stared at him for a moment, then turned and surveyed the moonlit sea ahead. It was clear. He said no more and settled himself to watch.

Hector managed the boat perfectly, turning her to ride the mounting waves so that it appeared they really were gaining some shelter from the proximity of the windward crags.

"A bit less than a mile," he whispered to Murdo. "Remember to loosen your sea-boots."

The coast crawled past. The waves, meeting the off-shore current, sucked and seethed along the fangs of broken rock — glinting where the black water climbed a sheer cliff face, shining white as it swilled in tumult over ragged outcrops.

Hector's face brushed the back of Murdo's hair. "Coming up now," he breathed. "When I give the word try to keep them back."

"All right," Murdo whispered.

Wide-eyed he stared at the little bay slipping towards them. The entrance was flecked with white. Beneath his feet the little boat leaped and fell, holding back the bottomless water beneath. Never had the boat's planking seemed so frail and so precious.

The rocks at the mouth of the bay came nearly abeam, thirty yards off to starboard.

"Wait . . . wait." Hector's breath was warm in Murdo's ear, "Wait. Right! . . . Now!"

Suddenly Hector flung the tiller hard across and kicked the throttle wide. The engine roared and the little boat swung in a tight circle to starboard, heeling over, heading straight for the rocks.

With cries the Germans leapt to their feet. Someone cannoned into Voss as the boat tossed, and they fell. Another man was struggling forward. Murdo rushed towards him, trying to block the way with his body. A heavy fist crashed against his ear. He felt something soft against his legs and kicked it. There was a shot and a cry of pain from in front of him. The boat lurched with the struggle and dipped violently. Someone clambered past him over the engine casing. He flung out a hand, caught the man by the ankle and heaved. The man slipped and fell half on top of him. He fought to regain his feet. Then suddenly, with a sickening crunch, the *Lobster Boy* ran headlong into a wicked fang of rock.

Waves flooded in, men staggered with the impact and fell in a tangled heap. Murdo saw a figure lurch backwards and go over the side, head-first into the black rock. All was confusion. Waves swilled, foaming to his knees. Then the boat was gone, and he was struggling in the icy water.

His clothing hampered him, the great boring waves thrust him downwards, tumbling and fighting, unable to breathe. Water everywhere. Suddenly his head was clear for an instant and he gasped a lungful of air, and half a lungful of water as the waves tugged him down again. He struggled with his sea-boots; one came off, the other stuck. With bursting chest he kicked out wildly and his head rose above the surface. He opened his mouth, but before he could breathe another wave swept over him, bearing him down, a wild jumble of arms and legs and clothes, spinning helplessly, not even knowing where the surface was. Still he kicked out. Thick seaweed brushed around his face. He pushed it away, but it was everywhere, all around him, trapping his hands, arms, legs. Down, down, down the waves bore him. His head reeled. His lungs were on fire. Blind in the black water, choking, writhing, he felt his senses slipping away. A warm glow started somewhere at the back of his brain, sliding down into his muscles, comforting, easing — peace. He gave himself up to the water.

A Bay Sheathed in Ice

Suddenly, with a shocking pain, something smacked Murdo across the front of his face. His back wrenched and twisted. Again the hard thing struck and ripped him across the ear like fire. Blindly, instinctively, he flung out both arms and encountered rock. Unaware of razor-sharp barnacles he clung tight. His head was clear of the water. Lungfuls of sweet air struggled into his body. The waves poured, foaming, across him. He hung on, every muscle forcing, clinging, against the rock. The water receded. Flashes of sense glimmered at the back of his brain and he crawled higher. More waves seethed around him, no longer cold. Flashes of vision — black rocks, tumbling water, white hands. The waves dropped away and he crawled higher still and clung there, mouth and face against the harsh stone, shuddering violently.

He had panicked, and it came again, gluing his arms and legs, stomach and chest and face to the streaming rock. But slowly it passed, very slowly, ebbing like a spent flood from mind and limbs. The waves no longer broke over him. Raising a streaming head, Murdo looked around the terrible place. He breathed convulsively, nearly sobbing. The beautiful air pumped into his lungs. He peered into the moonlit darkness. Cliffs rose sheer from the tossing sea thirty yards away. He was on a rocky outcrop, the black surging water all around. Something palc and sluggish, a lolling white face and shoulders, washed heavily on the waves a few yards off. It disappeared. Further over, to the left of the exploding crags, the waves broke with a roar on the boulders of a small beach.

His stomach cramped and more than a pint of water came gushing from his mouth.

For minutes he clung, shuddering, to the peak of rock. A semblance of thought struggled into his mind as the blanket of fear slowly withdrew. Two smaller outcrops spanned the stretch of water between the beach and himself. He could swim to one, and then to the other. He had to get to the shore, and soon. The cold was eating into him; with his returning senses he could feel it now. He could not last there much longer. He kicked off the remaining sea-boot and tugged at his oilskins. They clung about his body but at length came clear and he tossed them aside into the sea. For a minute longer he hung on, waiting for the sea to level, building up his courage. The moment came. With gritting teeth he launched himself into the water, striking out strongly towards the first outcrop. Now the boy had overcome his panic he was in control, his body rising with the surging wave, sinking back into the trough behind. Suddenly his arm struck something soft and yielding, and a dim shape rolled over against his face and chest. With a disgusted cry he thrust the thing from him and swam from it in horror.

Then the first rock was before him. For a moment he trod water before it, and as the wave lifted him forward, grabbed and clawed for a handhold, his feet trailing in the weed. The wave sank and his body sank with it, his wrists tearing on the barnacles, hip crashing against a little bulge of rock. But he was held, and was again clear of the water, more than a third of the way in towards the beach.

When he had regained his breath he launched himself once more into the glinting water. The thick trousers clung awkwardly about his legs, his battledress jacket hoisted itself beneath his armpits and hampered his movements. But a minute later he was swimming past the second rock and striking in towards the shore. The waves rose in the shallow water, broke and foamed. A current bore him towards the bottom of the crags thirty yards to his right, and for a moment Murdo felt the under-tow tugging at his feet. He redoubled his efforts and broke clear of it. Eight or ten yards out he reached for the bottom, but the water was still too deep and he sank for a moment, the foam swilling over his head.

Then the boulders of the beach were beneath his feet. As he tried to stand a wave came and banged him forward off balance, sprawling in the shallow water. He clutched at the smooth rocks, but the retreating wave sucked him back again. Another wave broke over him. As his body lifted he rode the crest and in a moment was dumped unceremoniously higher up the boulders. This time the back-wash was weaker and he crawled forward. The next wave lapped round his body for a moment, then was gone. He tried to stand, make his way clear of the water, but his legs would not support him and he fell back. On hands and knees he crawled a few yards further, then collapsed on his face. And there he lay, in the shadow of the cliff, sprawled among the rocks like so much trash washed up by the high tide.

Slowly Murdo pulled himself to his knees and stood up. He was very shaky. He leaned a hand against a rocky spur that rose from the boulders a few yards from the cliff. There was a taste of blood in his mouth. He spat, and wiping his lips on a sodden sleeve raised his head and looked wretchedly about him. It was a small rocky inlet. Cliffs rose on either hand and a gentle snow slope, gleaming in the moonlight, rolled up behind to the white moors. The wind, slight in the bay but cruelly cold, blew straight from the sea. Two figures moved slowly over the rocks below the cliff at the far side of the beach, another staggered about in the froth of the waves.

"Hector!" His voice sounded strangely loud and not like his own voice at all. "Over here!"

He let go of the rock and took a step forward. The figure at the water's edge looked all around unable to distinguish where the cry was coming from.

"Over here," Murdo called again.

"Is it you?" The old man stumbled across the awkward boulders in the direction of the voice. He had still not seen Murdo in the shadow of the crag.

"Here," Murdo said. He stepped out into the moonlight and nearly fell.

Hector clasped his arms about the boy's shoulders. "God be thanked!" he cried. There were tears in his voice. "You're not badly hurt?"

Murdo swallowed and shook his head. It was the first time he had even thought about Hector. Over the old man's shoulder he saw the two men along the beach joined by a third, who appeared at the foot of the cliff on the far side of the bay.

"The sea was too strong," Hector said. "You went out into deep water. I saw you go down." For a moment he was nearly overcome, then he sniffed hard and pulled himself together. "You're shaking like a leaf, boy. Come on, get walking. Warm yourself up a bit."

He took Murdo's arm across his shoulders and together they moved up the beach, slipping and stumbling on the boulders. It was hopeless, for they kept tripping each other up and moved so slowly that there was no warmth in it. Murdo removed his arm from Hector's neck. He flapped his arms about his chest and rubbed the thick sodden cloth of his trousers. A little warmth stole into his shoulders but otherwise he remained as cold as ever.

The Germans crossed the cove towards them. Despite the brightness of the moon, Murdo could not distinguish who each man was until they came close.

Carl Voss was in the lead, limping slightly from a twisted knee. He walked up to Hector and stopped. Then he struck the old man full force across the side of the head with his fist. It was a terrible blow and Hector reeled to the ground. Shocked, Murdo turned to face Voss himself. He saw the arm swing back and before he could move there was a flash behind his eyes and a loud noise, and he found himself lying on the boulders beside his friend.

"Pigs!" The German's boot lashed into Hector's side. "Stupid, stupid pigs!" Again the boot thudded into the old man.

Twisting like an eel Murdo grabbed Voss's foot as he drew it back, and wrenched it round, digging his fingers in. It swung near to his face and he bit savagely into the ankle, as hard as he could. The cloth was in his mouth, the kicking leg dragged him over the rocks till it broke free.

With an oath, for the struggle had hurt his damaged knee, Carl Voss turned on the boy, and the heavy boot hacked time and again, with sickening force, into his stomach and ribs.

Then there were raised voices, a scuffle of feet by Murdo's head, and a man landed heavily on the boulders a dozen feet away. It was Carl Voss.

Murdo felt an arm round his shoulders. It raised him until he was sitting, coughing, slumped against the cloth of a man's jacket. Flashes of red and black came and went in the darkness. There were dim voices. Slowly the waves of nausea and dull pain rolled back and he became aware of Hector bending over him.

"You're all right," he said. "It's all right."

Murdo pressed his lips together and nodded slightly. Then the man who held him tightened his arm and lifted him to his feet as easily as if he had been a child. Looking round Murdo saw that it was big Bjorn. The German looked down into his face. Murdo saw the tangle of wet blond hair, the blood of a deep scratch down the side of his eye.

"I am sorry," Bjorn said. "We are not all like that." He glanced contemptuously to where Carl Voss was pulling himself to his feet, one hand carefully holding the side of his face. "I hope you are not too much hurt."

Murdo shook his head and pulled his shoulders from the clasp of Bjorn's arm.

"I'm all right," he said.

When Bjorn saw how Murdo turned away from him he stood for a moment, then walked across to Henry Smith several yards along the beach. They were joined a minute later by Carl Voss, still feeling the side of his face.

119

Slowly Murdo made his way to a rocky outcrop and sat down, sheltered from the wind. As the dizziness passed off he became aware once more of the terrible cold, and the water still draining through his clothes.

A rattle of stones at the head of the cove made everyone turn. A dark figure was silhouetted against the snowy slope, which he had clearly just descended.

"Gunner?" Henry Smith called.

"Ja."

Murdo watched the man stumble down the beach on the treacherous boulders. As he approached there was a rapid exchange of words in German.

"Nein . . . nein," he said.

Whatever the three had been saying, Henry Smith was now very angry. He struggled with his life-jacket but the knots had jammed. Leaving it fastened he thrust a hand beneath and pulled the heavy service revolver from inside his coat. He crossed to where Hector was standing and levelled it at his chest from point blank range, finger on the trigger.

"I could shoot you," he said. His face was very still, his voice tight, as if he was holding himself in control against his inclination. "Right now!" He pushed the muzzle of the revolver into the old man's ribs. His breathing grew hard. "You would make fools of us! Well, two of my men are missing — Dag and Haakon. They might be dead, *You* might have killed them. They might be drowning at this very minute! So, we are going to look for them. You and the boy will come with myself and Bjorn Larvik. We will go that way." He nodded in the direction of Strathy Point. "But you have had your last chance. You tried, and you failed. Any more trouble — *any* more trouble — and I will shoot the boy." He turned to Murdo. "Up, on your feet!" he said roughly.

As they walked the few yards to the shore at the north end of the beach, staring towards the wave-swept rocks and calling, Murdo could not rid his mind of the soft yielding figure with a moon-white face that had bumped against him in the water. It must have been Haakon, Haakon with the big hands and big

120

features, prematurely balding. Now a waterlogged corpse. The thought made him sick, but he said nothing.

He turned back to the beach, and looked across the cove at Gunner and Carl Voss clambering over the rocks at the far side. Suddenly, forty yards away, a dark shape rolled sluggishly at the edge of a wave, bumped over the stones on the backwash and vanished among the breakers. He pointed. The others turned and Bjorn Larvik started forward, but by the time he reached the spot the body had gone. Heedless of the waves he waded in, peering about him. He saw nothing and moved along a few yards, the water to his thighs. Suddenly he stopped, then bent, feeling for something at his feet. A wave broke over his head and shoulders. As it retreated a dark heavy shape appeared in Bjorn's hands. He backed to the shore pulling the body behind him. As he came into the shallows Henry Smith joined him and took a grip on the man's shoulders and limp hanging arm. A minute later they laid him on the boulders well above the reach of the waves. It was Dag, young laughing Dag, with the red hair. He was quite dead.

Murdo had never seen a dead man before. He looked up at Hector. The old man's face was impassive.

For a long time nobody spoke.

It was Henry Smith who broke the silence. "What direction does the current flow here?" he asked.

Hector pointed out to sea, beyond Strathy Point.

Henry Smith followed his arm, looking past the high crag to the rolling swell and dim horizon. Slowly his gaze swept the bay, and he looked up at the stars. Then he looked down, and nodded. Crouching beside the dead man he began to go through his pockets. The blind white face rolled over against the stones as he pulled the twisted clothing this way and that.

"You go along the shore and tell the others, boy," Hector said quietly, with a knowing glance in the direction of the snowfield at the back of the beach.

Henry Smith looked up and carefully placed the revolver on a boulder beside his right hand.

"Bjorn, you'd better go and tell them," he said. "You two stand over there."

By the time Bjorn returned with Carl Voss and Gunner, Henry Smith had finished going through the young soldier's pockets. His few belongings lay on his sodden handkerchief beside his head. They were pathetic: a box of matches, a packet of cigarettes, a pocket knife, his wrist watch, and a wallet with a little picture of a girl on one side and a middle-aged couple on the other. Murdo watched, every detail burning itself into his memory. Could this awful, dead thing be the same Dag who had laughed and smiled and so merrily played the flute on that first trip to the island? Now the flute was gone. He stared at the wet hair and expressionless face, the stilled white hands fallen between the stones.

"You stay here with me," Bjorn said to him.

Gunner bent and took the body of his dead comrade over his shoulder. Supported by Carl Voss so that he did not fall, he made his way with Henry Smith and Hector around the foot of the cliff. A couple of minutes later the group reappeared in the moonlight on a little rock platform that jutted out above deep water. Gunner laid the body at their feet. The men composed themselves and Henry Smith said a prayer for the dead, though no word of it reached Murdo and Bjorn above the roar of the sea. Then Carl Voss and Gunner bent, took up the body of their friend and swung him far out into the waves, well clear of the rocks. For nearly a minute he floated, borne up by a balloon of air trapped in the wet clothes. Then the air escaped and Dag was gone, sunk into the depths of the Pentland Firth. Nothing remained but the few belongings gathered together at Murdo's feet. Bjorn tossed the cigarettes into the water, then carefully wrapped the other things in the wet handkerchief and put them in his pocket.

For an hour, then, they searched up and down the stony cove, and from the flanking cliffs and shores beyond, treacherous beneath the mantle of snow and ice, but there was no sign of Haakon. At length Henry Smith reluctantly admitted there was no more they could do, and the little band of men retreated to a corner of the bay to seek shelter among the rocks and boulders and wait for the morning light. According to Henry Smith's watch, which had survived the immersion and rough treatment, it was a little before three o'clock in the morning.

Murdo stripped himself of his trousers, battledress jacket and sweaters and wrung them as dry as possible, then put them back on and huddled beside Hector for warmth. But soon his trousers were stiff with the frost, and the oilskin on Hector's back might have been pressed out of crumpled tin. Murdo tried to pull the trousers over his frozen feet, but it was hopeless. The cold was terrible, the hours dragged by like an arctic night. The Germans talked quietly among themselves, but between Hector and Murdo it did not seem there was much to say, and for the most part they were silent.

Some time in the middle of the long night, Bjorn Larvik rose from his comrades and crossed to the two Scots. Without a by-your-leave he seated himself next to Murdo in the shelter of their rock. The boy did not like it and wished to move away, but Hector was on his other side, and he was reluctant to disturb the small pockets of heat he had been nurturing for more than an hour. He remained where he was between the two men, and very soon the warmth of the big German's body began to steal through to his skin.

Bjorn rarely spoke, and was so still that he might have been asleep, yet each time Murdo stole a sideways look he was awake, his eyes glinting in the light of the moon.

"Close your eyes," the man said. "At least try to sleep. The night will pass more quickly."

But sleep was impossible. Murdo nursed his damaged finger, which sometimes ached with the cold, and his mind was full of confused thoughts. Larvik was a German, an enemy, one of Hitler's men, a commando come to overthrow Britain. Yet he liked him, he seemed a good man, very different from Henry Smith and Voss and all the Germans he had imagined and read about. It was a troubling thought, and led on to all kinds of complications. The only fact, after a time, of which he was sure, was that he was glad Bjorn had come across, and wished —

though there was no doubt he was a faithful German soldier — that he could have been on their side, to help Hector and himself in their present trouble. He stayed for more than two hours.

The moon slid imperceptibly around the sky, climbing, then dropping towards the white crown of moorland behind them. A hundred times the darkness over the sea seemed to be lightening, but the sky remained as cram-full of stars as ever. However, a pale light was clearly discernible in the south-east, and slowly the wintry colours, purple and pink and green and yellow, slid into the clean night-washed sky.

Painfully Henry Smith climbed to his feet and stretched his frozen joints. His wispy fair hair, dried through the night, blew in the wind. His spectacles had vanished in the sea and without them his eyes, watery-pale, were almost fish-like. Dark bruise-marks of tiredness beneath them told the strain of the past few days. His eyelashes were blond, almost white, and his eyebrows sparse and thin. He screwed up his eyes and took in the bitter landscape.

"Now then." He turned to Hector. "Where are we — exactly?"

Hector moved his stiff shoulders. "You know as well as I do, Strathy Point."

Henry Smith sighed. "Exactly," he repeated.

"I don't know," Hector said. "About half way down the shore I should think. You'll probably see the beach from the top of one of those headlands there."

"So. Would this be the place you call the Geo Borbh?"

Completely taken aback, Hector could not keep the surprise from his face.

"I see I am right." Henry Smith said something to Carl Voss, who passed a stiff, buckled map from the rocks beside him. With some difficulty, for the pages had frozen together, the leader unfolded it and carefully checked their position. Then, slipping on the rocks, he made his way to the edge of the sea and peered across the southern headland towards Strathy beach. His plump figure was small against the backcloth of ocean.

He returned, smoothing the dishevelled hair across his bald patch.

"Bjorn," he said.

The huge blond man stretched and rose smoothly to his feet. He had bathed the cut on his face with sea water and already it was healing beneath a long brown scab.

"We can all do with some food and a hot drink," Henry Smith said. "Go down to the cave and get what you can from Knut. It's not very far. And ring the Captain Ivy from the call box in the village. Tell them I'm staying away, but I'll be back in a day or two."

Bjorn nodded. "Right," he said briefly, and bent to tie his boots.

"Keep an eye open for Haakon," Henry Smith continued. "And see if you can spot a boat anywhere. I think we might need it tonight — for the guns. We've got to try to get this lot ashore." He indicated the waste of water at the mouth of the bay, where the *Lobster Boy* had gone down.

Bjorn looked up in surprise, but kept his own counsel and finished tying his laces.

"That's it, then," he said, standing. "I'm off. I'll be back as soon as I can." He glanced from Murdo to Carl Voss, then back to Henry Smith. "Don't be too hard on the boy," he said. "And keep that animal away from him."

"You just get the food," Henry Smith said to him. "That's your job."

"Just don't be hard on the boy, that's all," Bjorn said again. "There's no need for it." He regarded the dark sea, still foaming about the rocks.

Murdo looked at Carl Voss. His face was turned towards the spot where Bjorn had just passed out of view. His lips were set and his dark eyes glittered. With powerful fingers he massaged his twisted knee.

For a while nobody moved, holding on as long as they could to the little pockets of warmth which they all, like Murdo, had nurtured through the long hours. Henry Smith, still standing, surveyed the four remaining survivors. They were a bedraggled and weary group of men, unshaven, their faces pale and blotched with the cold, clothes crumpled and still wet, frozen where they were not touched by the heat of their bodies. He took the revolver from Carl Voss and shortsightedly lined the sights up with a rock ten or twelve yards away.

"I have been thinking," he said almost absently. "It would be better if you were both out of the way. The current here is very convenient, as we know."

Seconds passed, seeming like minutes. Then, very slowly, he dropped his aim, until the barrel lined straight up with the middle of Murdo's face. There it paused. Murdo's eyes widened, hypnotised by the small black hole with its rim of blue steel. Henry Smith's face was very calm, his breathing easy. His eyes blinked unemotionally. Then, relaxing, the arm fell to his side, and he addressed them in a detached and matter-of-fact voice.

"Yes, I feel it might save us a great deal of trouble in the long run — but yet again you can be useful to me. So I must, for the present at least, postpone that convenience. Possibly I might even overlook it. We will see how you get on."

Frozen though he was, Murdo felt a great surge of relief, prickling through his body from legs to scalp. He half relaxed, but still the German leader held his rapt attention.

"There are two things I want you to know, however," Henry Smith went on. "The first is to remind you that if you attempt to run away, or thwart me in any respect whatever, I shall this time shoot you dead. In the present circumstances I should think no more of it than if I was shooting a rabbit in the garden. The second is that I intend to raise the boxes of guns from your sunken boat." He shook his head. "No, no, Mr Gunn. It is no use looking bewildered. You know even better than I do, it is perfectly possible. That was not just any rock you ran your boat into, you know exactly where she is lying. And with that weight in her she will not have moved much. Now, with the full moon we all saw last night, there will be big tides at the moment — if I remember the tide tables correctly, a rise and fall of about seventeen feet. It was nearly high tide when we crashed last night, and it will soon be low. So if the boat is where I think, there will not be much water above her even now." He looked across the wilderness of rocks. "Unless you have made a mistake and she is lying in a gully, it should be a relatively simple operation — and somehow I don't think you would make that mistake, not with the *Lobster Boy*, she means too much to you." He smiled. "That is the advantage of having 'the best seaman on the coast' to assist us."

He turned slightly to bring the two Germans into his sphere of authority. "First, however, we must look for Haakon. I do not think we'll find him, and we can't look for long. But there is the unlikely chance that he has survived and is hurt, or that his body has been washed up. So we must look. Voss, you come with me and these two Scottish . . ." he hunted for a word, then left the sentence unfinished. "Gunner, you can go that way. I will see you back here in forty minutes, that is at — eight thirty." He pushed the watch back up his wrist. "Right, on your feet, everyone."

Slowly the dishevelled figures pulled themselves from the boulders. The night had taken its toll and it was a painfully stiff and weary group of men that stood there, cautiously stretching and trying to rub some circulation back into joints and muscles which had frozen through the cold hours. One figure alone showed no signs of the ravages of the night — Hector. The sturdy old man stood there as solidly as if he had risen from his bed an hour earlier. His white hair was rumpled, the stubble thick upon his chin, but the clear blue eyes gazed out as steadily as ever. Even the blow from Carl Voss had resulted in only a slight redness on the side of his face. Murdo touched his own bruised eye and rubbed his frozen legs, and wished he was as tough himself.

The search along the coast revealed nothing. Haakon was certainly dead, for the water below the long line of cliffs to each side of the cove was bottomless, and the shore rocks beyond were empty. No tracks save those of a few sheep disturbed the mantle of snow. A Cambridge degree and engineering skills were no use to him now, for with Dag he was drifting through the weed and bumping over the stones on his way to the deep currents of the Pentland Firth.

At half past eight they assembled once more beneath the ice-sheathed cliff. Murdo gazed down at the beach. The tide was far out, a chaos of rock extending between themselves and the open water of the bay. He tried to pick out the pinnacle to which he had clung, and the two outcrops past which he had swum in the blackness of the night, but now the water had receded it was difficult to tell which they were. He thought he recognised them, rising from deep weedy pools, but he was far from certain.

"If I am correct," Henry Smith said, his eyes roving judiciously over the same sea rocks, "the boat should be lying about — there." He pointed to a ragged peak about thirty yards off-shore. "If the beach shelves at the same angle, there will be about five feet of water there right now. And I think the tide may have a little way to fall yet."

Gunner, the naval man, nodded.

"So." Henry Smith turned to Hector, blinking against the brightening day and high bank of snow. "Am I right?"

Hector shrugged non-commitally.

Henry Smith's voice was insistent and menacing. "Am I right?"

"It was dark, wasn't it?" Hector protested, "I don't know where she is. How could I? All I did was run her on the rocks where I thought we had a chance of getting ashore."

"And two of my men died. Oh no! You know where the boat is very well. And you know how deep the water will be." He stepped across to Murdo and raising the revolver pushed its icy muzzle into the boy's ear. "It did not take you very long to forget my warning, Mr Gunn. Now, do you want to see whether I am bluffing? I will ask you once more. Where is the *Lobster Boy*?"

Hector did not hesitate for a moment.

"All right," he said, drawing a deep breath. "Put the gun down."

With a smile Henry Smith removed the revolver.

"You see sense at last. I think that's the first wise thing you have done since we met. Now!"

"She's over there." Hector pointed towards a rock some thirty yards to the left of that indicated by Henry Smith. "She'll be lying on the bottom, the right way up I should think with all the weight in her. The tide is falling, it will drop another foot or so yet. By then you should be able to see her bows above the water."

"And how long will we have to unload her?"

"Two hours maybe."

"With the water at that temperature it will be long enough." The pale eyes turned to Murdo. "And now you can go out and see whether he is telling the truth. You have a choice. The water is cold, if you stay out there too long you will become unconscious: if you return without finding the boat, I will shoot you. It is up to you."

There was no arguing. Murdo looked to Hector for advice. With set and wrinkled face, the old man nodded back encouragingly. He began to rid himself of his clothes.

"No, leave them on," Hector said. "They will help to keep out the cold. Just take off your jacket."

Murdo's stockinged feet were numb; nevertheless the sharp rocks cut painfully into his soles as he limped across the lower shore, eighty yards below the boulders of the beach. Then he was stepping into the water, straight to his knees in a pool at the seaward end of a black weedy gully. A wave swept in, washing to his waist, fiery cold. Resting his hand against a side rock he waded out, feeling for footholds, the sea bed uneven and slippery beneath his feet. Then he was wading free, the rock Hector had indicated fifteen yards away. Half way there one leg skidded into a deep fissure, and struggling to keep his balance he stumbled and fell sidelong. He came up panting, his body burning with the cold of the water.

By the time he reached the rock the sea was to his chest, rising to his shoulders and lifting him as the waves rolled by.

He began casting around, trying to keep to the higher ledges — but there was nothing.

"Around the back," Hector called above the noise of the waves.

And almost at once there she was, the old *Lobster Boy*, her gunwale only a foot or two below the surface. He began to turn, to shout, then hesitated. Should he tell them? He looked back to the shore. There stood Hector, white haired and weather-beaten, flanked by the three Germans. He could not let his old friend down.

"Right there!" Hector's voice was anxious.

"There's nothing here."

"There must be."

"No." He pretended to keep searching.

"A little to the left, then."

Murdo moved away from the edge of the boat into open water, feeling around beneath the surface. His hands were numb, and he had difficulty in breathing.

"I'm coming out to you!"

"Oh, no!" Henry Smith motioned Hector back. "You stay here. One at a time."

For five minutes more Murdo pretended to search in the deep water. His head was spinning, he no longer felt the cold. He began to flounder.

"Go back where you were before."

Obediently, hardly knowing what he was doing, Murdo made his way back to the boat.

"She must be there."

Murdo put a hand on the bow for support.

"No," he shouted. "There's nothing here."

A big wave surged past, rising to his mouth and foaming on the rocks. In the deep following trough, the watchers on the shore saw the sturdy green timbers of the *Lobster Boy* rise from the water, gripped by the boy's hand.

"There she is!" Gunner and Carl Voss cried out simultaneously.

"All right, Murdo. Come on out. We've seen her." Hector's voice trembled. He turned to Henry Smith, "I'm going out there. Shoot me if you want. The boy's had enough."

Henry Smith nodded quietly, his eyes fixed with a look of unwilling admiration on the black-headed figure in the water. Two minutes later the white head joined him there. The Germans saw them talking briefly.

"Have a look in the boat," Henry Smith called through the breaking sea. "See if all the cases are there."

Slowly the boy's figure pulled itself clear of the waves as he climbed inboard, and dropped down into shallower water. His head was hanging low and he shook it as if to clear away drowsiness. For a moment he stumbled about, then straightened for a lungful of air and plunged beneath the surface. For several seconds he was gone, then suddenly burst into sight again, the icy water cascading from his shoulders. He turned to talk to Hector, who a moment later climbed into the boat after him. To the watching Germans it seemed they were arguing. Hector grabbed the boy by the shoulders and pointed emphatically towards the shore. Murdo nodded briefly, and clumsily climbed down from the boat. Slowly he set out for the beach. He had only gone a few yards, however, when he tripped and fell. Rising again from the water, he no longer seemed to know where he was going, and for a few paces splashed parallel to the shore. Hector shouted but he took no notice, his head hanging, almost touching the waves that rolled in from the bay. The next moment they had swung him about so that he was heading out to sea, still stumbling forward. Then he was reeling, floundering this way and that. With a shout Gunner leaped into the waves and forced his way through them towards him. He reached Murdo at the same time as Hector. The boy was unconscious, a limp shape swilling this way and that amid the tossing waves.

Switch Off the Moon

Murdo did not regain consciousness quickly. The men carried him out of the wind and chafed his arms and legs to bring back the circulation. Roughly they wrung out his clothing and covered him with their own jackets. But it was very slowly that some colour returned to his grey cheeks and his limbs lost their clammy chill. Gunner produced a small flask from his inside pocket and poured a little brandy into his mouth. Dimly Murdo felt the burning sensation in his throat, and a coughing, choking feeling, then a thin stream of fire coursed down his body.

"He is coming to." It was Henry Smith who spoke. "Give him some more of the brandy."

Again the burning in his mouth and the gasping. A radiant heat spread outward from his chest and stomach. Murdo breathed deeply and his eyes flickered open. What seemed a forest of men's legs hemmed him in. He looked up to their bodies and faces, and closed his eyes again. Then he remembered the sea, the dizziness, the lurching blackness. Hector was leaning over him, speaking, but he could not make out the words. He forced his eyes open.

"What . . ." the word was scarcely audible.

Again Hector's voice, and a hand on his shoulder. Then the old man stood up. They seemed so tall, immeasurably high, little faces looking down.

Henry Smith stood back a pace. "There is no more we can do until Bjorn comes back with the coffee. And before you ask — no, we are not building a fire. So we might as well get on with the unloading. The tide must be low now, you can see the bows of the boat quite plainly, almost between every wave." Without his thick coat he felt the wind icy and rubbed his arms vigorously, looking about in a business-like manner. "Right! Gunner, you get out there and take off the lashings. Voss, cut a length of rope and put a knot around this boy's wrists and ankles, there is no point in taking chances. Then give us a hand to carry the cases ashore."

Carl Voss loosened the catch of the big clasp knife that hung at his waist and turned towards the sea. He was soon back, binding the rough manilla tightly about Murdo's ankles, completing the work with a reef knot and whole series of half-hitches that would be impossible for him to unfasten. Then he lashed his wrists behind, the rope tugging at the skin. When he had finished he pulled the damp jackets over him once more, stood back for a moment, raised his boot as if to give the boy a parting kick, then laughed and went to join the others far down the rocks.

At first Murdo hardly noticed the new discomfort, so wretched did he feel. Gradually, however, as the worst of the weakness and nausea passed, he became aware of the harsh knots against the bones of his wrists, and the rope cutting into his ankles. He writhed his hands and strained his feet to try to get some relief, and with a little success, but the bonds were well fastened and there was no chance of working them loose.

The effort did Murdo good. As he lay back panting, the swimming specks cleared from his eyes and he felt rather better. By shifting his head a little he could see the men struggling in the waves as they carried the crates to the shore. It was a terrible task, for they were heavy and the sea-bed was treacherous. With an upsurge of concern and affection he regarded the stocky figure of Hector, his white hair blown by the wind, the sea surging about the case he clutched to his chest. Henry Smith stumbled and dropped his box, then had to

134

bend head and shoulders into the water to retrieve it. The day was brightening all the time, and as the boy watched, the first burnished dot of sun appeared at the rim of the tossing sea. Slowly it rose, dazzling and huge. A golden track spread across the water.

The sun brought no warmth, but Murdo felt it did and his spirits rose. Gunner had left the brandy flask on a stone beside him. He crawled across, picked it up in his teeth, and struggled back to his former position. Holding the flask between his knees he managed to unscrew the cap, then lost it between the stones. But when he came to take a mouthful of brandy, holding the flask tightly in his teeth, the spirit suddenly gushed forth, spilling down his neck and into the back of his throat, making him choke. Somehow he dropped the flask into his lap without wasting what remained, then leaned forward and coughed until his eyes watered.

The boat was nearly empty when Bjorn, accompanied by Peter, Sigurd and Arne, came down the slope behind the gully. They were carrying rucksacks of food, mess-tins and primus, and an assortment of dry clothes.

A word or two with Gunner was enough to tell Bjorn what had happened. He leaned down and unfastened the bonds from Murdo's wrists and ankles, and handed him a pair of dry socks, trousers and a sweater. While Murdo put them on, Bjorn spread those he discarded over the rocks where the low sun and wind might dry them a little. Through his youth and empty stomach, Murdo was half drunk with the brandy and smiled stupidly and light-headedly when the big man said something to him. But it was a hollow feeling of well-being that the spirit provided, and he needed the hot coffee and fried bully-beef and biscuit that came to him a quarter of an hour later. The healthier warmth sank into his stomach, and after a trough of sick weariness as the euphoria faded, a slow strength once more began to build up inside him. Soon, in dry clothes and sunshine, with the hot food doing its work, he felt a great deal better.

"How many cases left now?" Henry Smith asked him, as they huddled around a projecting corner of the crag out of the wind.

"Six."

The leader nodded approvingly, well pleased with the way the work had gone.

"Very good. One crate each and that is the entire cargo. Now we can get on with the boat. We will sink her in deep water where she will never be spotted."

Gunner turned enquiring eyes upon him.

"We need to get these cases down to the cave," Henry Smith explained, as though to a child. "Do you expect us to walk down the middle of the road? And someone might see the boat: do you want the police down here; do you want them to start a search?"

The last of the cases were soon ashore and the men gathered round the gunwales of the old boat. Breaking waves surged to their shoulders.

Tied up once more, Murdo watched as the strained command floated on the breeze.

"Right! Lift and — heave!"

Surprisingly easily, now the weight was out of her, the green timbers lifted and swung; the keel grated shorewards across the weedy rocks.

"Heave! . . . Again, heave!"

A figure stumbled and vanished beneath the waves, then reappeared streaming, and immediately resumed his place along the boat's side.

In thirty minutes *Lobster Boy* lay hauled up on a flat rock, clear of all but the highest waves. The last gouts of water spilled from a jagged hole at the bows. All around the planks were split and gaping.

"Can't do anything about that." Gunner, the naval man, shook his head. "Might put a patch on that; would keep the water out for a few minutes — but not with a cargo in her, not right the way down to the beach."

Henry Smith looked disheartened.

"When we came up from the cave," Bjorn said, "we passed a bothy. They had two little boats dragged up on the shingle. When it gets dark we could take one of those. It wouldn't carry all the boxes, though, we'd have to make a couple of trips."

"You're sure?"

Bjorn nodded.

"So all is not lost." Henry Smith brightened visibly. "We have no need of the old boat after all. Come on, Gunner, see what you can do about covering that hole, then we'll get rid of the wretched thing."

With canvas and nails Gunner set about his task and in an hour had covered the gaping timbers with a rough but workmanlike patch. The tide was rising and it was not too difficult to launch the boat into the weedy channel which ran alongside. The water seeped in and ran down to the stern. At once Peter took a small zinc bucket and started baling. Then the other Germans took heavy stones from the beach and flung them carelessly down on to the bottom boards. Steadily the old *Lobster Boy* settled lower in the water.

"Right." Henry Smith pointed to the platform of rock beneath the cliffs from which they had consigned Dag's body to the ocean. "We'll sink her out there. The water's very deep and we know the current flows straight out to sea."

While others made their way across the shore, Gunner took the oars, still lashed along the side thwart, and turned the boat in the channel. Heavily, as he rowed, the *Lobster Boy* made her way round the broken rocks. As Peter baled, bright streams of water caught the sunlight.

Soon they were there and Peter climbed ashore. Then Gunner stood and raised the oar like a pile-driver above his head. Once, twice, he drove it down. The little boat lurched, stricken, as the flimsy patch burst wide and the sea gushed in. Then Gunner passed up the oars and hands reached down to pull him on to the rock. With a heel he pushed the boat out from the crag.

A little apart from the others, guarded by Voss, Murdo and Hector stood together on the shore rocks.

"Forty years I've had her. Forty years! The best boat that was ever on these waters."

Murdo looked at Hector and saw tears swimming in the old man's eyes. Silently he remained at Hector's side, looking at the *Lobster Boy*.

The waves splashed up against the planking as Gunner and Arne heaved in boulders passed to them by the others. The little boat lurched like a stricken animal. The sea was almost in the gunwales, and suddenly the waves were over, spilling and spilling into the *Lobster Boy*. She gave one last heavy lurch, the stern sank, the green bows reared high, then she slipped below the surface, leaving not a trace on the dark-swelling sea.

The day passed slowly. Sigurd pronounced himself master of the primus. Broaching a case of provisions — most of the food was packed in waterproof containers — he provided a steady supply of hot cocoa and coffee, and twice a mug of soup and some hard biscuits. The men turned their wet clothes this way and that on the cold stones to catch the sun and the wind. The material froze, Peter, the fair young pilot, moulded his trousers and shirt into the shape of a man and stood him against the cliff, which even in such trying circumstances made them laugh.

Imperceptibly the sun moved behind the cliffs. Blue shadow settled over the beach; the temperature fell, Murdo handed back the warm clothes he was wearing, and put on his own which had been out in the sun all day. It was a difficult as well as a wretched task to thrust his limbs through iron-hard trouser legs and sleeves, and fasten the garments about him.

Bjorn Larvik and Gunner, each carrying an oar, set off up the snow slope once more, this time to borrow one of the bothy boats that Bjorn had discovered.

Huddled near the pile of crates beneath the cliff the others waited. The last traces of daylight sank behind the hill, and the long hours of darkness settled over land and sea. One shore light glittered, a tiny pinpoint far across the bay, where someone was not properly observing the blackout restrictions.

An hour passed. And then another hour. Henry Smith grew restless and sent Arne to look for the two men.

Wondering what caused the delay, they waited for his return. Murdo tucked his stockinged feet beneath him and pulled the collar of the battledress jacket close about his throat. He watched the thin veils of the northern lights flickering across the sky, white and pale green, like ghostly curtains and searchlights. Perhaps, he thought, if something had gone wrong, Hector and he would have a chance after all. He clenched his fists and flexed the muscles of his legs. He felt much better, strong enough to make a run for it if the chance arose. The hot drinks and food, and the enforced rest, had gone a long way to replace the energy sapped by his immersions in the sea.

The orange moon arose and swam low and hazy above the bay. They listened, but the soft roar of the waves drowned all other sound. Then at last, suddenly, Murdo spotted a small boat beneath the southern crags, silhouetted against the black and orange sea. He called out and pointed. The men stood, and swiftly Henry Smith made his way down to the shore rocks.

Carl Voss, whose revolver lay somewhere among the weed at the bottom of the bay, had taken a rifle from one of the cases during the day and filled the magazine. Watchful, now the darkness had returned, he motioned to Murdo and Hector and they descended the beach to join Henry Smith at the water's edge. The boat swung wide around the wilderness of shore rocks, then approached up the deep gully they had used earlier in the day. They heard the creak of wood and muffled splash of oars, and crossed to meet it.

"What went wrong?" Henry Smith called as Bjorn pulled close, shipping the oars and reaching for a knob of rock.

The big man looked up, holding the boat alongside as Gunner clambered out. "They were chained up," he said. "It was easy enough to smash the links, but I was afraid they would hear, so we waited until they all went out. They're off to the bar, I think. The path leads away from the shore, so they'll never know. Arne's gone round to the cave to tell Knut we'll be coming in an hour or so."

139

Henry Smith nodded. "Very good. Well, we'll get the boat loaded straight away. Gunner and Sigurd can take the first load and — " he eyed the rifle in Voss's hands " — Carl and I will take these two and whatever's left. The rest of you make your own way back to the cave around the shore."

It did not take long and soon the little boat was heading out to sea once more, rounding the cliff on the two mile journey down to Strathy beach.

Murdo settled himself once more in the shelter of the icy crag. He watched Bjorn and Peter make their way up the snow slope behind the beach and vanish, black silhouettes, over the crest of the headland. Now only Hector and himself, Carl Voss and Henry Smith remained in the cove. He shrugged his neck into his collar, tucked his fists beneath his armpits, and gazed out into the familiar night. The moon had brightened, a few small cumulus clouds had appeared. Beyond the bay, miles away, the inland hills gleamed with snow. He sighed and looked down at his jacket and legs, and thought about nothing.

In an hour and a half the boat returned, with Arne at the oars. Ten minutes were sufficient to load the last of the boxes and then Hector and Murdo were facing each other on the midship thwarts. Henry Smith sat with his revolver at the stern and Carl Voss and his Mauser rifle in the bow. They were heading out from the shore. Arne waved an arm and set off walking.

Briefly Murdo wondered about jumping, but it was a forlorn hope. Even if he had made it to the water, it was unlikely that he would be allowed to reach the shore, and it meant leaving Hector to face the wrath of the two armed Germans. Time was running out. Soon they would be captive in the cave, but even so he was not sorry to see the end of that frozen cove, and it was swiftly hidden behind the rising crags. Hector pulled strongly and half an hour later the line of beach was rising to meet them. As they came close three men appeared from the shadows under the cliff and made their way to the water's edge.

With a whispering crunch the boat slid to rest on the soft sand and toppled to its side, rocking in the following waves.

Hector and Murdo passed the boxes out, watched all the time by Carl Voss, the rifle resting easily in his hand. Then they stepped into the knee-deep water and pulled the boat a few yards up the beach. Bjorn and Gunner, still in the cave, would have to return it to the bothy — and with wire cutters and pliers repair the broken chain — since only they knew exactly how the boat had been lying.

For a while the five Germans stood beside the little pile of crates, talking among themselves. Then nodding, Carl Voss stepped aside. Knut, the bearded guard, with a duffle coat over his Royal Naval uniform, looked over at Hector and Murdo and said something amusing. Henry Smith laughed. The obvious insult made Murdo flush in the darkness and clench his fists. Then Peter and Sigurd shouldered a case each and the four strolled off up the beach in the direction of the cave.

The dark barrel of the rifle gleamed as Carl Voss turned to face them.

"All right," he said. "You know what you have to do. Carry the rest of these cases up to the cave. And make no mistake, if you lay one foot wrong I will put a bullet straight through you." He stepped back and motioned towards the crates of arms. "Right!"

Slowly Murdo trudged up the sands behind Hector. The moonlight streamed over the beach like searchlight. The flat sand spread out all around. Soon they would be in the cave — tied up, almost certainly. This was his last chance to make a run for it, and there was no hope. He glanced back at Carl Voss: alert as a cat the man limped behind them. Murdo settled the box more comfortably on his shoulder and pushed the harsh shaggy hair from his eyes. They passed through the high stacks near the cliff, dropped the boxes in the cave mouth and made their way once more down the long beach.

Fifteen minutes later only four cases remained. Murdo's arm ached, his shoulder was chafed and sore, but worse was the realisation that two more journeys would lead them into the cave, to an imprisonment from which he could imagine no escape. The thought brought the boy close to desperation. His wet socks, rubbed into holes by the day on the rocks, had gathered sand, which formed hard uncomfortable pads beneath his insteps and toes. He paused at the crates by the sea and pulled them off, shook out the crumbling sand and wrung them as dry as possible. Squinting up as he pushed his feet back into the gritty stretched wool, he noticed a couple of small but quite substantial grey clouds drifting towards the moon. Tugging the socks as comfortable as possible, he picked up a crate and hoisted it to his shoulder.

They were half way to the cave before Murdo realised the significance of what he had seen. If the beach was dark! . . . He bit his lip and glanced back again at Carl Voss. The watchful eyes glittered and Voss motioned him on with the rifle.

"I don't know what you're thinking of," he said, "but don't."

As they started down the beach again the moon was before them and he was able to observe it more closely. The clouds were moving up, diffusing and joining, but so slowly. Surely they were going to hit the moon, but would they be in time? Murdo's heart jumped in his throat.

All too soon they reached the last two cases, now almost lapped by the rising tide.

"Just a minute." As he walked Murdo had managed to kick his socks loose. He bent and removed them once more to shake out the sand. Slowly he pulled them on again, and squeezed some drops of water from the bottom of his trouser legs. Seeming to be brisk, but taking his time, he unfastened his jacket and tucked the shirt around his waist. From beneath his brows he glanced up at the clouds. They had united and now formed a single dark grey mass rimmed with white. And it was nearly to the moon, the first billowing waves suffused with moonlight. The shadow moved towards them across the sea and eastern headland. Murdo stood up, set his teeth, and heaved the last long box to his shoulder. The cool courage of the early evening had deserted him. His stomach turned over and he was trembling.

Slowly they began the final trudge up the beach. They were half way – they were drawing close to the crags. Then the cloud hit the moon. The white searchlight glimmered feebly then vanished, and darkness spread over the beach. On the instant Murdo dropped his box and sprang like a wild cat straight into the German's stomach. Carl Voss reeled backwards. The rifle went off with a cliff-shattering bang. Murdo struck him with every ounce of power at his disposal, with the pent-up rage of all that Hector and he had recently endured. The German fell. Then Murdo took to his heels and fled away seaward, into the deeper black shadows between the high stacks and the cliff.

Gasping for air, his nose and lip streaming blood, Voss picked himself up and snapped the bolt once. The boy had vanished, then he saw him, a dark fleeting shape against the sand. He flung the rifle to his shoulder and took careful aim. His finger tightened on the trigger.

The Road to the Hills

"No!" With a great roar Hector flung himself at the rifle.

Crack! The barrel kicked high and the shot whined harmlessly away among the crags. Carl Voss turned on him, his teeth bared, and savagely jerked the butt of the rifle into the old man's head. There was an ugly thud, his body jerked, and Hector slumped to the ground without a murmur.

But Murdo had gone. Voss stumbled to the edge of the rock, and as the moon appeared momentarily through a gap in the cloud, saw the boy's figure flitting along beneath the crag. Again he flung up the rifle. Crack! . . . Crack! The deafening reports echoed from the cliffs across the bay. Momentarily Murdo stumbled, then flung himself full length on the sand, out of sight behind one of the stacks.

"Stop it, you fool!" Henry Smith seized the bloody rifle from Voss's hands and threw it to the ground. "Do you want the whole village down here?" He looked across the moon-bright beach. There was no sign of the boy. He could be anywhere among those rocky pillars and shadowy crags. Then he saw the line of plunging tracks and pointed. "Get after him! And no more shooting." He turned on the men who had followed him out of the cave. "Go on, then! What are you waiting for? Good God, surely a whole squad of German soldiers can handle a young boy!"

They dashed away along the foot of the cliffs as the moon once more disappeared behind the cloud.

"No, Knut! . . . Knut!"

The guard stopped and came back to his leader.

"You see to the old man. Get those boxes put away. I'm going along to see those incompetents don't make a hash of it a second time." He turned and hurried across the beach after the others.

Murdo had left the sand behind and in the darkness stumbled on the weedy, sea-washed rocks. He could feel the blood wet down his right leg where the shot had clipped him and torn a groove across the side of his thigh. Already the numbness was wearing off and it hurt fiercely like a poker burn. His stockings gripped well; the soles of his feet, hardened from going barefoot in the summer, held on the barnacles. Twice his path was barred by rocky gullies, but he had crossed them a hundred times and there was no difficulty in descending to the glinting pools and climbing once more to the rocks beyond. As he went he scanned the dark cliff for a suitable place to climb to the headland. He made good speed, and four hundred yards beyond the beach came to the rocky fissure that was in his mind. He scrambled into the black shadows and began to climb.

He had been up the cleft a dozen times, but always in daylight when there was no need to hurry. Now, as he raced, the stone crumbled beneath his hands, scattering down the cliff to the pool and shore rocks below. Cursing beneath his breath he slowed his pace to take more care and not give his position away. He was still only half way up when the Germans arrived beneath him. He froze, there was a good chance they would not spot him up there. He was right, for they were more intent in catching him up than searching for him, and the leading men went straight past. But their way was barred by the deep inlet almost impossible to negotiate, and even as he watched, the moon reappeared from the far side of the cloud. He could see them plainly, though the fissure in which he clung remained black, steeped in shadow.

They paused irresolutely, looking this way and that for a spot where Murdo might have turned off the rocks. Henry Smith looked back, wondering if he could have travelled so far and so quickly without boots. Carl Voss scanned the ledges of the watery gully, and the shore beyond, lest Murdo should have swum across. Sigurd stepped into the mouth of the fissure and peered up, trying to penetrate the darkness. Staring down, Murdo could see him very clearly, the neat figure and handsome face.

Suddenly a rock shifted beneath Murdo's foot. He tried to hold it in with the pressure of his instep, but could not, and it rattled away with a little avalanche of pebbles almost to where Sigurd was standing.

The man shaded his eyes from the brightness of the moon and tried to make out the black shapes above him.

"Carl," he called. "Gunner."

"He is up there?"

"I think — just a minute. I — yes, there he is!" Sigurd pointed upwards and they all craned forward to see.

For a moment Murdo panicked. His legs trembled on the rocks and he pressed his face close, waiting helplessly for the smashing bullet. But it did not come, and he ventured to look down again. None of the men had produced the rifle or a revolver. What would they do?

Sigurd looked at Henry Smith. "Mine, I think," he said, with a smile. He was a mountaineer, the youngest of those who in the years before the war had performed such dazzling feats in the Alps and Himalayas for the glory of the Fatherland.

With an answering smile, almost as if he was sanctioning a theatrical performance, Henry Smith nodded.

Sigurd bent and tightened the laces of his boots, then stepped forward out of the moonlight. A moment later Murdo heard the clatter of stones below as the German started after him in pursuit. Swiftly he looked up, but the rocks were indistinguishable in the darkness. However they lay, there was no time to waste, and now heedless of noise he set off again, as fast as hand

and foot could find grips, praying that the sharp stones he sent down might hinder the man behind him.

But so great was his haste that he took a wrong lead, and before he knew it he was climbing out of the fissure towards the face of the crag itself. He cast about with his hand, but there was no way back except the way he had come. He glanced below — Sigurd was gaining, he had to go on. Soon he was out of the shadow, climbing across the moonlit rock face. Far below, amid the acres of dark rock mirrored with a hundred silver pools, the little white faces of the men peered up at the chase, the sea creaming at their heels. Murdo looked up, fighting back the giddy sickness, and felt steadily for hand-holds, for the shadows and moonlight were very deceptive. The ledges and crannies were covered with snow and he had to dust them bare with aching and almost numb fingers or with his stockinged feet, the snow spilling down the rock face and sifting into space. Once he came to a long run of ice and had to inch several yards across the sloping bulges of a thick-frozen ledge, holding fast to flutes of ice, like organ pipes glued to the cliff wall. Soon he was very high, nearing the crest, but as the rocks became more difficult Sigurd was gaining, gaining all the time. Glancing down again, Murdo saw him peering up as he reached for holds, so close that he could see the glint of moonlight on his teeth.

From below they looked no larger than two spiders, crawling infinitely slowly across the top of the sea-crag.

Murdo climbed on. He was nearly there. Just two feet above his outstretched hand the snowy grass commenced, sloping away to the top. Then, on the very verge of safety — there was no hold! Desperately he cast about, his belly crushed against the hard granite. But the searching fingers encountered no grip, his stockinged toes could find no knot of rock, no pebble to support him. He looked round. Sigurd was only a few feet behind him and coming up steadily. With a supreme effort Murdo flung his hand far out to the right, and with the very tips of his fingers encountered a tiny wart of rock. "It will have to do," he whispered in terror, and praying that his right toehold would support him, slid across, balancing against the rock, until he was able to grip the wart with the freezing tips of his fingers. His toes, having no other support, trembled with the strain, his leg began to shake. Then suddenly, as he reached up with his left hand, there was a good hold. He dusted the snow away and knotted his fingers in it, jammed his left toes against a tiny crack, and swung his other leg far out to the right where there was a solid sloping ledge. For a moment he hung there, spreadeagled against the very top cornice of the rock face. With a tremendous effort he pushed, praying that the sock would not slip on his foot. It held firm, and slowly he slid up towards the steep grassy slope. For a moment he hung in the balance, chin, arms, chest, knee, all pressed desperately against the snowy tussocks for support. Then he was up, and grabbing hold of the grass, dragged himself over the corner of the precipice.

Sigurd, with a longer reach, was only inches away. Skidding and sliding, Murdo hitched himself higher, clutching wildly at whatever met his hand, terrified of slipping backwards over the brink. But the German was too close. Suddenly Murdo felt his left ankle grabbed, and held in a grip of steel. He screamed. The hand pulled and he felt himself skidding back. One foot went over the edge. He looked down and saw Sigurd laughing through gritted teeth; his eyes glittered, thick snow powdered his curly hair and shoulders. Frantically Murdo kicked out. His left hand encountered a loose piece of rock, wedge-shaped and heavy, beneath the snow. He pulled it out and flung it down blindly with all his strength.

There was a sickening crack; his ankle was free; a loud, falling cry filled the air. Then there was a dull thud and the cry was cut off. A few stones and pebbles rattled away down the rocks. Trembling and sobbing, Murdo scrabbled and clawed his way up the snowy slope to safety. From below there came the sound of confused shouting, fading away in the direction of the cave.

For a full minute, Murdo was unable to move, panting and distressed, staring at the tracks he had made in the snow and the

149

terrible drop beyond. Then, hardly knowing what he was doing, heedless of the aching cold in his feet, he ran back along the top of the cliffs until he reached the gates of the wintry and deserted graveyard.

The cars were parked as Hector and Henry Smith had left them three days earlier, one on either side of the track, facing down into the dunes. The bonnets and roofs were piled high with snow and it had drifted against the doors. Quickly Murdo brushed the snow from the windscreen of Hector's old Ford, and scarred his fingernails across the hard granular ice. He could never clear it that way. He thought for a moment then hurried round the boot to see whether there was any petrol or paraffin there. It had frozen shut, but with a great wrench he managed to tear it open. Half a dozen bottles of whisky remained in a crate. He grabbed a couple and running back to the windscreen poured a whole bottle down the glass and over the headlights. The ice vanished as if by magic. He kicked the drift from the running-board, pulled open the driver's door and jumped in, flinging his tackety boots off the seat.

As always, the key was under the mat. He switched on and pulled the starter. The engine whirred. Again — the engine whirred discouragingly.

"Give it some choke, you fool," he said to himself, and pulled the knob full out.

Still no success.

"Come on! Come on!"

Again and again he pulled at the starter, his snowy stocking hovering above the accelerator, ready to catch it when the engine fired.

Nothing!

Reaching over to the back seat he grabbed the starting handle and dodged out to the front of the car.

"Come on! Where are you?" His numb fingers could not find the slot. "Ah!" He spread his legs and jerked the handle. Once — twice. The engine flopped over, completely dead. Again — his fingers slipped and gashed against the bumper, but

150

this time the engine choked. A fourth time — and suddenly the engine roared into life.

Snatching the handle clear and shaking his fingers with pain, he raced around the side of the car. But suddenly, through the graveyard gates, the Germans were upon him. With all his strength Murdo flung the iron handle at their heads and leaped into the car, slamming and locking the door against them. Swiftly he leaned across and snapped the locking button on the passenger door also.

They were at the window, hammering on the glass. Big hands seized the handles. He trod hard on the accelerator, making the engine roar, and flicked on the headlights. Dazzling bodies dashed across in front of the bonnet. Unshaven faces peered through the windows, twisted with shouting. Heavy fists pounded on the roof. The car lurched violently. Murdo flung it into gear, lifted his foot from the clutch and shot forward down the track. He had a brief vision of men leaping clear all round — then they were behind him. He braked, banged the gears into reverse, and spinning wildly, shot backwards. There was a heavy bump as the boot struck someone. The car swung violently and careered half way up the grassy bank, then came to rest and slid slowly forward. The Germans were in front of him again, dazzled by the headlights. Almost ignoring the clutch, Murdo crashed through the gears into first, trod down hard on the accelerator, and roared at full throttle straight into them. For a split second they wavered, then broke, and scattered from his path. Henry Smith, Carl Voss, Bjorn — he saw them all. They were there, they were gone — and the car fled on up the snow-covered road. Behind him there was the unmistakable crack of a rifle: instantaneously a bullet tore through the roof. Then he was round the bend and out of sight.

The windscreen was freezing on the inside. Murdo pressed his hand against it, but it froze over at once. Reaching across to the passenger seat he pulled the second bottle of whisky on to his lap and felt under the dashboard for a rag. Drawing the cork with his teeth, he slopped some whisky on to it and cleared the ice away. The road ahead was brilliant in the main beam of the headlights. The old car rattled and skidded through the dunes, leaping and spinning half out of control on the icy corners, wreaths of snow swirling from the bonnet and roof. In a few minutes, Murdo thought, he would be in Strathy. It couldn't be more than nine or ten o'clock. On a Friday night there would be at least half a dozen men at the inn; the landlord had several shotguns and a rifle. He had seen them in a glass-fronted cupboard.

Then suddenly his iced rear window was blinded out by the powerful lights of a car coming up from behind. As he swung round a tight corner he could see across his shoulder the blazing headlamps eating up the road at a tremendous rate. They could not be more than two or three hundred yards behind. He pressed his foot still further down on the throttle, the car would hardly hold the road. Still they came on. A sharp crest sprang up ahead, the car leaped, then he was slithering and snaking down the steep snowy brae that led to the narrow crossroads where he had to turn right for the village. Too late he tried to brake, jamming the pedal to the floor, but he was going too fast, the wheels had no grip. The car slewed wildly from side to side, the main road rushed towards him. For an instant he hesitated, then he was upon it, and over, leaping and bucking on the glen road beyond. He fought to keep the wheels out of the ditch. His speed fell. With numb horror he realised what he had done. There was no time to reverse. Already the German car was swishing down to the crossroads behind him. Bitterly he cursed his stupidity. Ahead — the road led miles and miles into the moors and the empty hills, to a deserted bothy, to nowhere. And behind, the German car crept up to his heels.

For the moment there was nothing to do but drive on. With his mouth dry, Murdo nursed the car up the rough snowy track, a twisting ribbon between the fringing clumps of moorland grass and heather. On his left the endless hills rose gently, rolling into the shadowy gloom of the night; on his right the land fell away to the frozen river in the bottom of the broad glen.

He had never travelled all the way up the strath before, only as far as Hector's peat banks, and the lodge and cottage at Bowside, three miles from the village. But the road wound on past these to the new forestry plantations, and beyond that again to the lonely shepherds' bothy at Loch Strathy. His eyes flickered down to the petrol gauge — at least the tank was full. For a moment he half smiled, remembering the deal Hector had made with some R.A.F. boys, trading whisky and venison for a drum of the pink high-octane aeroplane fuel. Then the smile faded and he wondered what had become of his old friend down there on the beach.

Behind him the Germans had stopped weaving, stopped looking for a place where they could nose past with their more powerful car. Quietly they came on about ten yards behind. Murdo shifted the driving mirror so that the headlights did not dazzle him.

In a few minutes they were at the Bowside turning. Looking across, Murdo could see that there was no-one at home. The houses were dark, hunched against the snowy hills. Nevertheless he jammed his hand on the horn and blew a long, harsh blast. The shocking sound reverberated over the silent moors. Down towards the river a herd of red deer rose to their feet, shifting nervously before they took to flight, springing in beautiful bounds almost parallel with the rocking cars. But no light or movement showed from the lonely buildings.

Mile followed mile. The bare hillsides suddenly became thick with trees as the cars lurched over a cattle grid between deer fences and entered the forestry area. Briefly Murdo thought of running for it, leaving the car and racing for shelter among the dense thickets of young spruce; but he had no chance of succeeding, not with the German car so close behind.

And then they were out of the forest again, pushing through the long, slanting snow-wreaths on the open moor. The moon was full in his face, white plains and slopes gleamed in the distance beyond the reach of the headlights. A range of hills ten miles away was clearly etched against the pale sky. Even as he strove to keep ahead of his pursuers, Murdo was dimly aware that the night was exceptionally beautiful. Life seemed very precious. He glanced back at the car behind. Inexorably it came on.

A blackcock clattered up with a harsh cry, almost it seemed from under his wheels, and circled away to the left. The hen bird followed at its tail and there was a sickening thud as it struck the wing of the car. Two or three feathers shone momentarily in the headlights. Murdo grimaced and drove on.

He tried to estimate how far they had come. Ten — twelve miles? It must be something like that, he decided. The end of the road could not be very far away. What would happen when they reached it? Would he be able to make a run for it, or would they simply capture him and take him back to the cave? It depended who was in the car. He would at least be safe, he thought, if Bjorn Larvik was there. But if he was not . . .!

He swung tightly round a banked corner and suddenly the road dropped steeply away. There, forty feet below him, was a wide ford, shrunk in the frosty weather to a narrow channel of black water between the banks of ice. He braked hard, but the descent was too steep. The old car bucked and skidded crazily as the patched ice shot up to meet it. Bang! The front wheels snapped up into the body like an explosion. Murdo crashed forward into the windscreen, the steering wheel thudded against his ribs. For a moment the car tottered on two wheels, then fell back, spun, and shot viciously at the far bank, slewing and snaking in the mud and ice. Crack! It hit the road again. The lights pierced the sky. The car fell heavily, rattling like a trailer-load of scrap iron, and fled towards the broad ditch. But miraculously the wheels held. It bounced off the verge, careered into a boulder, and skidded on up the treacherous road.

Murdo clung to the steering wheel and blinked dazedly and fiercely up the brilliant track ahead. His teeth were set, he sniffed back a trickle of blood from one nostril.

Slowly he became aware that something was different. The lights were no longer on his tail. Instead, the whole summit of a nearby knoll was illuminated. He slowed and looked more closely, swinging the driving mirror, then slowing still further, opened the car door and glanced back. Dark and indistinct, the great car lay helplessly on its side, lights blazing across the hillside and into the air. He stopped and waited to see what would happen. Slowly a door opened and a dim figure started to climb out. The lights went off, and he could see the car more clearly against the moonlit snow. Another figure emerged. From what Murdo could estimate it was hopeless, they would never get the car back on the road.

With unspeakable relief he pulled the door shut, slipped Hector's car into gear and rattled on up the road. The suspension had gone and every boulder jerked the body with a heavy 'clunk'.

But his relief was short-lived. Only a mile further on, the track ran out into a snowy space beside a small deserted cottage, and ceased. It was the Loch Strathy bothy.

Murdo switched off the lights and looked back. A frighteningly short distance away the inside light of the German car twinkled warmly amid the white wilderness. He could not distinguish the figures, but the light flickered time and again as if people were passing in front of it.

Swiftly he rummaged on the floor for his tackety boots. The Germans would not be long in following, that was certain. They must see the cottage, and Henry Smith would have binoculars and maps. Hastily he crammed his feet into his boots and dragged the laces together. What else? He pulled out the car key and pocketed it. The car itself contained nothing that he wanted except an old black and white toorie. He pulled it on the back of his head and patted the pockets of his trousers and khaki battledress jacket. His fingers touched his father's clasp knife and a screwed-up handkerchief — there seemed to be nothing else.

With a sudden clang something smacked into the car with enormous power, and the crack of a rifle echoed across the moors. There was not a second to lose. Murdo reached to the floor for the fallen bottle of whisky, slammed the car door and locked it. Then, crouching as he ran across the clearing, he put the old bothy between himself and the shooting.

Clearly it was no use hiding, they would be sure to find him. He must take to the moors. He looked from the neighbouring hills to Loch Strathy, a mile distant and covered with ice and drifted snow, trying to decide which way he should go. There was only one answer — upwards. Drawing a deep, determined breath he shoved the bottle of whisky down the front of his battle-dress, leaned momentarily against the gable wall of the cottage, then pushed himself off towards the foot of the rough slope.

After the comfort of the car the night seemed bitterly cold, but at least he had warmed through after that day on the seashore, and a few minutes' exercise brought the heat coursing through his body. At first his leg ached and burned like fire, but it no longer seemed to be bleeding, and when he felt it gingerly with his fingers the cold stickiness had gone, leaving a hard patch on the side of his trousers.

There was quite a lot of snow, but for the moment it did not seriously impede his progress and he made good speed. A few rifle shots rang out from below, whip cracks in the silence. They were shooting blind, he realised, but the thought gave him little confidence.

Murdo climbed with the accustomed stride of one well used to shepherding, and soon found himself high on the steep ridge that rose from the house to the rolling summits of the moor. Pausing for a moment to regain his breath, he looked back down his tracks, so clearly visible in the bright moonlight. A light was on in Hector's car, and as he listened intently, faint voices drifted up on the wind. Tiny figures, impossible to distinguish, moved in the circle of light. He turned again and pressed on up the slope.

Minutes later the roar of an engine caused him to halt a second time. They had managed to start Hector's car, and as he watched the lights went on, stabbing their golden-white beams through the dusky shadows. A door slammed. Slowly the car drew away in a circle, then gathering speed, headed off down the track towards the ford.

Briefly he watched its progress, angry with himself for not removing the distributor cap, then turned his gaze back to Loch Strathy cottage, scanning the slopes. He blinked and screwed up his eyes to see more clearly, for the icy wind was making them water. Two dark specks stood out on the near side of the bothy, moving slowly up the hillside after him. He imagined Carl Voss with the powerful rifle tucked beneath his arm, scouring the snowfields ahead for a sign of himself. He bit his lip, suppressing a shiver of fear, and looked around at the moors. Ten, twenty miles, they spread away on every side, to the very rim of the glittering sky. They were very empty, very big. Out there, you could die. But surrender was unthinkable: among those rolling hills lay Murdo's only hope of safety. He shrugged the jacket easy on his shoulders and headed out into the wilderness.

Full Moon

Three hours later the spread-eagled figure of Orion had swung far around the sky and the moon was at its zenith in the south, when Murdo stopped for the hundredth time and scanned the slopes behind him. For half an hour he had been climbing across the side of a mountain and its great flank stretched far down below. There was no sign of any movement upon the bright snow. Surely, he thought, he must be drawing clear, yet fear was so much stronger than hope that he could hardly believe it. He breathed deeply but easily as the wind blew cold on his damp forehead. He had plenty of strength left yet. He glanced up at the Plough and found the Pole Star, then set off again eastwards towards Strath Halladale. For more than an hour he had been heading in that direction. In the glen there were houses, and the little village of Kinbrace.

A snowy owl winging its way silently above hooted softly with surprise at the minute figure far below, toiling across the great slope like an ant on a sand dune. Far away, well beyond the foot of the mountain, the round wide-awake eyes spotted two more, even tinier figures, imperceptibly moving in the same direction. The white wings fluttered and it sailed back to the summit rocks to land without even a rustle, blinking in astonishment. The great head swivelled to look behind. Nothing moved, the shadowy moonlit hills rolled on until they vanished into the dimness of the horizon. The very mountain itself was lost in the landscape.

As Murdo climbed over the ridge the land fell away before him into a flat valley, the floor a gleaming level of frozen lochs, all pewter and silver, dappled with snow. Beyond, barring his path to the east, reared two imposing summits, even from that height outlined against the stars. It would take a while to climb through the steep pass between them. Still, that was the way he must go, and relieved that for the moment at least his path led downwards, he ploughed off, taking long, loose-kneed strides towards the valley bottom.

He thrust a hand deeply into the pocket of his blue serge trousers for warmth and encountered the comfortable haft of his father's knife. The contact gave him strength, and as he proceeded he thought of his father — and Lachlan and Maggie, but most of all his father — and the times they had all had together. Repeatedly, however, his mind returned to Hector and that roaring 'No!' on the beach, followed by a brief scuffle and then a long silence before the first of the shots. He tried to picture what had happened, and a hundred times in his mind's eye relived the nightmarish climb up the cliff.

As he descended, the hills rose ahead, and by the time he was skirting the first of the lochs, the nearer summit did indeed look formidable. It soon became apparent, however, that his track through the lochs would naturally take him between them, and that the slope to the pass was by no means as arduous as it had appeared earlier.

A few hundred yards brought him to a broad stream, half a mile in length, which linked two substantial lochs in the long valley chain. It must be crossed. Murdo looked at the ice, dusted and drifted with snow. It was impossible in the moonlight to judge how thick it was. Tentatively he slid one foot from the edge and leaned his weight upon it. The ice seemed firm enough. Then he thought of the black water swirling below. If he went through it might carry him beneath the surface — he would never get out. He withdrew and retraced his footsteps to the end of the loch. The water there would be stiller, the ice thicker. If he did break through, he should be able to clamber out again.

Cautiously he inched out from the shore. The ice was strong and apparently sound. Nevertheless he was careful, for there were sometimes springs in the bed of the loch that left weak patches, invisible beneath the snow. But he encountered none, and in a couple of minutes was on the further shore. The mountains lay ahead.

Murdo gazed up the slope he must travel, fingering the stiff patch on his trousers and testing the sharp, numb sensation of the wound beneath it. The pass was split by a deep rocky gully. On either side the ascent was rough, with steep slopes and tussocky grass. He decided to take the right hand rim, where there was more stone but less snow, and drawing a deep breath, trudged on.

Soon he had left the valley floor and was climbing. But in his choice of route he had made an error. As he went higher the gully deepened and pressed close into the side of the mountain, so that he was forced to watch how he went on the treacherous grass and strewn boulders. It was hard going and his legs began to tremble with the effort. Up and up he toiled, until at length he found himself on a steep slope beneath the summit crags. It was a landscape of snow and rock. A long run of scree swept from the foot of the cliffs into the stream below. The whole slope shifted beneath his feet as he started to cross, and little avalanches slid away into the shadows.

Beyond the scree the way was more difficult, winding along a broad ledge between boulders, with the snow-clad cliffs hanging above, and a rough rock-fall dropping into the gully below. His nailed boots struck occasional sparks, and skidded on the hidden stones. Then his right foot went from beneath him and he fell heavily, raking his damaged thigh against a corner of rock as he twisted to save the bottle in his jacket. The pain was acute, and it was long moments before he could grit himself to rising. A hot blade twisted in the wound. He felt the wetness on his leg as blood trickled past his knee and down into his sock. For some minutes, as he limped on, it seemed as though the ledge was merging into the crag, and he feared he would have to climb again or retrace his steps. Then he rounded a steep buttress, and suddenly the rocks were behind him. A gentle snow slope rose ahead to the crest of the pass. Relieved, but more slowly than before, he pressed his weary legs forward, and equally slowly the huge vista unfolded before him.

Featureless, shadowy, pale, mile upon mile, the moors rolled on ahead. No gleam of light, no sparkle from a lonely window, relieved the cold austerity of the scene. The thin, perishing wind blew through the funnel of the pass into his face.

A hundred times Murdo had pictured Hector's map, and travelled over the land in his mind's eye, for he knew the region well. Strath Halladale must be there — but there was no sign of it.

He was lost. A feeling of hopelessness and emptiness welled up within him. He had counted on the strath lying spread before him, or at least being in sight and not too far distant when he reached the top of the pass. Instead he was rewarded with an awe-inspiring revelation of the sheer immensity of the land.

For a minute he gave in. Anything was better than being lost and alone out there. Already the heat of the climb was leaving him and he shivered. He was tired, he wanted a rest, and thought longingly of the glowing fire and his warm bed in Hector's cottage. . . . Suddenly he was angry with himself. He would not give in — he would never give in! There was only one end to that kind of thinking. Strath Halladale lay to the east, there was no doubt about it. He glanced up at the North Star and took an easterly bearing, noting a long escarpment that must remain ahead. The full moon, dominating the night, would be slightly behind his right shoulder. He flexed the injured thigh. Then, denying the thoughts of despair and fortifying himself with images of the warmth and help that were waiting in Strath Halladale, only a few miles ahead, he pushed forward down the long slope.

Murdo was not the only person to be doubting himself on the moors at that moment. Even as he trudged down the hillside from the pass, Carl Voss and Peter arrived at the end of the loch below and crossed over the ice. Murdo's tracks led on ahead of them. Voss was sweating and he paused, pressing a hand to his knee, wrenched in the sea and bruised when Murdo struck him with the car. His face was twisted but determined as he gazed up the steep slope ahead. Surely the boy must be somewhere on that face, or in the gully, but he could not see him. He looked across at Peter, the young Luftwaffe pilot, who slowly shook his head in reply, never taking his eyes from the mountainside.

"He is some walker!"

Carl Voss pressed his lips together and snorted angrily in reply. "If it wasn't for this damned leg!" He massaged his knee gently and winced as the pain shot through it. "We'll never catch up with him like this. I'm only keeping you back." He slung the rifle from his shoulder and pulled a roughly folded map from inside his jacket. Shading a little torch with his hand he studied it carefully, comparing it with the land around them. "We are — here." His broad finger indicated the narrow space between a chain of blue lochs and the packed brown contours of a hillside. "And he has gone up here. Now . . ." Thoughtfully he studied Murdo's course and the lie of the land beyond the mountain. "If he has gone over the pass, and it looks as if he has, there are two possibilities. He will either keep straight on east, and in that case he has got a long way to go to — Strath Halladale, or whatever you call it, the God-forsaken place; or else he will see the road below him and drop down to this valley here, in which case he will see —" he peered closely at the map "— the Ben Crocach Hotel. It is only about two miles from the top of the hill there." He shifted a little to ease the weight on his aching leg and looked up the steep pass. "If I tried to climb that it would take an hour — more. I'd keep you back and that brat would get a bigger lead than ever. He's far enough ahead already." He thought for a moment. "The best plan is for you to go after him by yourself. I'm sure you can go faster than he can. I'll head round the side of the hill and cut him off if he tries to turn back to the hotel."

The young pilot nodded. "All right," he said. "I'll be following the tracks, so if you catch him I'll meet up with you. And if I catch him I'll fire two shots in the air." He lifted a foot and tried to squeeze some life into his frozen toes. In the cave on Strathy beach he had just exchanged his sodden boots for a pair of sandshoes when Murdo escaped. In the hurry and confusion there had been no time to change back.

"Never mind two shots in the air — two shots in the head. When you catch him, kill him," Carl Voss said. "No messing about. Just make sure he's dead, and leave him where he is. No-one will find him out here. If Heinrich hadn't been so squeamish we'd be back in the cave now."

"Mm." With some distaste, Peter regarded his dark companion. "It must be nice to have everything so simple in your mind, Voss," he said. "No indecision. Just 'kill him', and that's the problem solved. 'No messing about'."

Carl Voss pushed the map into his pocket and slung the rifle over his shoulder. "It's clean," he said simply.

"It's certainly final," Peter observed. "I'm afraid it's not my way, though." He looked up at the moon and ran a hand through his fair hair. "Well, I'll be off."

"Good luck," said Voss, with a dry smile.

Peter did not reply, and moving more swiftly than before, despite his frozen feet, settled down to following the footprints that led straight across the valley floor and up the side of the sweeping mountain ravine.

Carl Voss grunted, alone now, and gritted his teeth to make a further effort. Then, denying himself any respite for the sickening pain that lurched at every footfall, he strode off to the right, heading around the western flank of the mountain.

He kept high, and an hour later the hotel and scattering of outbuildings appeared ahead of him, far below. From what he could distinguish it was a good-sized place, an old lodge, probably used for shooting and fishing in the summer. But no lights were visible now, and there was no sign of the boy on the broad snow slopes above it.

He walked on, drawing closer. Suddenly he stopped. A line of footprints crossed the slope fifty yards ahead — but they were only the tracks of a deer. Then he saw the deer themselves, a herd of about fifty, moving quietly out of a hidden hollow not two hundred yards from the hotel. Clearly the boy was not there, the deer would have run off. There was no point in going down.

He pulled out his torch and studied the map again. Since the boy had not turned back to the hotel, then almost certainly he was heading for Strath Halladale. With his eye he drew a line east from the high pass and saw that it reached the strath near a loch, where there was a lodge. Four miles further south lay the little village of Kinbrace. Certainly he must prevent the boy from reaching there. He projected his own path south-east along the side of the hill, above the road, and saw that it led to a deserted stretch of strath between the village and the loch. If he continued he should be able to cut the boy off. It was a gamble, but there was not much else he could do except go back, and he had not trained for six months with the Alpenkorps to turn back now.

He looked up and ran his eyes carefully along the white crest high above him. Even yet the boy might cross the ridge and try to reach the hotel, or see the black splinters of telephone poles far below, marking the road. But the hillside remained empty, nothing moved. He returned the torch and map to his pockets and walked on, trying to ignore the pain, but gradually going slower despite himself. The weight of the gleaming rifle was a pleasure on his shoulder, the empty mountains were his own terrain. Like a wolf, he limped along the snowy slopes.

A third group of men were on the moors that night.

Leaving Peter and Carl Voss at the bothy, Henry Smith had driven Hector's rattling car down the track, back through the ford and snow wreaths, towards the village. He had not been going for fifteen minutes when car lights appeared more than a mile ahead, and the two met with dipped headlights, nose to nose on the narrow track. In the car were the last of his men, Arne, Gunner and Knut. Henry Smith was annoyed that Bjorn Larvik, the best countryman of them all, had elected to stay behind to care for the old man, who was still unconscious, and keep watch at the cave. They had all equipped themselves with rifles and ammunition, and set off in a 'borrowed' car just in case there should be any trouble. It was the work of a moment to push Hector's car off the road. Down the steep slope it went, bucking and tumbling over and over, finally crashing into the frozen channel of the stream. Then, with some satisfaction, they all climbed into the borrowed car and drove back to the bothy above Loch Strathy.

They set off immediately in pursuit of Carl Voss and Peter. Knut, with his tiny snub nose and beard, still in uniform and duffle coat, was returning the car. He leaned on top of the door smoking a cigarette, and watched Henry Smith lead Arne and Gunner at a fast pace up the long hillside. Soon they were dots cresting a far rise, and then they were gone. He turned the car in a heavy circle and set off for the village.

The three were only half an hour behind Carl Voss and Peter when they left the bothy, and by the time they arrived at the frozen loch they had cut this to fifteen minutes.

Breathing scarcely more deeply than normal, Henry Smith suddenly came to a halt and stood gazing in surprise at the three sets of footprints. Two led straight ahead towards the high pass, the other turned right around the side of the mountain. Slowly a rising fury took the place of astonishment.

"The fools! The incompetent fools!" He pointed. "What do they think are doing? Do they think that by going over mountains they will cut him off?" Trembling, he gnawed at one knuckle. But it was only for a moment that he hesitated. "Right! Leave them. We will follow him ourselves. Come. We must hurry!" He pushed his way past Gunner and strode off to the right. Angrily he crushed his map in a clenched fist, and beat it against his thigh as he walked.

The track led high around the mountain slope. Walking was treacherous, for the snow hid peaty hollows and tussocks of grass, and from time to time they fell. Unused to such haste on rough terrain their ankles ached, but Henry Smith would permit no rest, no respite, and kept pressing on, pressing on. They crossed the line of deer tracks and saw the herd far below, scouring the sheep fields for remnants of hay and oil cake. They saw the hotel, set back on the dappled plain. Left of the hotel, low down in the east, the stars had vanished, blotted out by a slowly advancing bank of cloud.

Suddenly Gunner exclaimed, and touching Henry Smith's arm, pointed to a tiny dot, slightly below them and half a mile further on. Short-sighted without his glasses, Henry Smith screwed up his eyes and peered across the slope, barely making it out. Even as they watched, it dropped from sight behind a shallow ridge.

Henry Smith was very calm. "All right, then," he said. "No talking."

With the quarry in sight they needed no encouragement. They forgot their tiredness and aching ankles. Arne shrugged the rifle comfortable on his back.

The land was levelling out ahead, dropping from the mountain to a rolling plateau of moors. The black figure showed again for a moment against the summit of a low rise.

Swift and light of stride, a few minutes brought them behind a small hillock, and cautiously they peered over the top, treading very softly. The hillside was empty. Then, over to the left and still far away, further than he had seemed before, a small figure appeared among a tumble of boulders, wending along the foot of a long gully. Arne reached inside his jacket and pulled out a sniper's telescopic sight. Carefully he clipped it home on top of his rifle. There was a loud 'click' as the spring lock snapped shut. He tightened the screws. Henry Smith reached out a hand and took it from him, passing his own in exchange. The rocks sprang forward as he raised the rifle to his shoulder and adjusted the sight. It took a moment to find the figure — then there he was. He seemed to be limping. Slowly he raised the fine cross of the sight until it rested, swaying slightly, on the dark body. But he was too far off, the sight would need adjustment for that degree of accuracy. Reluctantly he let it fall.

"He's hurt," he said factually to Gunner and Arne. "He has no idea we are here. So no noise — and watch the rocks down there. This is it."

Lips pressed tightly together, flared nostrils snorting slightly in the icy air, he strode forward down the far slope of the hill. Arne and Gunner followed at his heels. The sinister black rifles bumped heavily on their shoulders.

But the figure kept well ahead and it was nearly half an hour later when, dropping round a shoulder of the moors they suddenly came upon him, standing not four hundred yards off, looking around as if undecided which way to go.

Henry Smith sank to the ground, motioning the others to do the same.

"Sssh!" he breathed, his whisper scarcely audible. "Get yourselves down." Quietly he slipped the rifle from his shoulder. "Take a bead on him, just in case. If anything goes wrong, shoot." He settled himself on his belly in the snow, right leg in line with his target, and raised the rifle.

Gunner laid a hand on his sleeve. "He's only a boy. Give him a chance."

Henry Smith looked up, his baby face almost cherubic in the moonlight. "He's had enough chances already," he said. "I've lost three men, three vital men. We have ten miles to walk back over the hills to Loch Strathy, and another twelve or fourteen down the road to the village. And now they say it will be a week before the lorries arrive." He shook his head. "He is too big a risk."

Unhappily Gunner looked across at Arne.

His face long and thin, white hair bristling, Arne gazed coldly back at him. "I agree with Heinrich," he said shortly. "It is the best way now."

Helplessly Gunner turned away.

168

Henry Smith pulled the rifle into his shoulder and snuggled his cheek against the smooth butt. By now the figure had begun walking again. The dusky silhouette loomed before him in the telescope, stumbling a little with tiredness, feet slipping on the rough ground. Slowly the fine cross of the sight swung up the legs to the waist, and wavered a little. Then it was firm in the middle of the back. His finger tightened on the trigger.

CRACK! The deafeningly sharp report rang out across the silent moors.

Before the three men their quarry, without a murmur, flung up his arms and spun clumsily into the snow.

Henry Smith's face was grim as he rose and brushed the snow from his front.

"It is all over," he said. "The best way. Clean and finished."

Together they walked quietly forward along the line of tracks so recently made by a living man.

Before them the black figure lay twisted and quite still on the bright carpet. Henry Smith was a couple of paces in the lead. Suddenly he stopped, frozen in his tracks, his eyes wide with horror.

"No!" he breathed, "Oh, dear God!" and ran forward the last few yards.

Carl Voss was dead. His head hung heavily on the limp neck as they raised him in the snow. Lumps of snow adhered to his face and throat, and his clothes were covered with it. There was no mark on him, his dark face was quite calm.

Peter by himself made good speed, and although he could not see Murdo, was sure that he must be gaining on the boy. Up the long slope of the pass he strode, stumbling time and again, wrenching his ankles on the icy rocks below the crags. The stones rattled away into the gully, the moonlight glinted on the ice runs that sheathed the cliff face; the crest rose ahead and the huge vista unfolded below. Murdo's tumbled tracks continued straight down the far side of the mountain. Apparently he did not know about the road and the hotel.

Peter quartered the land below as he had been trained to do as a pilot, but it was no use, nothing moved on the smooth slopes. He set off again, almost at a run, slithering and sliding as his rubber shoes failed to secure a grip beneath the powdery snow.

It was a long descent, and he had nearly reached the bottom when, without really thinking about it, his eyes focussed on a tiny shape ahead. He paused; it was moving, and in the right direction. It might have been a sheep or a deer, but he did not think so. Cheered by the sight, and warming to the chase, he plunged on.

Reaching the flat he was almost running, jumping the little hollows, driving up the slopes and leaping clumsily down the far sides, the revolver bumping heavily in his pocket. His blood was up, and in the cold air he was hardly even panting as the rough land sped beneath his feet. It was like the cross-country races he had run at school in Aachen before the war.

His eyes sparkled as he crested a little rise and leaped from a small peat ridge into the hollow behind. But he landed badly, his right foot caught in something beneath the snow and he pitched sideways. There was a sickening 'snap'.

For a moment he lay still, shocked. But it did not hurt, and awkwardly he pulled himself round to try to release the foot. It had caught in a little hollow in the peat bank, and felt very queer. For a moment it would not budge, but turning again and using both hands he managed to ease it free. Well, that was that, he thought, and hoping that he had not sprained his ankle, scrambled to his feet. The blinding wave of pain hit him like an electric shock. He cried out aloud and fell forward into the snow. As the pain ebbed he sat up slowly and felt his foot and ankle with trembling fingers. Already the ankle was swelling, and when he tried gingerly to move his foot it only stirred a fraction and flopped over. The agony had ceased the moment he took his weight off it, but already the numbness was wearing off, and a hot pain stirred up in the middle of his foot like a little furnace. Frightened now, he sat back and looked around him. There was no sound, he was quite alone. The pitiless wind blew down the miles of naked hills and chilled the perspiration on his young brow.

Alone

Murdo, unaware of all that was happening, pressed on. For three hours he had seen no sign of his pursuers. When the shot came he stopped in his tracks, frozen, alert as a deer. But it had come from a completely unexpected direction, on the other side of the mountain. He did not know what to make of it. It could even have been a crofter after a stag for the pot. On the other hand — well, he was not going to investigate. Certainly it had been a long way off, and that was comforting.

As he continued he took a couple of small mouthfuls from the bottle of whisky. He had often heard Hector say that it was a good tonic, but it made his head swim and the taste was so vile that he pushed it back into his battledress blouse and left it there.

The hours and the miles passed, and it seemed that daylight was never returning when at last a faint greyness in the east proclaimed the approaching dawn. The moon had long vanished behind a rolling front of cloud that now blanketed the whole sky. Visibility had shrunk with the darkness, a mixed blessing, for while it hid him from the Germans, it made holding to an easterly course very difficult. Slowly, imperceptibly, the greyness became a definite lightening of the sky, and a rosy glow shone dull but encouragingly above the black and white landscape.

But with the dawn came the full realisation of his tiredness, and it was with a heavy tread that Murdo climbed the small hillock ahead.

Below him lay Strath Halladale. The rough hillside fell away to a broad saucer-shaped valley. A long loch gleamed icily in the half light, frozen from shore to shore. Beyond it, straight as an arrow, lay the single railway track, with the road running parallel on the far side of the fence. As the crow flies the line was no more than half a mile away, twice that around the southern end of the loch.

With tired eyes he gazed down the miles of white, seeking the little village of Kinbrace, or indeed any sign of life, but there was none. Beyond the loch the dark outline of a large house rose from a copse of trees, but no smoke drifted from the chimneys, no encouraging light shone through the leafless branches. The glen was deserted. As if to accent its desolation, the sudden wild, long whistle of a train echoed down the valley. Murdo looked up the line, and far away, beyond a bend, saw wisps of white steam curling into the air. The train did not seem to be moving. He screwed up his eyes, trying to make out the details. Only at the little moorland station and level crossing at Forsinard, from what he could recall, was a train likely to stop so far south, but he recognised nothing, though he had been there a dozen times. He could not remember the loch at all. Again the wild scream of the engine pierced the valley. If he could reach the railway line in time he might be able to stop the train!

Heedless of the weakness in his legs, Murdo plunged diagonally down the side of the hill, stumbling and rolling a dozen times in his headlong haste. The long slope flattened and he forced himself forward across the valley towards the southern end of the loch. The snow lay deep on top of tussocky grass, the most exhausting kind of walking, and though his heart and legs strove he made slow progress. But still there was no sign of the train, hidden around the bend at Forsinard. He dreaded its sudden appearance, racing down the track before him.

He stopped to listen, and in an instant all thoughts of the train were driven from his mind — for there, between himself and the road south to Kinbrace, a tiny group of figures was dropping from the moors. At the same moment they must have seen him, for they stopped, then abruptly began running down the slope towards him.

There were three men and they were fully a mile away. Yet Murdo saw that he would never make it around the foot of the loch, they would easily cut him off.

Again the train whistled, twice. He looked back in a panic of indecision. It was three times as far, well over a mile, to circle around the head of the loch. If the train came now he would never catch it. He looked at the railway line, so near across the ice, and yet so far. If only — he gazed at the ice. It appeared to be thick. Would it support him?

In two minutes he was at the water's edge. For a quarter of a mile the grey-white sheet spread to the tussocks of the further shore. Gently he tested it. The ice cracked, and held. Cautiously he inched out. It was taking his weight. With gathering confidence he moved forward until the rough granular ice spread out all around him. Through occasional patches, glass-clear, he could see the tips of a motionless forest of weed feet below. The men were still nearly a mile off. He saw them stop, then something whined off the ice ahead of him and there was the sharp crack of a rifle. The echo ricochetted from the hills at the far side of the strath. There was little chance of them hitting from that range, they must be desperate. The thought gave him slight encouragement. They must be as tired as he was, too, though it was difficult to believe. But there was no time to waste, every second brought them closer. Shuffling, so as not to strain the ice, Murdo made further out.

Then all at once there was a terrific snap and a splitting, pinging sound all around him. White lines exploded from beneath his feet. He froze, frightened to move. Then carefully he slid a foot backwards and drew the other towards it. The ice held. Again — suddenly the ice gave way, and in an instant he was plunged into the freezing water.

He was only beneath the surface for a moment, then he was thrashing about among the heavy floes, searching for a support. The cold tightened about his chest like steel bands so that he could scarcely breathe. For half a minute, as he struggled, he was overwhelmed by the old panic and despair, and panted for help from anyone, even the Germans. Then he knew once more that he was alone, there was no-one to help. No sooner was the thought in his mind than his teeth came together and his eyes grew fierce. Bracing himself, he caught hold of a jagged edge of ice. Immediately it broke away, but the next piece he grasped was firmer. He reached up and slid his forearm over the ice, then lying back, caught a foot over the edge further along. Slowly he inched forward, gripping in the granular snow, until he was practically lying on top of the water. Then very gently he pressed down and rolled his stomach over the corner. With no warning the ice collapsed and Murdo disappeared beneath the surface.

When he came up, the sheet of ice was over his head. Desperately he cast about, and one arm found open water. He hooked an elbow round the edge and pulled himself clear, forcing down the fear. The cold and confusion stopped him from thinking clearly, but he must try again. This time he found a straight side of ice, and using his flotation in the water, eased both arms along the surface, kicking against the floes. Pressing down with his forehead and finger-tips he hitched forward, trying to put no strain on the edge. Soon he was clear to the waist. With an inward prayer he spread his arms, eased his weight down, and wriggled forward on to his belly and thighs. There was another loud splitting noise, but the ice held, and moments later he had slithered clear of the danger spot.

The Germans had closed to something over half a mile. The train was in sight, stationary up the track, black smoke belching into the moorland air. Panting and shuddering, Murdo started to run towards it around the head of the loch. The wet trousers clung tight about his legs, his knees were weak and close to buckling. "I won't stop," he sobbed to himself. "I won't." The sodden black hair fell across his eyes.

Behind him the Germans were in little better shape. The rifles jerked awkwardly at each stride. Henry Smith had to stop, he could run no further, and leaned his hands on his knees gasping for breath. He waved Arne and Gunner on, but within a hundred yards they had slowed to a panting walk. They were exhausted. In wet boots their feet were numb and badly blistered; the night's relentless walking had reduced their legs to rubber and knots of aching muscle.

Murdo passed the head of the loch and was only three hundred yards from the railway track when with a great cloud of steam the train started up again. He forced himself, with the last dregs of his strength, into a poor imitation of a sprint, and hauled himself over the fence to the railway line.

The train roared past. He waved his arms frantically. At the steamy windows soldiers smiled out at him and waved back.

It was too much to bear. As the noise of the train faded and the last carriage receded down the track, heading south, he fought the tears of exhaustion and frustration that stung his eyes and mingled with the loch water that trickled down his face.

Twenty minutes later Murdo was more than a mile down the road and drawing close to the wintry copse and lodge that he had seen from the summit of the hill. The snow squeaked and crunched beneath his feet. There was no traffic, not even the roar of a distant tractor disturbed the soft rush and whine of the wind. The wheel tracks in the ice and snow looked as if they had been there for several days. To his left lay the open hills, to his right the railway line and loch; and half a mile behind, seen time and again as the road twisted, the three Germans followed remorselessly in his track. The leaden clouds shrugged low over the hills. The morning light was dim.

He hurried along the wall that skirted the stand of trees and turned over a cattle grid between grand ornamental gate-posts. The long drive wound ahead through leafless birches and dark twisted pines. He passed the end of a line of stables and other outbuildings, all in good repair, then the house was before him, a fine sandstone lodge with a gravelled courtyard. He ran to the big oak doors and thundered on them with his fists.

"Hello! Hello — quick! Quick!"

His blows boomed in the great hall, and faded into silence.

"Is there anybody there?"

There was no reply. Then he saw that all the windows stood bare and uncurtained. No tracks save his own, and those of one or two birds and some small animal, disturbed the snowy courtyard.

Quickly he circled the house, hoping there might be a keeper's cottage, but there was not. The lodge was completely deserted.

Briefly Murdo hesitated. He longed to hide, to give up the unrelenting effort and cast himself into the hands of fate. He had tried to the limit of his power, and he had failed; surely he was now entitled to the easy way out. But even as he looked around the buildings he knew that hiding was no use, for they would certainly find him. Then it would have been better, much better, to have given himself up on Strathy beach, or even at the graveyard. So much had happened since that he could expect little mercy. The time of second chances was long past, now they would shoot him on sight. He knew it, and in his mind's eye he saw the rifle and the finger on the trigger, heard the report, felt the terrible bullet and the black emptiness of falling. The image made him desperate. At that moment the German invasion meant nothing beside his own survival. He did not even think of it. What should he do?

The sight of his footprints gave him an idea. Since the lodge was deserted and they must know how tired he was, the Germans would expect him to hide. He crossed swiftly to the outbuildings and opened a couple of stable doors, leaving them just ajar. Then he climbed a flight of stone steps to a loft, and descending again ran on to other doors to confuse his tracks. Finally he returned to the lodge itself, peering through the windows. Drawing his jacket sleeve tight, he jerked an elbow through the pane of what appeared to be the dining-room. The glass tinkled to the floor. He reached inside, pushed back the catch, and heaved up the heavy window. A few seconds later he was standing in the room, scattering little lumps of snow on the carpet. It was the work of a moment to push the window down again and press the catch back, hard, trying to make it jam. Then, stamping the snow from his boots and taking great care not to scatter more as he went, he crossed immediately into the fine oak-lined hall.

His plan was to run straight through the house, but at once his eyes fell on the black telephone on a rosewood table. He seized the receiver and pressed it to his ear. It was stone dead. Angrily he banged the rest up and down, and dialled 999, but nothing disturbed the muffled silence. He put the receiver down again and started away, then paused. The Germans too would find it, and realise that he had not been able to summon help. With a fierce jerk he ripped the cable from the wall.

Swiftly then he continued to the sitting-room at the far end of the hall. He pushed the door shut behind him and crossed the thick, green and gold carpet to the window. It faced east, away from the courtyard and road, with a fine view of the hills on the far side of the valley. He eased back the catch, and being careful not to disturb the ornaments on the broad window sill, pushed the window up, scrambled through to the ground, and pulled the window shut behind him.

Then, keeping the house between himself and his pursuers, and avoiding open stretches of snow so that his tracks would not be too conspicuous, he made a wild dash across the end of the lodge garden, through the trees, over the wall, and away across the moors in the other direction, heading for a clump of conifers several hundred yards away.

He made it without being seen, and as he ducked and weaved beneath their sheltering branches, the first snowflakes of the day floated by, and fell softly to the ground.

The Germans came cautiously into the courtyard. They had no idea of the reception that might be awaiting them, and their rifles were at the ready. But a glance was enough to reveal that the buildings were deserted, and with relief that the chase must be nearly over, Henry Smith led his men forward. He saw the stable doors open and the scuffed snow on the window sill beneath the broken pane of glass. Leaving Gunner and Arne to keep watch, quickly he followed Murdo's initial circuit of the building. In the lightly falling snow he did not see the half-hidden line of tracks heading away into the moors, and a minute later was back in the courtyard. Sinking against a big dog kennel to take the weight off his weary legs, he dispatched Arne into the house and Gunner into the stables to hunt the boy out.

"Be careful, mind," he called after them. "Give him a chance and he'll put a pitchfork through you — young savage."

He reached into his pocket and pulled out a packet of cigarettes. It had been quite a chase, but they had made it in the end. The thought of shooting the boy did not appeal to him, especially a boy like Murdo, who he knew and reluctantly admired. It was one thing to hunt him down, quite another to kill him in cold blood. Still, it had to be, they could not take him all that way back. He broke open the breech of his rifle and snapped it shut again.

The snow was thickening. He looked around the grey-black buildings, imagining what they would be like in the summer, with horses and dogs in the courtyard, women and children walking about the lawns. It was good. He would like a place like that.

But they were taking their time about hunting that wretched boy out.

"Come on! Get a move on!" His voice was harsh.

There was a pause, then Arne flung open an upstairs window on the far side of the courtyard.

"I don't think he's here," he called. "The house looks empty."

An uneasy twinge made the hair prickle on the back of Henry Smith's neck.

"Have you looked everywhere?"

"Not yet. The place is huge, full of attics and cellars. Great big cupboards. But I'm sure he's not here."

"Look everywhere," Henry Smith called up to him, standing and brushing the snow from the seat of his trousers. "Everywhere."

"All right. Can I have the torch."

Henry Smith threw up the little flashlight he had used for map reading, and the window banged shut.

Gunner came out of the stables and sneezed. A few straws and wisps of hay adhered to his clothes.

"Well, he's not in there."

A stronger twinge of uncertainty passed through the leader. "You're sure?"

Gunner raised his thick eyebrows. "Yes."

"What about the other sheds?"

"They're not open."

"Look at the footprints! Check them!"

For a few minutes longer he waited. The snow settled on his jacket and tickled his face. He moved into the shelter of a projecting stable roof.

Arne pushed up the broken dining-room window of the lodge, and almost simultaneously Gunner came from the last of the outbuildings and pulled the door shut behind him.

"Well, he's definitely not here," he called across the courtyard through the falling snow.

"Have you looked round the back?"

"Yes, but there's nowhere to hide. He must be in the house."

"I'm afraid not," Arne called back. "And he's been at the telephone. Pulled the cables out of the wall."

"What!" Henry Smith was stunned. "Was it working?"

"I don't know."

"Can you fix it?"

"Yes. It will take a few minutes, though. I'll have to find something to take out the screws."

"Well you get on with that. Gunner and I will take a look round the outside."

"Right." The cropped blond head and red-rimmed eyes vanished into the gloom of the house.

"You stay here and keep your eyes open in case he is hiding, and tries to slip back to the road. I'll look round the other side again."

Moving more slowly Henry Smith followed the boy's footprints to the end of the lodge. As he rounded the corner the wind-driven snow struck in his face. He turned the top of his head into it and pulled his collar close. The visibility was deteriorating all the time. Carefully he made his way along the front of the lodge, between the broad bay windows and the lawn. Sheltering his eyes from the snow, a second time he failed to see Murdo's half-hidden tracks, and soon was at the far gable wall. He paused, dissatisfied. Clearly the boy had not gone that way, for a flawless stretch of snow-covered grass, broken only by their earlier prints, led back to the end of the courtyard. Henry Smith turned, and retraced his steps. Suddenly he spotted the ruffled snow on the window ledge, and looking below saw the line of footprints heading away from the house. Murdo had walked along the sunken edge of a flower patch beneath a high bank of rhododendrons, his tumbled foot-falls hidden between the edge of the lawn and snow-covered remnants of summer flowers. Already the snowflakes were filling them in, moulding the edges, smoothing them over. Silently Henry Smith looked away through the drifting veils of white. A few hundred yards off stood the dim silhouette of a copse of fir trees. Beyond that all was grey and blind.

A slow rage of frustration mounted within him, the culmination of all he had endured at the hands of the two Scots. He relieved it in a passionate outburst of oaths and curses, stamping his feet and beating his fists in the air. In a matter of seconds the stormy fit had run its course and he relaxed, panting and more calm.

Gunner heard the noise and appeared around the end of the house. Glad that the responsibility was not his, he shook his head half admiringly.

"He's some boy," he said.

"He's a damned pest, I know that," Henry Smith replied sharply.

Together they returned to the courtyard and waited for Arne beneath the overhanging stable roof. Impatiently the leader strode across to the dining room and shouted for him to hurry up.

Five minutes later Arne appeared once more in the window, a kitchen knife in his hand. "It's all right," he called through the thickening snow. "The line's dead."

"You're sure?"

"Yes."

A warm flood of relief made Henry Smith sink back momentarily against the stone wall. "Right. Come on over here, then."

Swiftly Arne tidied up in the lodge, pulled down the broken window, and joined them at the stable.

Henry Smith brushed some of the snow from his shoulders. "He's away again," he said with no preamble. "Out the far side towards the hills. I want you two to go after him. If you catch up with him you know what to do. Cover his body with a few rocks, or snow and heather: it will be safe enough for a week or two, that's all we need. I'll head down the road in case he tried to circle back to the village. The snow's filling in his footsteps all the time, so you'd better get cracking. We'll meet again here, in the stable. There's plenty of straw, and there might be some food in the house."

Arne nodded.

"What about Peter?" Gunner said.

"I'll keep a look out for him."

"And if we don't find the boy," said Arne, "and he doesn't cut back to the village?"

"In that case," Henry Smith replied, "he's probably dead. There's nothing out there but hills and more hills." He paused and made a rueful face. "But I suppose I'd better get in touch with the Colonel and let him know. See what he wants me to do."

Arne and Gunner exchanged glances, then looked back at their leader.

"Von Kramm?" Gunner said softly.

"Of course. Who else?" Henry Smith's voice was sharp. He felt the anger welling up inside him once more. He would cut a poor figure when the facts became known. "Still, that's my business. You've got your work to do, what are you hanging about for? Get moving."

Arne pushed himself from the wall, buttoning the collar of his jacket, and slung the heavy rifle to his shoulder. Gunner shook the snow from his hair and settled his own rifle in the crook of an arm. More hills lay ahead, more rough ground. He blinked with fatigue and braced his shoulders.

"Remember," Henry Smith told them, "he's quite as tired as you are."

"I wouldn't count on it," Arne said.

Gunner raised his eyebrows ironically, and thought of the warm comfortable straw in the stables, behind them. Not in the least encouraged by their leader's empty platitude, he clapped Arne heavily on the shoulder.

"Ah well," he sighed. "Come on."

Together they trudged away across the courtyard and round the corner out of sight.

For a minute Henry Smith watched the snow drifting and whirling by. Wearily he pulled the map from his inside pocket, unfolded it, and held it up against the stone wall. For a long time he pored over it, his brow wrinkled, trying to work out what route a resourceful but tired and frightened boy might follow. The great strath ran north and south. To the east, the way he was heading, lay nothing but a waste of hills, gashed with rivers, which beyond the watershed ran eastward into the North Sea, twenty miles away. Unconsciously and almost imperceptibly he shook his head. The boy had no chance. The only danger lay in the village of Kinbrace. If he saw the houses he might try to cut back along the foot of the hills and seek help there.

He folded the map and eased his aching legs. Then, wondering how he could explain to Colonel von Kramm, field officer in command of Operation Flood-Tide, the threat of a fourteen year old boy, he turned reluctantly from the lodge and made his way back down the long drive. The snow drifted through the trees. Already the tracks they had made twenty minutes earlier were almost obliterated.

At the same time Murdo was high above the valley, and climbing. Uncertain of his position, and doubtful that Kinbrace could really have lain round the next bend in the valley, his only thought was to keep ahead of the Germans. All his energies were directed into pushing on, pushing on, for the moment it did not matter where, so long as his feet might take him beyond the reach of those whipping bullets. But truly he did not have much strength left. He seemed to have gained a little time through entering the house and crossing the copse, but the nervous energy which had sustained him during the chase round the loch and down the road to the lodge, had gone. In its place a state of physical and mental weariness had settled like a blanket about his shoulders and legs. But his determination, though numb, burned as strongly as ever, and never faltered as he plodded up and up towards the shoulder of the long slope and the eastern summits.

Far below, the black clump of pine trees had long vanished into the swirling snow. His entire world had shrunk to a white circle of hillside two hundred yards across, flecked with black in the lee of rocky outcrops and clumps of heather. An arctic hare burst from under his feet and sprang off at incredible speed up the steep slope of the hill. A pair of grouse clattered away, calling loudly as they swung in a long low circle behind him, to settle again not very far from where they had risen.

He bent and broke a crust of snow from the edge of his footprint. The ice was beautifully sharp in his throat, and he crunched the aching-cold crystals in his teeth as he walked on.

Although only an hour or two after dawn, the morning was darkening as the clouds thickened and the snow fell still more heavily. The little world closed in upon him. The slight breeze drifted the flakes against his face, where they settled on eyebrows and eyelashes, cheeks and lips, tickling and bitterly cold as they melted. His toorie had vanished in the loch, and his shock of black hair, still wet from the ducking, was covered with a cap of snow. The whole front of his body, khaki blouse and thick blue trousers, was obliterated in a clinging white blanket that shivered off as the cloth wrinkled beneath it. Socks and trouser bottoms were thick with little balls of ice, moulded solid, packed tight around the gaps at the top of his boots. As he breathed, the whirling flakes pricked the inside of his nose and mouth.

And so he plodded on, unaware after a time how far he had come, thoughtless of where he was going. Behind him the moulding drifts filled in his footprints. The slope levelled out into a broad plateau. All around him the land spread out into the falling snow, flat and featureless.

After a time he noticed that his feet and ankles were black, smearing clots and stains of mud across the snow. He looked back at the line of inky footsteps, wondering which way to go to climb out of the bog. But there was no way of knowing, so he trudged on, noting the direction of the snowflakes so that he could keep a fairly straight course by the wind.

Abruptly, not a minute later, he fell sidelong as a leg was gone from beneath him into the mire. He struggled upright, trapped in the ooze right to the fork in his legs. He pulled his free leg beneath him, and levering with his hands and knee dragging the leg out. It was covered to the thigh with an evil-smelling mantle of black mud, which oozed down and fell in gobbets on to the snow.

Grunting, he pulled himself to his feet and looked for a way round the soft patch. He imagined it looked a little better to the left and turned his face in that direction. For a few steps the earth supported him, then again his leg slipped from sight and he lurched forward, wrenching his wounded thigh as he fell. For long moments he lay there, collecting himself, then a second time hauled his fouled leg from the sucking mud. Lumps of snow fell into the black crater. Panting with fatigue, he pulled the hair from his eyes with a muddy hand and peered once more into the veils of white.

How long that nightmare crossing of the bog took, Murdo never knew. Time and again he plunged into the mud. There seemed no way of telling the treacherous places from firm ground, for the frosts had covered the earth with a crust of ice and the snow was over all. At each footstep he hesitated, uncertain whether the ground would support him, or merely take his weight for a moment before he broke through once more into the soft mud beneath. At length he learned to steer clear of the smooth, level patches.

Half an hour — an hour. Murdo was panting. His sweat mingled with the melting snow in his face. His body was hot, burning — then chilled through and through, gripped down his back and across his stomach by the sodden clothes. He felt so weak. His legs trembled and would hardly go where he wanted them. He was frightened; he had never felt like that before. He cast about, this way and that; there seemed no way out of the terrible bog. He forgot to check the wind direction and retraced his steps, then circled and crossed them again. Where were the Germans? Where was he? No landmark, no slope of land. He might be no more than a hundred yards from where he set off. The stumbling, blind passage had completely destroyed his sense of direction. The very wind seemed to veer and switch direction as he stood still, the snowflakes whirling about him in the gloom of the morning. Morning — midday more like!

He forced himself to take ten deep breaths. "Your head, Murdo," he said out loud. "Use your head!" But he could not think straight, his head was swimming. For a long time he stood, and the wind froze him to the marrow, shivering and cramping. Vaguely he tried to recall the wind direction he had followed. Had the snow been into the left side of his face? He thought so, and turning once more so that the flakes drove on the whole in that direction, started forward yet again.

"One — more — step — Murdo. One — more — step — Murdo," he chanted underneath his breath at each footfall, forcing his uncertain legs to support him and carry him forward over the treacherous and uneven ground. It seemed as if he would never reach the other side, as if there *was* no other side. How he longed to lie and rest; how he mistrusted that wind. His struggle against the Germans seemed nothing compared with the struggle he was now having to put up for his life, against the Highland winter and the very mountains themselves.

But at last, when he felt he could surely stand no longer, he became aware of rising ground ahead, saw a little hillock, and dragged himself heavily towards it. The earth was firm beneath his feet. Too numb with exhaustion even to be thankful, he found a boulder and sank behind it into the drifts of snow.

The struggle was over. His breathing was deep. It was so warm and sheltered there. A comfortable glow spread through his body, and his relaxing legs trembled pleasantly as the heat stole through his muscles. It was so restful. He was so tired. His eyes slowly closed, and his head nodded on to his chest.

The rough, icy feel of the cloth jerked him back into consciousness, Black eyes wide with alarm, he pulled himself back from the brink of sleep. No — no sleep! He could die if he fell asleep, more than once he had heard the men say it: as you grew colder you sank deeper and deeper into unconsciousness, and did not wake up. But he must have rest, his body craved for it. Brushing the snow from beneath him, Murdo pulled his jacket close and huddled into the shelter of the rock.

His stomach ached, hot fires burned in his throat. Time and again he sucked a lump of snow to cool it down. It would have been good if he had held on to the whisky bottle to put some warmth into him, but that too was gone into the depths of the loch. He wondered where the Germans were. Wherever they might be, there was nothing he could do about it.

Murdo need not have feared. By the time Gunner and Arne had reached the summit of the slope above Strath Halladale, his tracks were no more than slight irregularities in the snow-smooth wilderness of heather and long grass. The bog had defeated them completely. Worn out and black to the waist, they had turned their backs to the wind and headed down into the comparatively sheltered country of the strath. An hour and a half before Murdo found shelter behind the rock, they were smoking cigarettes in one of the stables at the lodge, keeping themselves warm beneath a good thickness of clean straw. Two pairs of foul and miry trousers hung over one of the beams, frozen rigid and not drying out at all.

Henry Smith joined them an hour later, smothered in snow and in savage mood, though a second troop train had roared past him on its way south, revealing the success of the German plan. There had been no sign of the wretched boy or Peter. He had discovered, however, that the telephone was working in the village of Kinbrace, three miles to the south. Having heard Gunner's discouraging report, he set out after a short rest to report to Colonel von Kramm.

When he returned, late on that Saturday afternoon, his face was pale and pinched, from the conversation as much as the blizzard. He shook the snow from his jacket and flung himself down in the straw, too depressed even to swear. As he had anticipated, the colonel had not been impressed by his story. He had not said very much, that was not his way, but he had a certain way of saying it.

"I see. A boy of ... fourteen, did you say? ... And four men dead? ... You told him all about 'Flood-Tide' and now you don't know where he is. ... How old did you say? ... and there were ten of you. ... Yes, I appreciate there only seem to be a handful left. And Bjorn Larvik isn't with you — that's a pity. ... Well, there isn't much one can say. None of the other groups seem to be having your trouble: everything has gone splendidly. I'll get in touch with the Inverness group and they can come up and help — anyone who remains by then. ... I agree, one doesn't want to say more than necessary on the telephone. ... Yes, you can expect me tomorrow. ... There is no need? You realise, I take it, that there was a hold up in — down the line, and there are still seven days to go. The boy has to be silenced. If you can't do it any other way, take a leaf from Carl Voss's book. ... Oh, I see, he is no longer with you. Ah, a great loss indeed. ... I will see you at the hotel, then. I trust the food is acceptable. Do they have a good cellar?"

Henry Smith flushed as he recalled the cultured voice, and the fiery home-made whisky which was the best he had been able to scrounge from the innkeeper. For Colonel von Kramm, he had no doubt, the man would have been able to find something better. He was disgraced. When Arne asked how he had fared he was suddenly angry with his subordinate and told him to shut up and mind his own business. Burrowing into the straw, he pulled huge armfuls around himself and closed his eyes. At least he could get some rest. But for a long time he lay awake, remembering the events of the past ten days, cursing the boy and his old fisherman friend, the colonel's ironic words burning in his mind.

Meanwhile, out on the moors, a few hundred feet beneath the eastern summits, Murdo saw that daylight was beginning to fade and the snow was easing off. Guessing that it must be some time after three, he dragged himself to his feet. The world spun about him and his legs felt so weak that he had to steady himself with a hand against the rock. He brushed the snow from his jacket with vague fingers, and set off up the gentle hill ahead. His knees buckled and his feet dragged in the patched heather.

In an hour he made at most one mile of ground. The effort was supreme, but the snow was easing off and at length it stopped. Around him the landscape opened up to the last pale veils of the dusk.

He was standing on the top of the hill. Behind him a long curving ridge, miles long it seemed, swept down and around, its roots merging invisibly with a limitless expanse of shadowy plain — the bogs: far off, the advancing shadows welded sky and plateau, a dark barrier which made its awful size seem greater still. Ahead lay a huge valley, with an impressive mountain rising sheer on the far side, its ragged flanks heavy with the mantle of snow. Right and left the hillsides fell steeply away, down and down, until in the half-light they levelled into a desolation of moor. Through the opening clouds a bitter sky, ice-pale with frost and glittering brilliantly with a host of tiny stars, promised a blindingly cold night. It was very beautiful, and as inhospitable as the moon. Over the endless miles of waste, limited only by encroaching darkness, not one light gleamed, not one animal moved. Then a hundred yards below, a solitary red grouse burst noisily into the air. 'Go-back go-back go-back' it called, sailing over the valley towards the mountain beyond. In seconds it was gone, the harsh call faded into silence. The wind stirred the boy's hair, the dusk and mountain solitude closed round him once more.

Murdo was swaying where he stood, and sat sideways in the snow to steady himself as he surveyed the scene. He could not go much further, he had to have shelter for the night. But there was no shelter.

At length he chose the long hillside on the left. There appeared to be a sizable stream at the bottom, studded with rocks and half frozen over. With luck there would be sheep fanks or some old ruin down there. Slowly he headed across the shoulder of the ridge and began to descend the steep slope.

His legs would carry him properly no longer. Time and again he stumbled and fell headlong, sprawling head over heels down the hillside, landing with a sickening jolt against some boulder. The hidden stones tricked his feet so that he turned his ankles with a wrench. The angle of the slope taxed his already exhausted muscles, so that by the time he was halfway down his knees had lost the last of their strength and his legs trembled uncontrollably.

And then they would support him no longer. As he tried to stand his knees buckled and he pitched forward into the snow again.

Yet somehow, crawling and tumbling, he arrived at the bottom of the hillside and huddled, shaking, on the bare bank of the stream. His breathing was fast and shallow, and this time the shuddering did not pass, but grew worse as the cold of the night and the earth felt through his wet clothes.

He pulled himself to his knees. "I must get shelter," he whispered, his voice convulsive. Half rising he tried to walk up the bank. "I must get shelter!" Over and over the four words revolved in his mind and waves of darkness rolled across the sky. Painfully slowly, yard after yard, he dragged himself down the broad brink of the river.

He did not see the little suspension bridge at first. Then with wakening awareness, as his eyes focussed, there it was before him, two black stakes against the snow, a flimsy catwalk of boards slung across invisible ropes. Murdo looked across, and for a moment did not realise what he was seeing. Then his heart stirred, too weary to surge with joy or relief. There, half hidden among a few stunted trees, a little patch of light gleamed in the darkness.

"Help! Hello!" But his voice would not come. Desperately he struggled forward. Clutching the swaying ropes with all his little strength, he dragged himself over the stream and stumbled towards the light. A fallen stone wall was before him, Heedless of the snow he crawled over the rocks and fell through the rough, cutting branches of the old trees beyond.

It was a small croft house. The green-curtained window shone cheerfully in the gloom. Reaching the door, Murdo pulled himself up and banged on it loudly with the flat of his hand.

A dog within was already barking at his approach and now redoubled its noise. A man's voice told it to shut up and for a moment there was silence. Then there was the sound of footsteps and a light glimmered in the hallway. A bolt shot back, and an old man holding a lantern appeared in the doorway.

"I . . . I . . . Can you . . ." said Murdo. But the words were not there. He took a stumbling half-step forward, reeled, and fell senseless into the arms of the old man.

Blizzard over Carn Mor

When Murdo woke it was just getting light. He found himself in a small whitewashed room in the warmth of a clean bed. He blinked sleepily, and looked from the dark beams across the ceiling to the lightening, rose-patterned curtains over the little window. A table and chair stood against the wall beneath two framed pictures of Summery scenes. His white bed-spread was covered by a crumpled red eiderdown. He curled up in the luxury of the warmth and pulled the sheets and rough blankets closer about his neck.

Slowly the events of the day before came back to him, so vivid, but unreal, almost as if they had been bad dreams. The heavy lassitude of his limbs and the ache in his head were enough in themselves to assure him that they were not. Again he clung to the cliff, struggled in the icy water, stood to his shins in the mud looking into the swirling snow. The memories frightened him afresh, and he tried to think of other matters. What had become of Hector? He wished they could be back as they had been — fishing off the point in the *Lobster Boy*, running the old croft — before that meeting in the Captain Ivy turned their lives upside down. He remembered Hector's rash words, spoken so lightly: "Let's give him a run for his money." And he thought of his father, goodness knows where, and wished that somehow he could materialize to take the load off his shoulders. He would know what to do.

But his father was not there. The only help he was likely to get must come from the old shepherd in whose cottage he now found himself. Dimly he recalled his arrival the night before, the door opening and the old man standing there, a dog barking somewhere in the background. Even more dimly he seemed to remember shouting out in the darkness, and light coming, and somebody there beside him until he fell asleep again. He stretched his legs down the bed and pressed his feet against a still warm hot-water bottle, turned over, and closed his eyes.

He did not sleep, and fifteen minutes later pushed back the bedclothes and sat up, feeling the air of the bedroom chill against his bed-hot chest and shoulders. He had not considered what he was wearing, and was surprised to find himself in a pair of baggy blue-striped pyjamas. He felt a tight dressing about his leg where the bullet had struck him, and pushing down the pyjama trousers, found a broad bandage bound neatly over the wound. A blister niggled against his heel, and when he pulled up his foot he saw it was as big as a half-crown and dark with blood. All things considered, however, he did not feel too bad, though somewhat light-headed and swimmy. It was a sensation he had not known for years and took him back to days of childhood fever and sickness at his aunt's house. Unheralded he had a sudden vision of the bedroom and drawn blinds, and could almost taste the boiled fish and hated junket. With a new and unexpected affection he recalled his aunt's patient nursing. She had done her best for them all. The memory faded. He swung his legs to the floor: the feeling would soon go away, he thought. But when he stood up he found that he was weaker than he had realised, and had to sit on the side of the bed for a moment to let the dizziness pass.

A brown dressing gown, unexpected in a shepherd's house, hung on the back of the door. He put it on and fastened the frayed cord about his waist. Then, feeling rather shy, he padded barefoot on to the landing and down the steep flight of stairs to the hallway. He wondered how he had ascended the night before, whether he had been carried or had walked, for he had no remembrance of it. He scratched his head and brushed the hair from his eyes.

It was a little croft house, built to the same pattern as Hector's and ten thousand more, with the front door facing the stairs and a room at each end of the narrow hallway. A faded rag rug lay on the brushed boards. The door leading into the parlour was ajar, and through it Murdo could see a china cabinet and a little table with lace mats and ornaments upon it. The other door was closed. He knocked gently and pushed it open.

The old man sat at the far side of a dying peat fire. His face was Highland, brown and deeply lined, and he was balding. He wore a collarless shirt with the sleeves rolled back from his forearms, an old waistcoat, and thick baggy trousers. He looked up as Murdo entered, and though he scarcely smiled, his manner was kind.

"Come over to the fire," he said.

Murdo perched himself on the edge of an old leather armchair and leaned towards the grey ash. A fawning collie crept forward and sniffed at his foot. When he put a hand down it backed, then sidled forward again and allowed itself to be petted. Growing quite frenzied with instant pleasure, it jumped up and tried to lick his face.

"Get down, Corrie," the old man growled. "Go on!"

The collie backed away to a rough box in the corner spread with an old hair-covered jacket and some rags of curtain.

"Pull the chair in," the old man said. "Keep yourself warm." He stirred the cinders to a glow and reached across for some small pieces of peat to make the fire burn up quickly. Then he brushed the hearth tidy.

"Well," he said. "How are you feeling now?"

"I've just woken up," said Murdo.

"You'd like a cup of tea."

Without waiting for an answer he carried the teapot through to the back kitchen and tipped the slops into a waste bucket, rinsed it out, and brought it back dripping. A big kettle steamed on the hob. He reached for the caddy on the mantlepiece and soon had a pot of fresh tea standing on a trivet in front of the fire. Then he unhooked a couple of willow pattern cups from the dresser behind him and poured out. Without asking he added milk and two big spoonfuls of sugar to Murdo's cup, stirred it up, and passed it over.

"I suppose that's how you take it," he said. "I never met a boy that didn't."

Murdo's chest felt strangely tight. He swallowed and smiled. "Thank you."

"You're looking better, anyway."

Murdo pulled the dressing gown about his throat and sipped at the boiling tea. He looked up at his clothes hanging from a pulley above their heads.

"They'll be a bit wet yet," the man said to him. "They were lying there on the floor for a while and the snow melted into them. I gave your trousers a bit of a rinse out." He ran a hand over the weathered crown of his head and straightened the fringe of white-grey hair with his fingers.

Embarrassed by the trouble he was giving and the old shepherd's kindness, Murdo felt the tightness rise into his throat. He looked down at the hearth once more. His boots, thoroughly cleaned, stood at the side drying slowly.

"I'm sorry to be such a bother," he said.

For several moments, regarding him, the old man was silent. "I think maybe you were lucky to find the house," he said at length.

"Yes — very."

"Do you have any idea where you are?" he said gently.

"No." The tears rushed into Murdo's eyes and he turned swiftly away so that the old man should not see. But his shoulders shook. He saw the cup of tea spilling on to the dressing gown and could not stop it. A hand took it from him. A huge lump welled up in his throat and the tears streamed down his face. Two or three drops landed on the arm of the chair and he wiped them off with the sleeve of the dressing gown.

A minute later, ashamed of himself, he rubbed the back of a hand across his cheeks and turned back, keeping his eyes fixed on the hearth and fire.

"Sorry," he said, his chest still jumping a little.

"That's nothing to be ashamed of, boy," the old man said. "Anyone worth calling a man will have a cry sometime."

Murdo sniffed and picked up his cup of tea from the hearth.

"You can take some breakfast, anyway."

Half smiling, Murdo glanced quickly across and nodded. He rubbed again at the streaks his tears had left on the old leather arm of his chair.

"Well you get yourself away back to bed and I'll bring it up. Take the tea with you."

Murdo protested. "No, really, I can't . . ."

"Off you go. You're worn out, boy."

And no sooner did Murdo's head hit the pillow than he was sound asleep again.

He was woken three hours later by a hand gently shaking his shoulder. Startled, he struck it off and leaped up in the bed, his eyes staring, not knowing for a minute where he was.

"All right, all right, son. It's only me."

His heart still thudding, Murdo subsided into the blankets. The old man pulled them straight. Murdo smelled bacon, and saw a breakfast tray on the little table against the wall. He propped himself on the pillows and the old man brought the tray across and set it on his knees. It was loaded, a large plate full of crinkly bacon, with two eggs and a slice of fried bread; another plate piled with toast made at the fire, with fork marks in the middle and a lick of soot around some of the crusts; a dish of home-made butter and a pot of marmalade.

"You tuck in, son," the old man said. "You'll have a fair appetite, if I'm not mistaken." He turned back to the table and poured them both a large cup of tea, put Murdo's on the tray and seated himself on the little chair against the wall. "Don't worry yourself about my ration book. There's half a side of bacon down there, and I've got two cows and a dozen hens. It's a relief to get someone to eat it all up."

Murdo took him at his word, and soon the plate of bacon and eggs was empty. He made a start on the toast and marmalade.

For a while the old man watched him, saying nothing. He observed the yellowing bruise across his cheekbone and eye. He wondered at the watchful, half wild expression that had come into Murdo's face. He recalled his collapse at the door, the torn leg, his crying out in the night.

"Where do you come from, son?" he said at length.

"Strathy."

The man nodded. Silence returned. Murdo wanted to tell him everything, to pour it all out, but normally a boy of few words he did not know how to begin.

"And what — are you staying in Kinbrace and went out after the sheep? Was there some trouble?"

"Not like you mean." Murdo shook his head, stumbling over the words. "It's the men, they were after me. And the snow came on, and I didn't know where I was. You couldn't see anything."

"What men?"

"I don't know how to tell you." He hesitated. "It's Germans. They're here. And me and Hector were bringing rifles and explosives from Island Roan and . . . and then I got away and they were chasing me. And they had guns."

The words were incredible, but Murdo's sincerity and distress were beyond doubt. The old shepherd questioned him and bit by bit the whole story came tumbling out. His tea cooled on the tray, the slice of toast remained half eaten on his plate.

At length the story was complete and they both fell silent. Murdo realised he had become cold sitting up, and balancing the tray on his chest snuggled down beneath the blankets, taking the half eaten slice of toast in his hand.

The man moved his empty teacup aside on the little table and reached into a waistcoat pocket for his pipe and tobacco tin.

His face lightened as he pushed sombre thoughts behind him for the moment.

"Well!" He laughed shortly. "I've told yon Hector often enough that he would end up in trouble one of these days."

"You know him?"

"Aye. He's a well-known man, that. I used to be down in Helmsdale at the fishing when I was first married. He had a little boat there. He wasn't much more than a boy like yourself then. But he was wild. Everybody knew Hector Gunn. The things he could do with that boat — the things he got up to! We joined up together in the First War — went to the Navy." For a moment his old eyes were reflective then he returned to the present. "I still see him from time to time at the sheep sales. I used to see your dad, too, come to that. Not that I knew him well. But next time you see Hector Gunn, you tell him you were talking to Duncan Beg."

Murdo buttered another piece of toast and spread it with marmalade. But he had no sooner bitten into it than he knew he did not want it. A lurch of nausea went from his stomach to his head and he thought he would be sick. He took another bite of the toast, but it was suddenly uneatable, like cardboard in his mouth. He chewed it into a paste, but only by a great effort got it down his throat. The sweat broke out on his forehead. He laid the toast on his plate and put the tray on the floor. As he lowered his head the nausea swept through him again and he pulled himself up quickly. As soon as it had passed he slid down under the blankets.

For a while the shepherd did not notice. He shook his head slowly from side to side.

"Well, they might find the cottage by accident, I suppose, if they're still searching after the blizzard — but I doubt it. You came an unlikely way from the lodge. You can't see the cottage from the tops, you have to walk down the ridge a bit and know where to look. But if they have a map — and they are bound to, I should say — well, Corriebreck is the only cottage west of the clachan at Braemore. It's the only shelter. They'll have to look. But if you're not here . . ." He paused and thought of Murdo's condition when he arrived the night before. "Aye, they'd be right enough to reckon you are probably dead. The snow started again about an hour after you came in. It's snowed off and on all through the night. There'll not be a trace of your footprints anywhere now."

"Would they get across the bogs?" Murdo asked.

Duncan Beg nodded. "It's not so bad when you can see and just keep to the high ground. But if they want to come to Corriebreck, the best way is to take a car round to the east coast, and then come up from Berriedale. If the roads are clear, that is. They might even get as far as Braemore, then it's only a six mile walk up the track."

"Corriebreck?" Murdo said.

"Here. This croft."

Murdo pictured Henry Smith and his men trudging up the snowy glen towards the cottage, rifles on their backs. And he lay in bed, waiting for them.

"You'll have to be careful," the old man said. "If they bring up one of the other groups to help in the search, you won't know what they look like. All the army boys from round here are being sent south now — you saw one of the troop trains yesterday. And every news is full of the build-up on the French coast. It could hardly be bigger. And you know the plan for the whole invasion. With knowledge like that you can't afford to take any chances. Nor can they."

Murdo's face was pale, his hair and eyes black on the white pillow. "What do you think they'll do?" he asked.

"It's hard to say. I think they've got to look for you before the snow starts again. If the roads are clear they will probably drive round to the east coast and come up the glen. If they are not, then they'll have to come over the hill. But I wouldn't like to do it, not with the hills the way they are now — and then have to walk back again."

Fingering the tight bandage as he listened, Murdo got a sharp nip from his wound.

"What do you think I should do?" he asked.

"If you are up to it, I think you should make your way down to Braemore and see Johnny Murray. There's a phone there and one or two people who could give you a hand. If the phone's off with the snow, and it usually is, he will run you down to Berriedale on the tractor. It's only another six or seven miles down the river."

Murdo looked at Duncan Beg. Clearly he was well on in years, but many of the old shepherds were fit and strong.

"You couldn't come with me?" he said.

No sooner had he spoken than he regretted the words. A shadow settled on the old man's face.

"I would if I could, boy. I'm sorry. A mile down the road when the weather's warm is about all I can manage these days."

"It's all right," Murdo said. "I'll manage fine."

"You're sure?" For the first time the old man seemed to see the perspiration on Murdo's brow, the heavy look in his eyes. "If I was five years younger I would go with you in a minute. If Angus was here he would be halfway to Braemore already. But I'm afraid you're on your own."

"Angus?" Murdo said. "Is that your son?"

The shepherd nodded. "Away in the army — in the tanks with Monty. Only the two of us left now, since the wife died and Mary and Hughina went off to get married."

Murdo looked away sympathetically, and the old man got up.

"Well, if you get dressed," he said. "I'll show you the way. From the look of the sky over Carn Mor, I don't think you should waste any time."

He went out, carrying the breakfast tray, and Murdo climbed out of bed. His clothes were downstairs. The shepherd had lowered the pulley before the fire and they were nearly dry. Even though he had been put into pyjamas the night before, he did not like unnecessarily to change before a stranger and carried them back to the bedroom. Five minutes later he was dressed and ready to leave.

"How's the leg?" the old man asked as he limped into the living room fastening the buckle of his jacket.

"It's a bit stiff," Murdo replied. "It'll loosen up with walking."

"Do you want anything to eat with you?"

"No thank you," Murdo said. "I'm full, And it's only — six miles, you said?"

"That's right. Come here, and I'll show you."

He led the way to the front door and round the end of the barn. The river which Murdo had crossed the previous evening wound down the glen, shrunk to an irregular black ribbon between the banks of ice. On either side of the valley rough slopes, heavy with snow, rose to the high crests of the moors. Beyond, four or five miles downstream, a massive white mountain hunched its shoulders beneath a weight of clouds. Dark blue and black they reared and spread above the white slopes.

"Aye, it doesn't look too good," the old man said, following Murdo's eyes. "We're always in for a bit of dirty weather when it comes in like that over Carn Mor." He looked critically around the sky. "But I think you'll be all right as far as Braemore. Look, you see the track." He pointed to a white path that wound through the heather and away down the glen. "Follow the track all the way, it will take you straight to Braemore. If you lose the path with the snow, just keep to the left hand bank of the river until you reach the loch, then cut straight across the side of the hill — it will bring you out just the same."

Murdo eased his legs and picked at his damp trousers. "Well, I'll be off."

"Now remember," the old man said. "It's Johnny Murray you want to see. He won't be far away from home on a Sunday. Tell him that Duncan Beg sent you."

Murdo nodded.

"Look after yourself, then." He clapped a wrinkled hand on Murdo's shoulder and stood back.

"I'll do that," Murdo said. "Thank you for the breakfast and everything."

The old man smiled at the boy's embarrassed politeness and waved him on.

"Good luck," he said.

Murdo turned and made his way across the sheep-stained snow to the level track. Two hundred yards downstream it wound round a spur of the hill and passed out of sight of the cottage. He turned at the bend and saw the shepherd still at the corner of the barn, watching him go. He waved and the old man waved back. A moment later the rocky hillside had risen between them.

Walking was hard work, for even on the level track the snow was deep, and time and again long wreaths swept down from the hillside so that Murdo found himself ploughing thigh-deep through the drifts. Before he had gone half a mile the wound in his leg began to throb painfully, but as his muscles loosened it eased off to a dull ache. The bandage fell slack and slipped down his leg, coming to rest in a tangle above his sock.

The cold air chased away the dizziness, and the food in his stomach began its good work. But still he felt much weaker than he had expected. His legs lacked their customary strength and did not respond to the uneven ground; his arms and shoulders swung too lightly as he tramped along.

The clouds were piling up. Darkness upon darkness they marched above the moors until the whole eastern sky seemed ready to fall. The summits of the mountains were shrouded and the distance grew dim as evening.

But the storm held off, and in less than two hours Murdo saw the loch lying ahead in a little hollow. It was about a mile away and completely covered with ice. He looked beyond it, across the slope of the hill, for a sign of Braemore.

Suddenly he stopped. On the near side of the loch, threequarters of a mile away yet, three men were moving up the track towards him. His stomach sank. Duncan Beg had said nothing about meeting anyone. The Germans must have done what he thought, driven round by road to come up from Berriedale and Braemore. He gnawed his lip. On the other hand they could be shepherds, searching for strays before the storm broke. They might be the very help he was seeking. But how could he know? For long moments he stood, torn by indecision, then realised that he could not take the chance. Even if they were shepherds, he did not need their help, he could reach Braemore by himself. He must avoid them — but how? He could not hide, he could not return to Corriebreck. And whatever he did, they would see his tracks. The only answer was to cross the river. If they were shepherds they would not follow him. If they were the Germans, at least he would have a good lead.

He plunged off the track and as fast as possible made his way across the glen towards the river. Black and dangerous it swept along beneath shells of ice. A quarter of a mile above him the channel twisted beneath a steep bluff. If he could reach it before they saw him — but the thought was no sooner in his mind than a long shout reached his ears, and then another. He looked back. The tiny figures appeared to be running. Moving as quickly as he could across the rough ground, Murdo reached the bluff and was hidden from their sight.

Ahead of him, just two hundred yards further on, a suspension bridge, similar to the one at Corriebreck, trailed its flimsy catwalk of planks above the river. As he hurried towards it he was struck with an idea and patted his trouser pocket to make sure of the clasp knife. If the ropes were of manilla and not wire, he could at least prevent them from following that way. He reached the posts and examined the cables. They were of heavy tarred rope. Hanging on to the slack hand lines, he wobbled across the old barrel-stave planks, swinging above the icy water. In half a minute he was on the opposite bank. Reaching into his pocket, he pulled out his father's knife and flipped up the blade. The rope was hard, but the well-honed blade, though rusty from its recent soakings, had kept a good edge. A few moments of heavy sawing was enough to sever the four stout ropes and send the whole structure flopping into the river with a great splash, sprawling across the white banks and broken ice. The dark current caught at the planking and tugged the free end into the water, sweeping it away downstream. Suddenly appalled at what he had done, Murdo stared at the two stark, snow-plastered posts, and hoped ironically that the men he had seen were not simply shepherds. If they were the Germans, however, it should hold them up for a while. No-one would choose to cross that stretch of river without a bridge.

He turned to face the slope above him. Up and up it reached, heavy with drifts, and overhead the inky clouds pulled themselves together for the onslaught that could only be a few minutes away. Low black tatters writhed and swirled beneath. Their message was unmistakable: 'Keep off the mountain,' they said. 'Don't be foolhardy.'

Murdo looked down the river. Still hidden beyond the bluff, the men could not appear for several minutes yet. But again their shouts rang up the gusty stillness of the afternoon. What if they *were* only a group of shepherds, warning him of the blizzard about to descend? He must assume they were not, and turned his attention to the side of the glen. East and west the rough slope, devoid of trees and shelter, rose steeply into the edge of cloud. There was only one solution, he must climb. The snow would soon hide him from their eyes, there was plenty of shelter high up on the mountain.

Staring up with considerable fear at the heavy slopes and black sky above him, he tugged the khaki jacket over the waistband of his trousers, and began to climb.

Later, Murdo could remember little of that nightmare ascent. It could not have lasted more than three or four hours, for he reached the further glen shortly after it grew dark, but in that time as many years grew on his young shoulders.

The river fell away below. His lungs were bursting, his heart surged into his throat it thudded so violently. Waves of dizziness swept over him, making the hillside reel. Drift followed drift, fall followed fall: the breath rasped in and out of his throat, numbingly cold. Slowly the rolling moorland beneath him flattened. Tiny figures clustered at the bridge posts, minute in the landscape, pointing, gesticulating, uncertain what to do. A few soft flakes of snow fell through the air. The whirling, spinning tails of cloud, the ragged ends of that black, all-engulfing darkness, drew close.

Then suddenly the storm was upon him. The wind sprang out, and snow, thick as feathers, beat in his face, choking, smothering. Horizontally the flakes whipped past, and each flake stung like a needle. They stabbed his eyes and cheeks, burned his ears, so that he turned the crown of his head into the heart of the blizzard. The cold gripped his skull, contracting and contracting, tightening about his brain.

He struggled up the exposed slope where the snow was thin on the ground, and the storm raged against him: he sought shelter in the gullies, and floundered to his waist in drifts. There was no landmark, nothing to see but the snow; nothing to hear but the wind and the noises he made himself; nothing to remember but the struggle and the pain. At times no more than half conscious, only something within Murdo himself refused to submit, and he fought on. Upwards — ever upwards.

And then at last came a time when the slope flattened, and in the dim roaring whiteness that was his world, he staggered to a little cliff and fell beside it. For a second, a minute, an hour, he may have lost consciousness completely. Later he recalled opening his eyes to find himself sprawled in the snow, one arm flung out, his head half buried in a drift. He turned his face into the rock face and lay there for a long time without moving while the blizzard swept past, massive and endless, yet left him alone save for a few soft flakes that drifted down.

Then he was out in it again. The malevolent wind screamed for him in the summit rocks. His hands and face were numb. On he trudged, and on. The ground tilted. Staggering like a drunken man, he half walked, half fell, down from the high pass. Time and again he tripped and lay where he fell, motionless, as if life had departed.

And then, suddenly halting, he realised that the snow had eased. Slowly his eyes swam into focus. The peaks were left behind, a great cliff hung above his right shoulder. He could see the moors and the river below.

With dismay he stared — it was the same glen!

Or was it? He rubbed a sodden red hand across his face to brush off the plastering of snow and slithering gouts of slush.

He tried to read the landscape — the river, mountains, moor. Was it the same glen? Surely it was not — no, definitely it was not!

"Oh, thank God!" he mumbled, and sat down abruptly in the snow.

It was dark when he reached the river. He peered at the glinting black water, trying to see which way it flowed. It ran to the left. In the little light that filtered through gaps in the cloud, he followed the river down the broad empty glen.

Some time later — he never knew when, or how far he had walked — there, far over to the left, stood the squat shape of an old house, almost indescernible in the gloom. But there was no welcoming, beckoning light this time.

He crossed the quarter mile of heather and rough pasture. The house was deserted. His knocks returned a hollow echo from the empty hall.

It was no time for respecting property. Kicking beneath the snow, almost at once his boot struck an old fence post. With some difficulty he pulled it from the frozen ground, a clumsy weapon covered with grass and snow. A crude blow smashed in the window and sent the glass tinkling to the floorboards inside. He reached through and pushed the catch back, then heaved up the window. For a moment it stuck, then shot up half way and jammed solid. A sharp pain in his frozen hand told him he had cut himself, and putting the palm to his mouth he felt the taste of warm blood. He squeezed through the gap and pulled the window shut behind him.

Inside the house all was black, but slowly his eyes adjusted until he could distinguish dim shapes. He was in what had once been the living room. The place was not very long empty, for paper still clung to the walls and it was dry. A few sticks of furniture remained, and bumping into something soft he discovered, with a feeling almost akin to pleasure, that it was an old burst sofa. He swept some scraps of gritty paper and wood to the floor and slumped heavily upon it. Heedless of the ice and snow that still clung to his clothes, he drew up his legs. Minutes later he was sound asleep.

Outside the clouds were gathering again. The last stars disappeared behind an advancing storm cloak, and the moors resigned themselves to darkness.

Gone to Earth

Dawn came late. It was preceded by no lightening in the east, no glow in the sky: it came, if you could say it came from anywhere, from the ground. Imperceptibly the night gave way to dimness, and dimness to an endless waste of moors, over which the clouds lowered and the snow drove in wild, fierce blasts.

The cold half-light filtered into Murdo's cottage and stole about the bare rooms, revealing the filth of desolation. He tossed fretfully in his sleep, muttering and half crying out as the dreams raged inside his head. Mountainous black seas, crags, dead men, Hector, tearing hot bullets, the blizzard, Carl Voss, his father, exhaustion throbbed and swam. More and more, as the dawn lightened, he turned and flung his head from side to side. His breathing quickened almost to panting, then suddenly, with a choking cry, he sat bolt upright and woke.

Where was he? Shutting his eyes for a moment he tried to steady the trembling and sickness that convulsed his whole body. But he could not control himself. Rushing to the door he flung it wide, and heedless of the blizzard and icy gale that beat against him, vomited down the side of the house.

It seemed as if he would never stop. Long after there was nothing left his stomach kept heaving, and the sweat stood on his forehead, icy cold in the wind. At length, shivering and weak, he turned back into the hallway and closed the door behind him.

He was ill, really ill this time. Again his stomach cramped and he leaned against the staircase, pressing his brow to one of the struts of the bannisters. Slowly the confusion in his head quietened. Heavily Murdo pushed himself back and made his way to the sofa once more. For a while he just sat, staring wretchedly at the damp soot and rubbish in the fireplace, numb to everything but his own misery. At length he raised his head and looked towards the window. Through the broken pane and narrow strips of glass that were not covered with drift he could see the blizzard. Horizontally, blinding, the flakes swept past. No matter how he felt, he could not go out in that; no-one would venture forth in such conditions. It was a relief. Unless there was another house close by, and he was sure there was not, he must stay where he was. Try to get a fire going, dry out his clothes.

Shivering, he pulled his shirt and jacket tight to the throat, draped a filthy rag of sacking about his head, and ploughed through knee-deep snow to the end of the house. This way and that he peered through screwed-up eyes into the veils of grey, searching for any sign of life. Up and down the glen nothing was to be seen but the empty hillside, the shrouded river sixty yards away, and the driving snow. The wind rushed and whined about the house and few small out-buildings, the cold cut through to his skin. Abruptly, as he forced the front door shut upon it, the noise was cut off. For a moment he stood in the hallway, and his eyes closed. Reluctantly he opened them again and dragged himself on an inspection of the house.

Although it was dirty with the grime of desertion, the building was in good repair. The last occupants could not have been out for more than a year or two. Save for an empty window in the back kitchen, where a pane of glass had fallen out and let the rain in, and two extensive wet patches on the ceilings, there seemed little wrong with it. The black grates were messy, and the second downstairs room had been used by a shepherd, for a couple of liver-fluke tins stood in one corner, and the high mantlepiece was littered with some empty beer bottles, candle stubs and a bit of stained rag. Struck by an inspiration, Murdo poked about among this rubbish, and almost immediately his fingers alighted on a packet of Woodbines with two left in it, and an old match box. He shook the box and it rattled. With a sinking heart he tipped the charred sticks into his palm, but there among the dead matches were half a dozen or more with pink tips, and they were dry.

Almost hopefully he gathered together some paper — a dusty yellowed copy of the *Daily Record* dated the previous summer, some old paper bags that rattled with dry crusts, a *People's Friend Annual* that had been kicked into a cupboard — and carried them through to the room in which he had slept. The dried-out corpse of a rook straggled awkwardly in the grate. Taking it by the wing tip Murdo tossed it into the far corner. Then he felt up the chimney in case it should have been blocked for some reason, but it seemed perfectly clear. He raked away the damp soot and old ash with his hands, laid the paper in the grate, and smashed a broken chair to a bundle of sticks and splintered wood. Soon a bright yellow fire was leaping up the chimney, smoking heavily as the remaining soot smouldered and the varnish flared on the wood.

One chair, however, will not keep a fire going for long, and hunting through the house, Murdo dragged everything burnable into the living room. It was a pitiful collection. Carefully he fed some more into the blaze. His trousers and jacket began to steam. With the warmth the fever drew on again so that his head swam, and he had to put out a hand to steady himself.

But before he lay down, he needed more wood. There was no shortage, for the whole house was lined with wood, but he felt too weak even to think of how he might tear up the floorboards. There were the doors, however, and going upstairs to a bedroom, he took hold of the door of a small cupboard and wrenched it back against the hinges, then slammed it hard. Again and again he twisted and slammed. The catch broke and the metal buckled. He took the flat of his foot and kicked against the hinges, his head thudding with every blow. The screws gave and the cream-painted door skewed awkwardly to one side. A few more wrenches and it came away altogether. Murdo propped it against the wall and jumped on the boards, then the split planks, and soon had reduced the neat door to burnable pieces. He carried them downstairs and laid them at the side of the fire.

In a while he had built a reasonable stack. It was still not big enough, but for the moment he felt he could do no more. He dragged the sofa across until it was only a foot or two from the blaze, then took off his heavy wet clothes and hung them around to dry. Wearing only his damp underclothes, he huddled towards the fire.

He had shut the door to keep the room as warm as possible, but the back and sides of the sofa gave little protection from the arctic gusts that blew through the broken pane. For a time he tried to put up with it, turning first one shivering side then the other to the flames, but it was impossible. He padded through the dust of snow to the window, and with the faded curtains and two or three splintered boards managed to rig a rough patch. Then he hurried through the hall to the other downstairs room, tore down those curtains also, and carried them back to the fire.

For a few minutes he crouched to the blaze, trying to dry out his underclothes. His shins and chest scorched, his back and the backs of his arms and legs remained cold as ice. Piling the fire as high as he dared he stretched out on the sofa, and lifting the curtains from the hearth carefully arranged them on top of himself like sheets. They were damp against his legs and bare shoulders, but at least they were warm and would soon dry out. On top he pulled a bit of ragged carpet he had found upstairs. Turning to face the fire he twitched the curtains about his chin and drew up his feet. The flames danced and flared; his eyes began to slip out of focus. The heat, gathering in the cocoon of the sofa, made the room swim about him. He closed his eyes.

For three days sickness and fever wrapped him in their web of sleep; not a sound, healing sleep, but a burning unconsciousness that inflamed his mind into grotesque nightmares and dreams that racked his mind as much as the fever racked his body.

Periodically he woke and stacked more wood on the fire, or gathered a handful of snow to drink, moving about the house in a daze of heat and cold, so that when again he collapsed heavily on to the couch and fell asleep, he might never have risen.

If the Germans had arrived at the door, he was theirs. He might not even have woken as they carried him off. But they did not come, indeed they could not come. For two whole days the blizzard blew and the moors were quite impassable.

But the third morning dawned fair. The snow had ceased during the night and the wind had shifted to the south. No longer were the clouds lowering and slate-grey, they were white, and as the morning wore on, chinks appeared and patches of sunlight moved across the moors. Some of the snow on the roof of Murdo's cottage slipped and fell to the ground with a hiss and a thud. By the evening a listener in the silence might have heard the tinkling of water about him as the frozen runnels began to flow, and a tiny rustling as the snow slumped more heavily on the grass, and clumps of heather broke free from its weight.

That same Wednesday evening brought Murdo's fever to its climax. The fire was out and the room very cold. But he had put on his clothes the day before, when they were dry, and beneath the covering of curtains and carpet his body was burning hot. The sweat streamed off him, beading down his face and making his hair wet. From head to toe his body shivered violently.

But by ten o'clock his breathing was easier, the trembling had quietened. By midnight he lay calm. The furrows left his brow and the wet hair dried across his face.

It was daylight when he woke. The nightmares were gone. For a long time Murdo just lay there gazing at the ceiling. Brilliant sunshine flooded through the window, revealing all the cobwebs and dust and the filthiness of the rags that covered him. But he was accustomed to them and kept them tucked about his face, for it was warm underneath. A musical noise of trickling water came from the window, and further off a heavy splashing roar like a waterfall.

At last he pulled an arm from beneath the curtains and scratched his head. His hand was filthy, smeared with soot and ash, and a scratch across the back was ridged with grime. The deep cut across his palm made him hold the hand half closed, and when he stretched his fingers slightly the black scab, already cracked open a dozen times, tugged sharply against the flesh. For a while he amused himself with it, enjoying the sensation as his fingers tugged gently against the cut. But the skin of his hands, apart from being dirty, was of a different texture. Normally weather-beaten and rough, it had become smooth and soft, slightly damp.

Carefully he pushed the coverings back and swung his legs to the floor. Immediately a trace of the old dizziness made him blink and lean back for a moment against the arm of the sofa. Then he rose, feeling very weak, and tentatively stretched himself at the fireplace. His clothes were twisted and uncomfortable from having been slept in, and he unfastened his battledress and trousers to tuck in the shirt and sweater. As he did so he became aware how hollow and empty his stomach felt, and for a moment pulled up the clothes to examine himself. He was thin as a rake, his ribs stood out sharply and his stomach had sunk almost out of sight beneath his chest,

"It's food you need, Murdo," he said to himself, tucking down his clothes once more and fumbling with the buttons.

He crossed to the window. A few sheep huddled under a wall in the sunshine a few yards away, their droppings scattered across the melting snow. The crown of the wall and the roofs of the outhouses were thickly covered: their long blue shadows reached across the dazzling turf. But the snow would not last very long if the thaw continued at its present rate, for the sun struck warm through the glass, and all the way along the roofs dripped, the sparkling drops carving caverns for themselves in the drifts below. As he stood there a great slab of snow, too wet and heavy to adhere any longer to the sloping roof of the barn, slid over the rone pipe and thudded to the ground in a long crumpled heap. The river, sixty yards beyond, gushed brown and brim-full between the snowy banks and roared over the boulders of a salmon pool.

Food! Murdo looked at the sheep. There might well be a stack of turnips in one of the sheds.

As he opened the front door the mild air surprised him. It was warmer outside than in. The sheep scattered, tails swirling, as if scenting danger as the boy appeared in the doorway. Blinking in the brightness, occasionally putting a hand to the rough wall for support, Murdo began searching through the old croft buildings.

At the end of the house was a lean-to, bare and deep in sheep dirt. Obviously the animals used it as a shelter in bad weather. A few yards away stood the barn and shed. The shed was locked, though through the window it appeared to be empty save for a few rusting tools. The barn, when he had unfastened the cord that held the door shut, proved to have a stack of hay in it and a few sacks of oil cake for the sheep. Not a sign of turnips, or any human food. Murdo fell in the hay and gnawed a corner of one of the drab cakes. It tasted terrible, like dust and dry grass, and made him cough. He lay back and closed his eyes.

He may have dozed a little, but slowly, as half an hour slipped by, an idea germinated in his mind. At first it seemed horrible, and he rejected it: then it came to seem only too realistic. He had to have food, and there was one food only — the sheep. Rolling over on his hip he dug the clasp knife from his trouser pocket.

At first his fingers could not open it, but with a black thumb nail he managed to push up the blade enough to grip it. With a snap it flicked open. The edge was still good, but it could be better. Picking a smooth stone from just inside the barn door, he spat on it and carefully whetted the concave blade back and forth until the edge gleamed steel-white, and satisfied the delicate tip of his finger. He laid it on a ledge, and gathering a big armful of hay, carried it outside and strewed it widely on the ground. From a safe distance the sheep watched with interest, looking from one to the other as if seeking an opinion. Around the hay Murdo scattered a few scoops of oil cake, leaving a trail to the door of the barn. Just outside he spread them more thickly, tempting the animals through the entrance to a positive feast on the barn floor. Then he settled himself out of sight in the hay and waited, fingering the sharp blade and planning how he would do it. Even in proper conditions, he knew, it was a bloody business, for over the years he had helped his father and Hector to kill several sheep, and a pig too.

It was a long time before the animals came up, then suddenly they were there, more than a dozen of them. The poor creatures were starving and tore at the hay ravenously.

Murdo stationed himself just inside the barn door and prepared for what he must do, trying to blind his thoughts and make it an instinctive act. The barn was well built and there were no chinks through which to peer. He waited for what seemed a long time, but at length a shadow appeared in the sunlight that streamed through the doorway, and then another one. He cautioned himself: 'Don't rush it, wait until you are certain.'

The shadows grew as the sheep became bolder and drew towards the doorway, until one must have been at the very brink, for in the low sunlight he could see the shadow beneath its knees. He drew a deep breath and set his teeth, gathering himself like a cat. Muzzling at the oil cake the leading sheep came closer still, and Murdo saw the tips of its ears at the edge of the door. He shuffled his feet slightly, gripped the knife like a dagger, and launched himself round the corner.

Before the sheep could move he was upon it, the sudden fury of his attack bowling it to the ground. It bleated despairingly and rolled its eyes. Murdo knotted his fingers in the wool and flung himself astride the creature, feeling for its throat with the knife. But the fleece was thick, and the knife not very big. Time and again he thrust into the wool. The animal kicked wildly and he was nearly flung off. Then suddenly the knife slipped home and the hot blood gushed over his hands and arms, swamping the blood from his own burst palm, drenching the snow scarlet.

Still the animal kicked and he hung on tight, but slowly the struggling lessened and the kicking became spasmodic. In a while it no longer fought to raise its head. Finally the beast lay still, and the pumping blood subsided to a trickle. Murdo fell in the snow across its flank, exhausted and drained.

When he had recovered somewhat, he wiped the sweat from his face with a bloody hand and dragged the sheep through the entrance of the barn. Then he set to with the knife. In half an hour he had several juicy joints of mutton laid out on the hay. It was enough. Taking the partially dismembered sheep by the front legs, he started to drag it towards the river. The animal was heavy, and dragging it through the wet snow it became a dead weight. For thirty yards Murdo struggled, leaving a bloody trench across the pasture. But the effort was too great. He dropped it where it lay and walked back to the barn. An old twist of cord lay on one of the ledges. He tied up three of the joints and slung them over a rafter, to keep them fresh in the cool air and free from rats and insects. The fourth joint he had to cook. Taking it in his hand, still warm, he tied up the barn door and turned back into the house.

The sheep shifted nervously, looking from the carcase to the shredded armfuls of hay and oil cake, and at the door into which he had disappeared. At length one, bigger and bolder than the rest, walked forward cautiously and began to tug at the remains of the hay. The others moved closer.

There were still three matches left and it did not take Murdo long to get a good fire going. The wood he had broken in the house was finished, but there was no need for more destruction since he had discovered some ready sawn logs and the remains of a small peat stack in the barn. He brought a couple of armfuls indoors and piled them at the side of the hearth, then lay back on the sofa to wait until the fire had built up enough heat to grill the meat.

An hour later the peat and spitting logs had laid a foundation of ash, and the heart of the fire glowed white and crimson. Carefully Murdo adjusted the small logs and flaming cinders to expose the heat. He skewered a thick slice of mutton on a

215

length of fence wire which he had twisted off to use as a poker, and gingerly laid it across the gap. Almost at once the smoke blackened it, but slowly the juices ran down and droplets of fat hissed and flared in the flames. The smell was good and his mouth watered so much that he had to keep swallowing. Time and again he turned the meat, doing his best to ensure that it was cooked right through.

At last it seemed to be ready. He laid the hot mutton in his lap on a corner of his shirt, then skewered another slice and set it on top of the fire. Ravenously he bit into the meat. The taste was smoky, but it was very good. The middle was still pink and largely uncooked, so he ate all the edges and threw the remainder into the back of the fire.

Twenty minutes later he started on the second slice, but after a few mouthfuls his appetite deserted him. He wanted no more. Nevertheless, he knew that he needed the food and forced himself to take a few more bites. Mechanically he chewed on the roast mutton but it was tasteless, and he was hardly able to swallow it. He regarded the third slice, oozing its juices into the fire. It nauseated him, and pulling out the wire he dropped the meat into the flames along with the piece he had been eating. Slowly the red-brown slices curled up and fizzled among the burning logs.

For a while he thought he would be sick again, then the feeling passed and the strengthening warmth of the food began to radiate from his stomach. He set a good log on the fire and packed the edges with scraps of peat. Then he pulled off his boots, unfastened his jacket and stretched out on the sofa.

He did not sleep at once, and as he gazed at the ceiling he thought of nothing — just drifted in the still aftermath of the fever and slaughtering the sheep. Now and again he seemed to feel the animal buck beneath him and saw the rolling eyes and dead mouth. Then from the mist of a thousand dormant memories, prompted possibly by some pattern in the plaster, he remembered his old schoolroom, the carved brown desks and curling maps, the sharp smell of the chalk dust, the voice of the dominie as he rapped on the table and thrust the pointer like a billiard cue in his own direction. How familiar it all was, how comfortable and secure, yet how far away those days of childish jokes and irresponsibility. Wryly he half smiled, wondering what the dominie would have to say about his present predicament. His smile broadened as the thought expanded to include his Aunt Winifred. "I knew, Murdo; I knew where you would end up one of these days. Chased by Germans! The idea! Well, you've only got yourself to blame, you and that father of yours." He slipped a hand into his pocket and pulled out the black and white knife. He had scrubbed the blood away in the snow. Holding it in his palm he wondered, as he had been wondering since he woke three hours earlier, what the Germans were doing. Were troops still gathering on the coasts of France and Belgium? Were the British forces still moving south? Had Operation Flood-Tide already begun? There was no way of knowing. And if it had not, what of Henry Smith and his men? He recalled the figures clustered at the bridge below Carn Mor; one of them, he was sure, had been the German leader, and another was Gunner. But he could have been wrong, the memory was vague.

And slowly all his memories became vague. His eyes closed, his breathing was deep and even. He fell asleep.

It was the coldness that woke him. A concave shell and a dust of grey ash were all that remained of the big log. The room was in shadow. Going to the window, Murdo saw that the sun had swung far round in the sky. He estimated that it was mid afternoon, probably about two-thirty. With distaste he surveyed the slabs of red meat, laid out in wet piles at one side of the window ledge. A pool of blood had dribbled over and made a dark patch on the floorboards. Though his stomach called out for food again, he thought he would postpone cooking more until later in the day.

The short sleep had done him good, and though he could expect to be weak for some time, he was sufficiently recovered to start taking an interest in the world around him. He felt filthy. Going outside he pulled up his sleeves, turned down his collar, and scrubbed his face and arms vigorously in the icy melt-water that trickled from the drain-pipe. It was crystal clear. When he had finished he cupped his hands and took a long drink. The water was achingly cold against his teeth and in his throat, and chill in his stomach, but it made him feel clean.

After that, being naturally of a tidy disposition even though he was living roughly, he straightened up the room which he was using. He hung up the curtains again, so far as he could, and made a neater patch over the smashed window; stood the meat on a sheet of paper and rubbed the ledge clean with a rag; got rid of the broken glass and dried-out corpse of the rook; tidied the hearth and stack of fuel, and pushed the few sticks of furniture straight.

It occurred to him that if the Germans should come looking up the glen — assuming that 'Operation Flood-Tide' had not already commenced — it would be to his advantage to let them know as little as possible about the house. So he drew the faded curtains across the window, and did the same in the other downstairs room. The glass in the front door and the little back kitchen was already covered with old net curtain to above head height, and when he put his eyes to it from outside, he could not see through.

Finally he had to get rid of the sheep's carcass. Lacing his boots he crossed the pasture, sending the sheep scurrying from their sunlit wall. Briefly he regarded the butchered animal. He was sorry he had killed it, and for so little — but it was no good being sentimental. Bracing himself, he grasped one of the front legs and began hauling the carcass behind him towards the river. It had stiffened, and the second front leg and already eyeless head kept catching the back of his knee, so that once he fell. The haunches, where he had removed the joints of meat, were dark and bright red against the snow. Grey links of intestines trailed behind. He reached the brink of the river and rested for a moment. The torrent of water had risen above the banks of ice and largely washed them away. Peat-dark and brimming it swam through the sheep pastures. Half a dozen gulls and a few crows that had been hopping about the sheep's carcass when he came out, circled and crossed back and forth overhead. Standing back, he heaved the sheep the last couple of feet and let it fall into the river. The wool filled with water, the swollen current sucked it away in a trice. Jostling and swooping for some morsel of flesh as it washed to the surface, the wheeling gulls followed its progress downstream. Their cries grew fainter.

Murdo rinsed his hands at the bank, and taking a few deep breaths of the sweet air, retraced his steps to the house. Before he went indoors he lingered for a while in the last of the sunshine, looking up and down the glen. It was broad and bowl-shaped. Upstream the mountains gathered close, dominated by the great white flanks of Carn Mor, and another rugged mountain almost directly behind the cottage. Downstream, towards the coast, the land flattened, the moors rising no more than two or three hundred feet above the valley floor. Trees covered the opposite, southern slope. When he went down the next morning, that was the route he must take. The going would be harder, but the trees would give him protection.

High over the wooded ridge a large bird was circling, too large for a buzzard and to his sharp eyes with the wrong silhouette. It was joined by a second. They could only be eagles. For several minutes he watched as they passed slowly upstream, and vanished towards a high spur of the mountain.

The afternoon was drawing on. Already the sun was dipping behind the peaks of the moor and the glen was filling with blue shadows. The warmth that had been in the air was gone. A bank of rain clouds was gathering in the west. Murdo shivered, and turned indoors to warm himself at the fire.

It was an hour later that the thunderbolt fell.

Wild from the Hills

The room was dark, though enough daylight still lingered to brighten the shabby curtains that Murdo had pulled across the window. The fire glowed hot, and yellow flames licked around the edges of a new log. The smell of burning mutton was in the air. A scrap of whittled wood, showing the rough outline of a deer in flight, lay broken in the hearth. Murdo had taken off his jacket and sweater and lounged on the sofa in grubby shirt sleeves. He felt dispirited and washed out, and thought gloomily of the long night ahead. Idly he scratched at the sheep-blood stains that had dried stiff down the leg of his trousers. If only it was morning, he hated hanging about; and sitting there in front of the fire made him feel worse, as if the fever was returning. Bleakly he regarded the half-eaten slice of meat that lay beside him on the arm of the sofa.

Suddenly, on the edge of his awareness, there was a faint whisper of sound from outside. He sat bolt upright, and froze. Eyes wide, he stared at the window. His ears strained. Nothing was to be heard save the deep drumming of the river and tinkle of water from the drainpipe. Perhaps he had been mistaken. Then again there was a muffled sound, the soft swish and crunch of a boot in the melting snow. A moment later the footstep was plain and a dark shape passed across the light of the curtains. Murdo's heart thudded. The silhouette returned and lingered at the window for two or three seconds, then passed on. There was silence. He waited. Abruptly there was a loud knocking at the front door.

For a moment Murdo could not move, then forcing himself to overcome the weakness of instant surrender, he rose and crept cautiously to the window. There was a little chink at the top of the curtains. Pulling himself to the broad window ledge, he peered along the side of the house. A man — at least he could only see one — stood at the front door, looking this way and that as he waited for an answer.

It was no good pretending there was no-one in the house, for there were his tracks criss-crossing the snow half a dozen times behind the man's back, and he would have seen the smoke from the chimney too.

Again the man rapped on the door with his knuckles and the noise boomed in the empty house.

"Hello!" he called loudly. "Is there anybody there?"

For a desperate, confused moment Murdo could think only of escape, climbing from the little window at the back and running away across the snow. But he could scarcely have run a hundred yards, he had not the strength. There was no hope of escape that way. He climbed down from the window ledge, and as he stood he felt the panic ebb away, drain from his head and neck and arms, and he grew still. It was strange, something beyond determination: in that moment of crisis, though his heart still pounded, he found himself possessed of an icy inner calm. Quietly he crossed to the stack of wood beside the hearth and picked out a short branch the thickness of his arm. Then, pulling on his unlaced boots, he walked into the hallway and opened the front door.

A big man stood on the step. He was quite young and wore a heavy jacket and rubber boots. His hair was dark and cropped short. Clearly he was not a Highlander.

Murdo stood in the narrow gap of the doorway and grasped the hidden branch tightly in his hand. He was a wild sight, with burning black eyes and shaggy hair, his shirt crumpled, trousers torn and stained.

"Yes?" he said enquiringly.

The man regarded him closely. "I'm sorry to bother you," his English was very precise, "but can you tell me whether there is another house further up the valley?"

Murdo looked up the deserted, snowy glen to where it turned out of sight behind a long ridge of the hillside.

"Just ours," he said, "and a couple of old ruins."

"Oh." The man seemed nonplussed. "You don't live here, then?"

"Hardly." Murdo opened the door a little wider so that he could see into the deserted hall.

"I saw the smoke from the chimney and I thought . . ." his words trailed away.

"No, the place has been empty for years. Dad and me use it when we're down at the sheep sometimes, that's all." Amazed at the ease with which the lies were springing to his lips, Murdo waited for a moment. "Why? Are you looking for somebody?"

The man considered the tousled figure before him, trying to read the face that regarded him with such disconcerting frankness from the half-open doorway.

"Yes, we are, as a matter of fact," he said at length. "There's a boy missing. We think he might have been lost up this way in the snowstorm."

Murdo shook his head. "We haven't seen anybody at all," he said. "Not for a week or more. Not even Davie with the sheep." One of his legs was beginning to tremble. He fought to keep it still. "Who was it? No-one from around here?"

"No, a boy from Berriedale."

Murdo knew Berriedale, or at least he had been there a couple of times when his father's regiment was on manoeuvres nearby.

"Oh? Who?" he said.

The man was taken aback momentarily. "Oh, well, he's not a local lad. Up here on holiday."

"Ah!" Murdo shifted his feet and cleared his throat. His voice felt none too steady.

"Is your father about?"

"Yes, somewhere. He went out the back a while ago. Do you want to see him?"

"No . . . No, it's all right."

"Are you sure?" Murdo drew a breath and gripped the branch tightly. "Come in for a minute, if you like, and I'll see if I can find him." He opened the door a little wider.

"No. I must be getting back. It'll be dark soon."

Murdo looked up at the sky. "Yes, it's going to rain, too. It's always bad when it comes in black like that over the hill — my father says." He bit the inside of his lip — he was overdoing it.

The young man followed his eyes and smiled wryly. "You're probably right." He eased his cold feet in the snow.

Murdo waited and did not speak.

"Well, thank you for your help."

"It's no trouble," Murdo said. "I hope you don't get too wet."

The man nodded and made his way back between the house and shed towards the white track that ran down the side of the glen. Murdo raised a hand in farewell, and closed the door.

For a moment he slumped against it, too stunned to move. Then pulling himself together, he hurried into the back kitchen where there was a good view of that side of the valley. His visitor was stepping out as briskly as the ground permitted, moving from side to side as he picked his way through the melting drifts. But two hundred yards on he paused irresolutely and looked back. For long moments he stood there, then stepped off the track into deeper snow and began making his way towards the river, looking this way and that as if he was searching for somebody.

The view from the window was limited in that direction, and quickly he passed out of sight behind the end of the house. Murdo moved back into the room in which he had been living and pulled the curtain aside. A minute or so later the man reappeared, moving along the near bank of the river and heading towards the barn. Nervously Murdo passed his tongue across cracked lips. Another fifty yards and the stranger would see the track where he had dragged the sheep through the

224

pasture, and the blood in the snow. He leaned across the window to see clearly, and the movement must have caught the man's eye, because he stopped for a moment, then waved a casual arm and turned up towards the front door. As he came forward he felt unconsciously at the belt of his trousers, then pretended he was tucking in his shirt, but the movement was not lost upon Murdo. His heart began thudding once more, and there was a burning, sick feeling in his gullet. He took deep breaths to calm himself, and a few moments later opened the front door as the big man came up smiling.

"I thought I had better have a word with your father after all," he explained. "But there seems to be no sign of him."

"Oh, most likely he'll be in one of the sheds," Murdo said as casually as he could, "or down behind the sheep fanks. Come in for a minute, and I'll fetch him for you. Have a warm at the fire." Again he opened the door wide, and tightened his trembling grip on the rough club.

"Well, I must say I could do with a sit-down," the young stranger admitted. "Thank you."

Ducking his head in the low doorway, he stepped through into the dim hall. Even before he had a chance to turn, Murdo slammed the door behind him, and raising the heavy branch, thrashed it across the side of his dark head. And the German saw him — a glimpse, forever photographed into his memory, of the boy's face, savage as an animal — fierce black eyes, bared teeth, his whole stocky body twisted with effort. His hands went up too late, and the vision shattered in a blinding explosion of red and black and a great pit down which he was falling, falling — and that was all.

Appalled at what he had done, Murdo looked down at the sprawled figure on the boards at his feet. The man seemed to take up the whole of the narrow hallway. He had fallen awkwardly across the foot of the stairs and his face was hidden against the bottom tread. Murdo bent and tried gently to turn him over, to see how badly he was hurt. But the limp German was a dead weight and he had to grasp the front of his jacket and use all of his strength to haul him on to his back. The man's head knocked heavily against the bottom post of the bannisters. Anxiously Murdo examined the body for signs of life. He did not seem to be breathing. Perhaps he had killed him! Murdo pressed his ear against the German's chest, but nothing was to be heard. He grabbed his wrist and searched for a pulse — and abruptly he found it, strong and steady, throbbing powerfully beneath his fingers. With a sigh of relief he sank back on his heels. Then suddenly he was frightened that the man might recover too quickly. He ran out to the barn for the length of cord he had used to tie up the joints of mutton. Dragging meat and all with him, he raced back to the house and bound the man's wrists and ankles tightly.

When he had finished he felt inside the young German's jacket, and removed the heavy service revolver from the holster at his waist. The magazine was full. Feeling through his pockets in case he carried any other weapon with him, Murdo came upon twelve more rounds of ammunition lying loose. The only other items of interest were a map, a wrist watch, and the greater part of a large bar of milk chocolate. He laid them on one side and replaced the other odds and ends in his pocket — a handkerchief, a comb, an assortment of small British coins, and a nicely marked pebble from the beach.

The young man still showed no sign of coming round. It was cold in the hall. Taking him again by the front of the jacket, Murdo dragged him into the living room and laid him on the old length of carpet beside the fire. Five minutes later he groaned and began to stir. His eyes flickered open. Murdo rolled up his own jacket and sweater and placed them under the German's head.

The interminable hours of darkness drew on. A rattling, gusty rain set in and the wind roared about the house, making the windows shake and the doors tug against their fastenings. The barn door slammed back and forward, so loud and insistent that at length Murdo had to go out through the pelting rain to tie it shut again. Half a dozen sheep, which had been feeding on the hay and oil cake, burst past him through the black doorway

226

and ran away bleating. Throughout the night they gathered for shelter in the lean-to, their coughing and low notes comforting and familiar sounds in the darkness. It was cold, and Murdo kept the fire stacked high with wood and peat. The wind sucked the flames up the chimney so that the sparks flew and little flames at the back burned green and blue.

Murdo stuck one of the old candle stubs on a piece of wood and pored over the map. He was, so far as he could tell, at a cottage named Dalgarbh, and the mountain which rose above was called Sgorach. Below it the glen wound six miles through descending moorland to the east coast, reaching the sea at Berriedale. Just above the shore, where the river was crossed by the road, it was joined by the stream he had followed from Duncan Beg's cottage beyond the mountains. He traced them down with a black forefinger. Clearly, he thought, 'Operation Flood-Tide' could not yet have swung into action, for if it had they would not still be searching for him. All he had to do, once daylight came, was follow the river down to Berriedale, then telephone the police. As he travelled through the trees on the southern slope of the glen he must keep his eyes open, for when the young German beside him did not turn up, they would be sure to send out a search party. He broke off two more squares of milk chocolate, put one into the German's mouth and ate the other himself. It tasted much better than the mutton.

The watch Murdo had taken from the prisoner's wrist made the night drag by even more slowly. He tried to sleep, but was quite unable to do so. After what seemed hours of restless tossing and turning, another consultation of the watch revealed that its tormenting fingers had crawled forward no more than thirty minutes. At nine o'clock it felt like midnight, and at midnight it felt like four o'clock in the morning. Repeatedly he put the watch to his ear to make sure it had not stopped. He tried to talk to the German, but the heavy young man had nothing to say and either glowered back or ignored him, nursing his sore head and his self-contempt at having been knocked senseless and taken prisoner by a boy. Too late he saw that the end joint of the third finger on the boy's right hand was missing.

The heavy revolver fascinated Murdo. Time and again he broke it open, ejecting and replacing the cartridges, drawing beads on marks on the wall and imaginary pursuers. He spread the map and traced his track, so far as he was able, from the bothy at Loch Strathy to his present shelter at Dalgarbh. He read advertisements and recipes and scraps of the romantic stories in what remained of the old *People's Friend Annual*, leaning forward to get the light of the fire, for there were only enough candle stubs to last a couple of hours. He closed his eyes and dozed fitfully. He grilled some more of the mutton and offered a slice to the German, who refused to eat it and looked on disgusted as Murdo chewed his way around the edge of a smoke-blackened cutlet.

At last the fourteen hours of murky night passed by, and going to the window for the twentieth time, Murdo perceived a definite lightening of the landscape outside. He could distinguish the black shape of the barn and see a dim outline of hills against the sky. It was seven o'clock.

Low in spirits, but relieved that the night was over and at last he was able to take some action, he began to prepare for his departure. He buckled the heavy revolver about his waist and pulled his sweater over the top. He put on his battledress jacket and boots, and laid the things he was to carry on the window sill — map, pocket knife, a handful of cartridges, a couple of slabs of cooked mutton, and the remains of the chocolate.

Kneeling then, he struck one of the two remaining matches and examined the young German's head. There was little to see, for the wound was in his hair and he pulled his head away as Murdo's fingers touched him. A long trickle of blood down the side of his neck had dried during the night. There was nothing Murdo could do.

The match burned low and nipped his fingers. He threw it into the fire and turned his attention to the prisoner's bonds. Unwrapping the last of the cord from the joints of mutton, he put another turn around his wrists and ankles. After that he rolled the man in a length of rick netting and tied down the end with tags of mesh. Finally he threaded a piece of old rope through his legs and arms, knotted it in the mesh, and with a multitude of tight knots secured it to the thick shaft of the hob at the side of the fire.

"Are you sure you don't want me to run away?" the German said ironically.

Murdo smiled. He remembered a rusty old basin in the barn. Filling it at the sheep trough, he carried it carefully into the house and poured the water on the fire. There was a fierce dying hiss and clouds of steam and ash puffed out into the room. He repeated the performance until he was sure the fire was completely extinguished.

"I'm sorry," he said, "you might be a bit cold. But you could have burned through the ropes or cut them on the window glass."

His apology did not help the young German's feelings. He gave Murdo a single glance, eyes full of self-reproach and disappointment, then turned his face to the wall.

Without the flicker of firelight the room was dark, and Murdo drew back the curtains to get the benefit of the faint dawn light. Roughly he scoured the bowl at the sheep trough, then filled it with clean water and carried it into the living room. He laid a piece of cooked mutton beside it on a corner of the hearth. Then he filled his pockets with the items from the window ledge, and was ready to leave.

"As soon as I can, I'll tell someone you're here," he said.

There was no reply.

Feeling miserable and guilty, Murdo shrugged, then turned away into the empty hall. A moment later he passed out into the cold wet gloom of the morning, and pulled the front door shut behind him.

The deluge during the night had cleared away much of the snow, and sodden patches of black loomed among the white, dappling the hillsides and broad floor of the glen. The wind had died down and it looked as though the rain, which already had eased to an intermittent drizzle, would soon stop altogether. The dark clouds were lifting and pale channels, like water among pack ice, were opening in the east above the North Sea.

From beyond the barn and sheds came a deep roaring as the brimming river poured over the salmon breaks. Murdo trudged towards it through the slush and flood and soon stood on the brink. The water raced by, earth-dark and glinting in the light from the sky. The weight of the current was in the middle, but at the edges the water lapped over the bank and flowed away across the lower pastures. Acres were under water, and downstream a great flood spread threequarters of the way across the valley. Murdo regarded the clots and rafts of foam as they sped past. The broken bridge upon which he had relied to make his crossing flipped and lurched dangerously, as the hanging planks snicked the crest of the current not six inches below.

Irresolutely he paused, but yet again there seemed no choice. He could not risk going down the near side of the valley, for a search party must certainly be sent out before long, and there was no shelter or protection. If he crossed, on the other hand, the river in full spate was the best protection for which he could ask.

The wooden spars were rotten and slippery, and he stood with his feet on the wire cables at either side. Slowly he edged along, holding tightly to the hand lines. With his weight the bridge gave a little, and dropped until the middle planks dipped clear below the mid-stream current. The whole structure leaped dangerously and snapped back and forth. Murdo locked his hands on the ropes and felt forward with his feet until he was actually walking into the water. Icy with melting snow, the current bore powerfully against his calves and swelled above his knees, tearing at him in the half-darkness. Murdo hung on, forcing his legs against it and managing to keep the instep of his boots hooked over the cables. The wires sank deeper, then began to rise, and in two or three minutes he was past the worst part. Momentarily he relaxed — too soon. Instantly his feet were gone from beneath him, his legs trailed in the current. But he had tight hold of the hand lines, and ignoring the pain in his split palm managed to struggle along, hand over hand. Then the cables were above water once more, he regained his feet — he was over! With a tremendous feeling of relief, exhilaration overcoming his weakness, Murdo stood panting on the river-bank.

Briefly he examined his bleeding hand, then reaching into his trouser pocket for the knife, turned his attention to the bridge. The original cables were of wire, now rusted and ragged with age, but the upstream suspension cable had recently been replaced and was of rope. That, at least, he could cut, and in a few moments he had sliced through the tough fibres. As the last strands snapped the rope flew out and the flimsy footbridge slipped sidelong into the racing current, throwing up a great curling wave in the middle of the river. With some satisfaction Murdo regarded it, then turned to the wires. Clearly he could not sever them, but the lashings were of twine. He crouched beside a heavy iron ground pin and sawed at the ancient coils. Inch by inch they fell apart and he peeled them from the rusty end of the wire. With his heel he kicked at the rigid stub and slowly it bent back. But it was hopeless, no matter how he kicked and tugged he would never be able to unbend the half hitches; even with a hammer and marline spike it would have been difficult. With a sigh he picked the knife from the ground and stepped back. It was fortunate that he did so, for he had not considered the tremendous power of the current, bearing full against the catwalk, all borne by the second suspension cable. Suddenly the rotting post beside him snapped under the strain. There was a loud crack, a jerk, a flying tumble of ropes, and it was away. In the slow wintry dawn the destroyed bridge jumped and flapped in the brimming river, held by a single wire.

Murdo folded the knife shut and set his face from the flood. Conscious that pursuers might see his footprints from the further bank, he trod a line of plunging steps through a patch of snow, as if he was heading towards the south-western hills. Reaching a stretch of pools and boggy grass, however, he turned back and carefully made his way east along the bottom rim of the glen, towards the trees that lined the escarpment.

The way was unpleasant among the gnarled and mossy branches of the birch trees. They were saturated and spilled showers of heavy drops upon his head and shoulders. Sometimes, too, a little snow remained, that landed with a slap and slid down his neck and sleeve. Underfoot the snow was deep in places, and the wet ground made the going heavy. He was sodden to the top of his legs and his feet were very cold.

To make up for these discomforts, however, the trees, even though they were sparse in some parts and naked of leaves, gave excellent cover. Higher in spirits than he had been for a long time, Murdo pulled a slab of smoky mutton from his jacket pocket, picked away some khaki fluff, and began to chew it as he went along. It was good to feel the strength coming back into his legs, and the cool air was sweet to breathe. The revolver hung heavy at his belt, and he pulled up his sweater to feel again the sharp bulk of the butt in his hand. It made him feel tough, like a soldier; then he wondered if he would ever dare to use it.

Time passed, daylight grew, the clouds opened to admit a promising morning, and he made good progress. Occasionally a white hare or some rabbits and birds darted away as he disturbed their feeding. A herd of fifteen hind, alarmed, raised their slim heads to regard his passage. Stamping uneasily they turned and swept off in a stream, running and springing, down through the trees, and up the further slope. Murdo paused to watch them go. They were beautiful. Suddenly they checked, swerved, and streamed back down the hillside, vanishing into the trees further down the glen. There on the road, where he had not seen them before, were two men. Their voices now came to him across the valley. Relying on the trees to mask him, though soon he could see them plainly, Murdo froze where he was. Slowly they passed on up the track and finally disappeared behind a clump of fir trees.

If they were looking for the young German they had two or three miles to go before they even reached the cottage, and then the same back again. That gave him well over an hour's lead, and they had to cross the river and follow his trail on top of that. Nevertheless, there was no time to be lost, and he pressed on as quickly as the woods would allow.

An hour and a half later, when the hands of the German's wrist watch showed the time to be just after eleven o'clock, a large grey roof appeared through a gap in the trees on the far side of the glen. Hot and panting from his exertions, Murdo climbed to a vantage point and examined it closely. It was a huge, stone-built lodge surrounded by a high wall. Cheerful lights shone in the windows and smoke curled from the chimneys. This time the owners were at home. As he watched, a young girl came running round the end of the house pursued by a puppy, and disappeared in the front door.

Carefully he checked up and down the glen, then slithered through the trees to the foot of the wood. Where there was a house there should be a bridge, he thought, and a few minutes later spotted a sturdy wooden structure over a little gorge a hundred yards downstream. The road was still clear. Quickly he ducked out of the trees, slid down the bank, hurried across the bridge, and scrambled up the far slope.

Danger had made him cautious and at the top of the bank he paused, raising his head very carefully to survey the road ahead. It was empty. He was just preparing to make a run for the lodge entrance when two soldiers — of all things two British soldiers — came walking briskly through the gates and turned away down the road.

"Hey!" He leaped to his feet. "Hey, stop!"

The soldiers paused and looked back. Murdo scrambled over the edge of the bank. Knees half buckling as he ran, he hurried down the stony track to where they stood. In a matter of seconds he was beside them, and with a hand knotted in one of the soldiers' sleeves was pouring out his tale, incoherent, stumbling over the words, his face ill and eager and desperate.

Astonished, the two soldiers regarded him. At length the taller and senior of the two, a corporal, cut him off and pulled his arm free from Murdo's grip.

"All right!" he said, half laughing and half concerned. "All right! We're on our way down to Berriedale this minute. You can tell it all to the Colonel."

They were on foot, and the three set off together down the road. The second soldier felt in his breast pocket for a packet of cigarettes and lit up. He remembered he had some chocolate, and unbuttoning the flap again, rummaged inside to produce at length a crumpled half bar of Cadbury's Milk. He passed it over.

"Go on," he said. "Take it."

Unenthusiastically Murdo popped the battered squares into his mouth. Suddenly he felt very tired. He didn't feel like talking. For so long he had looked forward to that moment, and now it had come he just wanted to be left alone, to sleep. There was too much to explain. He had carried the burden, let somebody else take it now.

In twenty minutes they reached the crest of the slope above the shore. Beneath them the North Sea was blue-grey and flecked with white horses. Through the tree tops, where the narrow coast road crossed two stone bridges, Murdo could see a scattering of army cars and trucks. A few men stood about, chatting in small groups, smoking and gazing at the twin torrents that gushed from the hills to converge in a tumult fifty yards below. Briefly he paused to take in the scene, and a shiver of relief ran down into his legs. The nightmare, the flight, the pursuit — it was all over.

A few minutes' descent through the wood, and the three emerged between the grey stone bridges at the shore. A dozen heads swept in their direction. Men shifted, as if glad of the diversion, and watched them with interest.

A man of distinguished appearance was leaning on the parapet of the southern bridge studying a map.

The taller of the two soldiers addressed him as they drew close.

"Colonel," he called.

The man looked up, then turned from his map and regarded with attention the little group that approached him. His cap was in his hand, his silver hair stirred a little in the breeze.

Murdo hurried forward. Anxious to get his tale told, he had eyes for no-one but the Colonel. But something in the attitude of one man, half seen, stopped him dead in his tracks. The blood drained from his cheeks. Spinning round, he found himself staring straight into the face of big Bjorn Larvik. Beside him stood Arne, the half-albino, pink-eyed and alert.

It hit Murdo like an electric shock, and he reeled visibly.

Not five yards away, Henry Smith, dressed in the uniform of a British officer, relaxed and broke into a broad smile. Other men were smiling too. One stepped forward and took him by the arm.

In an instant Murdo burst from him and dashed away across the second bridge — but men were coming towards him from the far side.

He was trapped, completely.

Terrified, like a wild creature facing capture, he sprang on to the parapet of the bridge. The peaty waters leaped from the confines of the arch beneath him in a dizzying torrent that redoubled in turmoil as it poured headlong into the second flood fifty yards below. For an instant he poised there, fierce and wild-eyed, heedless of the revolver hanging at his waist. Then they were upon him. Hands reached out to pluck him back, and he sprang forward. For a moment he fell, then the raging, icy waters twitched him away and closed over his head.

Down towards the sea he swept, tumbling over and over in the savage current. Sharp rocks dashed against his body, the huge muscles of water thrust him now to the very bed of the river, now to the surface. He could do nothing, his struggles were futile. Down and down he tossed and rolled, numb, choking, half-paralysed with the cold. On — and on. Then almost abruptly the waters slackened and levelled as the flood ran into the body of the rising tide. Through glazing eyes Murdo found he was near the bank, and somehow managed to writhe and drag himself half out of the water among the boulders at the river mouth. Then he collapsed.

And there he lay, face downwards in the weed and mud, limp as a sodden sack, as the soldiers came up to him. They looked down, nobody was smiling now. Then bending, Bjorn lifted him in his arms and carried him effortlessly up the shore to the twin bridges. Too weak to struggle, too shocked to protest, Murdo slumped against the man's shoulder. He was numb, his mouth hung open, his dark eyes were blank with despair. A car door opened, they laid him inside, it slammed shut. And a moment later off they set with him — back, towards Strathy.

The Smoking Cliffs

It was a fifty mile drive from Berriedale to Strathy, for the road had to circle the mountains. But as the clouds rolled back and the sun shone forth on that early February afternoon, Murdo had no eyes for the road he was travelling. Slumped in the back of the car he had given up all hope, and made no effort to pull himself together. The cold water drained from his clothes, gobbets of mud slid down his chest and legs, his mouth was gritty from the river sludge. After all his efforts, all he had endured, in the end they had been too clever for him. Everything had been a waste of time. The thought weighed on him like a leaden blanket. It was too much to bear. His lips trembled, from disappointment and shock as much as the cold, for the car was warm. Periodically his stomach cramped, making him shudder.

Mile followed upon mile. They passed through the fishing village of Helmsdale, and turned inland up the broad deserted straths of Kildonan and Halladale. The car bucked on the bad road, swerving and braking for occasional sheep and snow patches that impeded their progress. From the front seat came the intermittent murmur of German voices, but Murdo paid them no heed; everything was swamped, drowned, in the feeling of utter defeat that enveloped him.

Eventually he had to move, however, and pushed himself up into a sitting position. He was half surprised to discover that he had been sprawled across the knees of Bjorn Larvik, which now were smeared with the same cold mud as himself. The German was dressed in the uniform of a British army sergeant, his own equivalent rank, with three chevrons on his muddy arm. Gingerly Murdo removed a clot from his own jacket, looked for a place to deposit it, then smeared it against his knee.

He indicated the mess on Bjorn's uniform. "Sorry," he said.

The big man looked at him, then smiled wryly. Leaning forward he pulled a sergeant's greatcoat from behind his back.

"Put this around yourself," he said.

Murdo fumbled with the stiff, mud-caked buttons and tugged off his sodden battledress. Then he peeled off his ragged sweater and shirt. At the bridge he had forgotten the revolver, and now the holster was empty. It had slipped around his belt so that he was half sitting on it. He pulled it back to the front where it was more comfortable. Bjorn looked down and regarded it with interest, but said nothing. Murdo did not explain. He pulled the khaki greatcoat around his bare shoulders. It was blanket-thick and scratchy, but immediately he felt better. Holding it close with one hand, he pushed the hair from his eyes and rubbed a sleeve over the steamy window.

They were running parallel to the railway line. Already they had passed Kinbrace and the empty lodge, the loch into which he had fallen through the ice, and the spot where he had stood and watched the troop train roar past. Gentle hills rolled up from the valley floor, blotched with snow and sparkling in the winter sunlight. Occasional cataracts foamed in the gullies.

In the front seat of the car sat Henry Smith and the distinguished man whom the soldier had addressed as 'Colonel'. Clearly he was the officer in charge of the present operation. Henry Smith was driving, but it was the colonel who attracted Murdo's attention. Among his men on the bridge he had seemed a figure apart, and now there was something about even the back of his neck that displayed authority. He sat easily, like

...quire being driven over his estate, as if he had a right to be ...here. He seemed to be enjoying the drive. Scraps of their ...ragmentary conversation reached Murdo's ears, but it was all in German and he could not understand a word.

Bjorn gazed out of the window beside him, broad-chested, great spade-like hands resting in his lap. Murdo's glance flickered across the side of his good-natured, peasant face. A fading pink scar near his eye bore witness of the deep scratch he had received when the *Lobster Boy* went down. He was a fine man. Since they first met on Island Roan, Murdo had admired him. He seemed more like a friend than one of the enemy. Twice the boy drew breath, on the brink of asking a question, then let it go again, too sick at heart to make the effort.

Realising something of how he felt, after a time Bjorn said, "You have led us quite a chase."

Murdo looked across and half nodded, wrinkling his brow. "It didn't do much good."

"But it is remarkable. Did you have no help — apart from the old shepherd at . . . I forget the name of the place?"

"Corriebreck. No, only him."

"No-one else?"

"No."

"But that was before the blizzard. Where were you then?"

"In an old house up the river."

"For all that time — by yourself. What did you eat?"

Murdo told him about the sheep. There was even a scrap of meat in the pocket of his discarded jacket. He produced it, grey and sodden, and dropped it out of the car window with disgust.

"And you saw nobody. What about —" Bjorn's eyes turned towards the hidden holster at Murdo's waist.

"Well, I meant no-one . . ." Suddenly Murdo saw that he was being led on to divulge information the Germans did not possess. Angry that he should have been betrayed by feelings of kindness and sympathy, he turned and looked out of the window beside him.

"I am a German soldier," Bjorn said simply. "That is all I wanted to know."

He waited for a minute to let the justice of his words sink in then said, "You have been ill, I can see it in your face. But your eye, where Voss hit you, that is better."

Still looking out of the window, Murdo put up dirty fingers and probed his yellow cheekbone. Only a faint twinge remained.

"It's all right," he muttered, then half turned round. "That man, Voss, was he at the bridge? Will he be coming up with the others, after?"

"No. I am afraid he had an accident — on the moors. You have no more to fear from Carl Voss."

Murdo's eyes opened wide in an unspoken question.

"No, don't ask. He was shot, I will tell you that."

Murdo remembered the unexplained crack of the rifle he had heard on his flight to Strath Halladale.

"Somewhere near two high hills and a pass?"

"I believe so, yes. And Peter is still missing."

Though they did not know it, the likable young pilot was never to be heard of again. Nor was his body found. Only crows visited his remains in the heathery gully where at length he had crept for shelter from the blizzard and numbing wind. The empty moors keep their secrets well.

For a few moments they were silent, lost in private thought. Then Bjorn said. "You will be wondering about your old friend, Mr Gunn."

Eagerly Murdo looked up.

"He is all right," Bjorn reassured him. "A prisoner in the cave. I am afraid Carl Voss hit him rather hard when you escaped, but he came round. He is a tough old man."

"He is that."

"He is a relative — your uncle perhaps?"

"No, just a friend of my dad's — and me now."

"Your father, he is in the army?"

"Aye, a sergeant in the Seaforth's," Murdo said proudly.

Then with genuine interest Bjorn asked about all the members of his family, and produced a wallet to show Murdo a

240

well-thumbed photographs of his pretty wife and two young children.

They were passing along a particularly desolate stretch of road when the Colonel glanced at his watch and Henry Smith pulled into a passing place beneath a bank of heather. As he switched off the engine a soft roar of water rose on the moorland air. He walked back to the boot and a moment later appeared carrying a coiled up aerial and grey steel radio, similar to the one Murdo had seen in the schoolroom on Island Roan. Soon it was set up on a rock a dozen feet away and he ran the aerial to the car. The Colonel joined him, leaning with casual elegance against the bonnet and smoking a cigarette. Bjorn returned the wallet to his breast pocket and turned down the window. As Henry Smith tuned in Murdo heard the hissing crackle of the set and passing scraps of other programmes. At last he found the station he was seeking and stood back as the last bars of 'Workers' Playtime' rang cheerfully across the glen. They were followed by the weather forecast and programme news, then the chimes of Big Ben. The Colonel checked his watch as the last notes faded, to be followed by the single reverberating stroke of one o'clock.

In that lonely setting the familiar sound — a symbol of British character and resistance during the dark days of the war, and heard by Murdo almost every morning and evening of his life — seemed strange and unreal. So did the well-known voice of the announcer.

"This is the BBC Home Service. Here is the one o'clock news for today, Friday the fifth of February, 1943, read by Alvar Liddell.

"News now coming in suggests that the build-up of German troops along the Channel coasts of France and Belgium is nearly complete. RAF reconnaissance aircraft report that roads inland, which for the past week have been heavy with infantry, artillery, armoured cars and tanks, are more quiet. It is estimated that the invasion force presently assembled along the hundred mile stretch of coast between Dieppe and Ostende numbers 200,000 men, supported by flotillas of ships, landing craft and other vessels. More than 2,500 bombers and fighter aircraft of the Luftwaffe are believed to have assembled at airfields within a hundred miles of the coast.

"British troops throughout the country have been withdrawn from their camps and drafted to the Kent and Sussex coasts to resist the threatened invasion.

"In a speech from his underground headquarters in London last night, the Prime Minister warned of the very real threat posed by the German build-up, and counselled families throughout the land to prepare their weapons of defence. For the details of his speech I hand you over to Nicholas Abbot . . ."

Henry Smith raised his eyebrows and glanced towards the Colonel, who did not respond. At Murdo's side Bjorn Larvik was very still. Their expressions were sombre as they continued listening to the news, inwardly considering its implications and visualising all too vividly the struggle and bloodshed that lay ahead. The invasion of Britain now seemed inevitable, either from within or without. It only remained for the guerilla groups to trigger it off by supplying the German prisoners — at that moment working on the farms and roads of Britain — with rifles, ammunition and explosives. Then they would storm the armouries, and in a matter of hours an army of tens of thousands would be unleashed within the heart of the country. Swift strikes, as Henry Smith had foretold, at the radio stations and telephone exchanges, key bridges and roads, and in little more than a day the country and its defences would be brought to a standstill. Chaos would reign. While across the Channel, like a pack of wolves, the might of the German army was gathered ready to attack.

Without speaking they listened until the end of the broadcast. Then Henry Smith coiled up the aerial, replaced the radio in the boot, and they drove on. Bjorn wound up the window.

Half an hour later the first patch of the North Atlantic appeared, dark blue and still a good way off, between the dappled ridges of the glen. The Colonel murmured a few words to Henry Smith, who half turned his head and spoke to Bjorn.

He says you are to get down on the floor," Bjorn translated. We will soon be in a village near to your home. There must be no chance that you will be seen."

There was no arguing. Murdo pushed his muddy clothes out of the way and settled himself on the floor of the car. There was a smell of old cigarette ash and mud. The hard road struck up through the matting and the door handle pressed uncomfortably into his back. 'No chance of being seen — huh!' he grumbled under his breath. 'Fat chance it would be with my luck. Just rotten uncomfortable, that's all.' He shifted and wriggled his shoulders, but still the door handle jabbed into his spine. In the cramped space behind the front seats there was no option but to put up with it.

The idea came out of nowhere. Soon they would be in Melvich. Hidden from Henry Smith's stare in the driving mirror, he glanced up at the soldier beside him. Abstractedly Bjorn gazed out of the side window, watching the countryside pass by. Murdo examined the door handle beyond his big legs, noting which way it opened. The handle at present sticking into his back would turn the same way. Pretending to make himself more comfortable, he drew up his knees and twisted his shoulders a few inches, ready to make a grab for it when the time came.

Unfortunately he could not see out of the window, but a moment later the car swung heavily to the left and accelerated down a slope. Clearly they had just hit the north road, a single track even though it was the principal route of the district. With a rattling jolt they swept on to the Halladale Bridge, and Murdo saw the iron girders flash past above him. 'Now up the hill again . . . and to the right,' he murmured beneath his breath. They were only four miles from Strathy, he knew every turn in the road. Henry Smith accelerated: imperceptibly Murdo nodded — everyone took the straight bit fast. He waited. 'Slow down at the thirty mile an hour limit . . . now the sunk bit of road at the drain — there!' He looked through the opposite window and saw bare tree-tops swish past — they were in the village. He prepared himself, waiting for the power lines. There they were! . . . 'Now!'

In one leaping movement he twisted, wrenched the door handle at his back, and tried to fling himself into the road.

"Help! Help!"

For an instant he saw the crossroads and the Melvich Hotel, then powerful arms plucked him back, a hand of steel clamped over his mouth, and the door slammed shut. He could not move. There had been no-one there, anyway.

Ten minutes later the car drew up at the graveyard gates above Strathy beach. Far across the water the hills of Orkney were blue on the horizon. They descended the dunes to the deserted shore, and on white sand passed through the stacks and outcrops of rock beneath the eastern crags.

The mouth of the cave was piled with boxes and crates. While the Germans lingered in the wintry sunshine, Murdo was led into the chill darkness. Soon Knut was putting the finishing touches to knots that bit painfully into his ankles and wrists.

"You'll not get away this time," he said viciously, looping the end round yet again and jerking it as tight as it would go. "The lorries will be here in a couple of hours."

Murdo did not speak. After all he had been through he no longer felt frightened. He looked up at the guard's bowed silhouette, almost invisible outside the circle of torchlight, and kicked his bound feet against the man's legs as hard as he could, raking his studs across the shin. Knut cried out and stumbled, then replied by hacking his own boot into Murdo's hip and side — once, twice.

"Kick me, would you!" he snarled. "You animal!"

"You're just like Carl Voss," Murdo cried, and spat up at the dark shape. "I hope you end up like him, too, with a bullet in you."

Knut's boot struck him again with vicious force. Then he bent and caught at the ends of rope and pulled them tight. The gold buttons and braid glinted on his naval uniform. His fair hair, snub nose and dark curly beard moved in and out of the shadows. In a minute the work was finished. Taking Murdo by

lapels of his greatcoat, Knut dumped him against the wall of
e cave and stood back.

"Now, let's see you get out of that," he challenged. "The old
man's been in here for a week and he hasn't moved." He
cleared his throat noisily and moved away down the cave, a
lean shape behind the torchlight. For a moment his body
blocked out the patch of light that glimmered at the narrow
turning, then he was gone.

Murdo stared about him, but the darkness was almost
complete and he could distinguish nothing.

"Hector?" he said.

The only sounds were the drip of water, the soft roar of
the sea, and the murmur of men's voices at the cave
mouth.

"Hector! Are you there?"

This time a long grunt issued from the blackness at the other
side of the chamber.

"Hector, it's me — Murdo. Are you all right?"

There was a slow, rattling cough and the noise of laboured
breathing before the words came.

"Yes, I'm fine." His voice was choked and weak. "How are
you boy?"

"I'm all right," Murdo said, his own voice strong in
comparison. He squirmed across the pile of smooth boulders
that blocked the inner end of the cave.

"What — happened?"

"Nothing," Murdo said, his eyes still unable to penetrate the
gloom, though Hector could only have been an arm's length
away. "They were after me and then the snow came. We were
in the hills. I didn't see anybody."

"Two men dead and one missing . . . it sounds like a
bloodbath. Anyway . . . you gave them a run for their money."
The old man's voice was little more than a wheeze, and broke
off into an uncontrollable fit of coughing that left him
struggling for breath.

Murdo was alarmed. "Have you been lying here all this
time?" he said.

"Aye," said Hector. "I'm a tough old nut. Don't wo. yourself, I'm not as easy to finish off as all that."

"Have you had any food?" Murdo pictured the slabs o. smoky mutton that apart from a few squares of chocolate were all he had eaten in the past five days.

"Oh, aye — dribs and drabs, you know. Yon Bjorn fellow was very good . . . while he was here, but I haven't seen him for a few days. And the others brought a bit. I'm not very hungry."

After a while Murdo said, "Has nobody in the village missed us?"

"No, he's been very clever, that Mr Smith. Still at the inn — large as life. Put it out that we were staying a few days at Donald's house in Clerkhill. . . . Took our ration books and told them in the shop that the old Ford was iced up. And the Clerkhill people think . . . we're back in the village. With the bad weather nobody's thought anything about it."

"But it's eight days now."

"It wouldn't be the first time I've . . . been away without telling everybody where I'm going. You know that yourself."

It was cold and damp on the rocks, and despite his thick coat Murdo felt the chill creeping into his bones. He twisted and gazed up at the shelf where they had stacked the crates of guns and ammunition. The shadows were impenetrably black.

"Did they move it all down the cave?" he said.

"What?"

"The guns and that."

"I think so. It took them a long time, anyway." Again Hector struggled for breath. "All down there in the cave mouth, is it?"

"Uh-huh. They're waiting for the lorries now."

"What day is it?"

"Friday."

"Well, the balloon goes up tomorrow. . . . All over the country."

"What — 'Flood-Tide'?"

"Aye, Saturday. Try to catch us on the hop. . . . Sunday would suit them better, with everyone off their guard . . . but all the prisoners will be in camp then."

Murdo listened to the low drone of speech at the entance to the cave, and a man's sudden laughter.

"Is yon Colonel chap still with them?" Hector said.

"Yes — well he was when I came down," Murdo replied. "Who is he?"

There was a thick chuckle beside him. "They've been fair worried about you, boy. I'll tell you who he is. Colonel von Kramm, leader . . . of the whole shebang."

"What, the whole operation?" Murdo was astonished.

"That's right. Hitler's big hope. The leader of the German invasion — in a cave on Strathy beach!"

"He came up because of me?"

"He did. From what I can make out . . . everything was going well with the other groups, they were all straining at the leash . . . but you were missing." Hector's voice was growing weaker. "He was so disgusted with our Mr Smith . . . that he came up to take charge himself."

"And I walked right into his trap," Murdo said disconsolately.

"It looks like it."

Again they were silent. Murdo's mind went back over his run. He remembered the old shepherd at Corriebreck.

"Do you know a fellow called Duncan Beg?" he said.

"Up by Kinbrace? Aye." But Hector was not interested. "Why?"

"I'll tell you about it later," Murdo said.

Time dragged by. In Murdo's side the pain of Knut's final kick had quietened to a dull ache. To have done so much, and be defeated now! He writhed his hands at his back, but the knots were too firmly tied. He strained and tugged. The ropes burned and slipped a fraction, but whether it was with sweat or blister marks, Murdo did not know.

He remembered the knife in his trouser pocket.

"Hector," he whispered. "I've got Dad's knife here. Can you reach it?"

He wriggled close until the old fisherman's hands were at his hip, but Hector was bound too tightly and his fingers were

numb with the days of captivity. It was all he could do to p
the greatcoat back. The trouser pocket was wet and stretch
tight, the knife well down against Murdo's thigh.

If he could not use the knife, Murdo thought, perhaps he
could chafe through the rope against a rock. The boulders on
the cave floor were round and worn smooth by the sea, but the
walls were rougher. He scrambled down to the sand and
fumbled along the invisible rock for a place where he could get
a good rub at the ropes on his wrists. There was no sharp edge,
nevertheless he picked a rough corner, and kneeling awkwardly
began sawing his wrists up and down behind his back. The rock
caught his bones and scraped against his skin. The position was
so twisted that even before a minute was up he had to
straighten to ease the cramp in his back and shoulders.

Suddenly there was the chatter of louder voices and laughter
at the cave mouth. It sounded as though new men had arrived.
The lorries must have come. Leaving the sawing, Murdo
humped himself down the cave with his legs, keeping his head
ducked in case he struck it on a projecting rock. Soon he could
see through the narrow neck towards the entrance. Most of the
men were hidden from his sight, but beneath an overhanging
buttress he could see one figure in army overalls, and the legs of
two more. The man in overalls pulled off his cap and sat down
with his back to the cave wall. Someone handed him a tin mug,
then an arm appeared, filling the mug from a large enamel teapot.

Murdo scrambled back up the cave. There was no time to rub
the rope through against a rock. Was it not possible to get the
knife out somehow? Then there might be a chance to run for it
while the Germans were carrying the cases up the dunes. He
pushed his hip against a protruberance of rock, but everything
— knife, pocket, trousers and greatcoat — moved up and down
in one lump. Frustrated, he gnawed his bottom lip. From a sea
of confused ideas, two rose uppermost. Even though his feet
were tied, if he could push down his trousers he might manage
to take the pocket in his teeth and shake the knife out. Or, if he
could prop himself upside down, it might drop out of its own
accord.

At least it was worth trying. He wormed across to a fairly straight stretch of rock, turned on his back and shuffled close in. Then he propped his feet high against the black wall, and with a great effort jerked them a few inches higher. But it was no good that way, with his arms tied he could not get his feet high enough. He let himself fall heavily to the sand.

When he made a second attempt he lay alongside the wall, and rolling backwards swung his feet high. At the top of the arc he caught his heels against the rock, then hitched and shuffled higher and higher, until it seemed that his bound arms must dislocate with the strain. At length, propped nearly upright on the back of his neck, he arched his body straight. The skirts of the greatcoat fell about his face. The knife slipped a little in his trouser pocket. He shook himself slightly and it slipped some more, then stuck. Two, three times he jerked his hips. Suddenly, with no warning, the knife fell free and landed in the sand beside his ear with a little thud.

Murdo slumped sideways and lay for a moment while the ache ebbed from his shoulders and bruised ribs. Then sitting up, he scrabbled behind his back for the knife. The sand was wet and hard from the last tide, and almost at once his fingers fell upon the smooth warm haft. The spring was stiff, but it opened under the force of his big thumb nail, and a few moments of awkward sawing brought the ropes falling slack over his hands. With relief he rubbed his chafed wrists and brought the blood tingling into the tips of his fingers.

To free his ankles was the work of a few seconds, and scrambling quickly up the rocks, a few swift slashes brought the cords tumbling over Hector's hands and feet too.

The old man eased his joints and squeezed his numb fingers in the darkness. He coughed convulsively, but a trace of the old spirit showed through his wheezing words.

"Tie the ends in a knot," he gasped, struggling for breath. "Wrap them round again in case they come to check. There's nothing you can do while they're all here."

It was as well they did so, for a minute or two later Knut came back up the cave, feeling his way against the wall, his eyes dazzled from the sunshine outside.

"Ah," he said, his torch picking out Murdo who sat dejectedly on the rocks a few feet below Hector. "There you are." He rolled him back and felt the ropes at his wrists. Murdo strained them tight with all his strength, holding the loose ends in his fists. Knut shone the torch on his ankles. Satisfied, he moved on to Hector. The old man wheezed noisily and closed his eyes. For a moment Knut shone his torch on Hector's face, then turned away down the cave. "You won't be here much longer," he called back over his shoulder. "They've come for the — " he struck his head a resounding crack on the roof and issued a string of oaths. Rubbing his scalp with one hand, he passed out of sight.

There was a hubbub of voices and the sound of boxes knocking and scraping at the cave mouth. Grunts followed, and a certain amount of scuffling, then slowly the voices and sounds faded into the distance. Murdo strained his ears, but beyond the far murmur of the sea and the cry of a gull there was silence. Swiftly he slipped the ropes from his hands and feet and stood up. The smooth boulders slipped and grated beneath his heels. Hector covered the noise with a fit of coughing, and in a moment Murdo had scrambled down to the carpet of sand.

Heart pounding, he listened — still no sound. Then there was a faint rustle at the mouth of the cave and the sound of a match striking. Slowly he crept to the neck of the inner chamber, and an inch at a time peered around the corner. Framed in the entrance twenty-five yards away, sitting on a box with his back towards him, was Knut. He seemed to be alone. A thin trickle of smoke drifted from his hand. A few paces away his Mauser rifle was propped against the sunlit crag.

Softly Murdo returned to Hector, and in a few whispered words told him what he had seen. The greatcoat and boots were too clumsy for what he now must do. Impatiently he pushed them off. The clammy air of the cave struck chill against his

250

...in and damp vest. He bent and very quietly picked up a heavy rock from the foot of the pile, one that he could carry easily. It was sea-smooth, cold and gritty in his hands. He swallowed and ran a tongue over dry lips. It was hard to control his breathing. Softly he crept forward.

In a moment he was at the turning. Trying not to let his trousers brush against the rock walls, he eased himself through the narrow neck. He was in full view. One slip and the man must see him. Surely he must turn round. Cold sweat trickled down Murdo's face. Nearer he crept — and nearer. Like a cat he placed his stockinged feet delicately in the sand. Fifteen yards, ten, seven, five. The man flipped the butt of his cigarette away and shifted in his seat. Murdo froze. Surely he must sense him right there behind him. But Knut ran a hand through his fair hair, scratched his beard, and settled down again. For ten seconds Murdo could not move. He wanted to swallow but dare not. Forcing himself, again he inched forward. Four yards, three, two. He could almost reach out a hand and touch the dark uniform. There was the purple mark of an old boil on the back of the man's neck. One yard. He was right behind him. The rock was poised. Murdo's face was in agony. Could he do it? Yes, he could — he had to! Shutting his eyes, he drove down the stone against the back of the man's head. There was a sickening crack. Slowly, like a rag doll, Knut slumped from his seat to the wet, footmarked sand. Still, save for one terrible twitching arm, he lay there with the boulder beside his face.

Numbly Murdo looked down at his handiwork. Twice in two days. He wondered whether the man was dead. There was no shadow of movement save in the last shivering of his hand, like a trout after you have struck it against a stone.

"Murdo!" Hector's voice came from behind him. He was clutching a corner of the rock wall for support. "Get him back here."

"I think I've killed him," Murdo said.

"Nonsense! Get him back here."

Bending, Murdo took the limp figure by the shoulders a.
dragged him backwards into the shadows of the inner cave.

"Is he right out of sight?"

"Yes."

"Come on, then." Hector began to stumble towards the
beach but after a few steps he had to rest. His grey, white-
stubbled face ran with perspiration. On his temple the ugly
contusion where Carl Voss had struck him with the rifle butt
was still swollen and blue.

"Lean on me," Murdo said, and took the old man's arm over
his shoulder. Hector's imprisonment and bindings had left him
so weak that he could hardly stand. Despite every effort he
hung heavily around Murdo's neck and gripped his arm for
support. Slowly they made their way past the great stack of
cases and along the bottom of the cliffs, away from the dunes.
In two minutes they had turned a corner and were out of sight.

Hector stopped, struggling for breath. His chest heaved.
"It's no good. I can't go any faster. You run ahead and get
help."

"What about you?"

"Never mind about me!" Hector's anger at his own
helplessness showed in the sharp words. "You're the only
chance we've got."

Murdo realised he was right and nodded.

"Get me yon fellow's rifle," Hector said. "You'll need all the
start you can get. I'll try to hold them back." His gnarled hand
gripped a knob of rock for support, the other leaned heavily on
his knee. "Go on, now — quick!"

For a moment Murdo hesitated, then ran back to the
entrance of the cave and grabbed up Knut's rifle. He was
turning away when his eye was caught, and hung for a moment
upon a stack of smaller boxes. Ammunition. Hector would
want more than a magazine full. A few swift blows with the
butt of the rifle and the wood split open. On pulling the planks
apart and tearing back the oiled papers, however, he was
confronted not by bullets but by long grey cylinders, with red
lettering on them and fuse wires at the end. Cursing, he

smashed open a second box, and this time it was grenades. Row upon row the criss-crossed little bombs lay stacked like metal eggs, gleaming a dull blue-bronze. They would have to do. Hastily snatching a couple, he thrust them into his trouser pockets and pulled the shattered boxes together.

He had turned to dart away, when suddenly there was a clatter of stones at the corner of the cliff and the sound of returning voices. There was no time to reach Hector with the rifle! Quick as a thought he ran to a small outcrop of rocks opposite the cave mouth, and crouched behind it trembling.

The soldiers came closer and closer. Their voices were casual and easy, he heard the soft crunch of their boots in the wet sand. Even as they approached the mouth of the cave they suspected nothing. Then abruptly, not ten yards away, they stopped and fell silent.

"Knut?" A questioning voice rang out. It sounded like Henry Smith. There was no reply. "Knut?" he called again, louder this time.

Then there was another, quiet voice, the Colonel's. In the silence that followed Murdo heard running footsteps which diminished up the beach — apparently into the cave. A few seconds later there was a muffled cry, and the man raced out again, calling loudly. Others shouted in reply, and there was a swift scattering of footsteps, right and left along the foot of the cliffs and back into the cave.

Henry Smith was furious. Harsh and loud his voice rang across the sands, directing, confusing, cursing them for incompetence.

Murdo waited to be discovered, but no-one came. Very cautiously he ventured to peer from behind his island of rocks. The Colonel stood quietly at one side of the cave, saying nothing, while Henry Smith stalked up and down, beating his fists against his sides in a passion of disgrace and frustration. Awe-struck, Murdo regarded him. Two men ran across the face of the cliff. Beyond them, far down a sandy inlet where Henry Smith could not yet see him, a soldier in overalls appeared, pulling Hector by the arm. Hector was resisting. A fist was raised and he fell to the ground. Another man emerged from the cave, not quite sure what to do next. Suddenly Henry Smith swung round. He regarded the outcrop behind which Murdo was crouching, and the high stacks twenty yards beyond. Seeing they were unchecked, he began striding down the beach. Murdo pulled his head back, but not quickly enough and the German leader spotted the movement. He called out sharply, and three soldiers came running towards him.

"I see you!" he cried aloud in English. "Now Knut is dead! You young savage — this time I will kill you!"

Murdo heard the heavy footfalls coming closer. Trembling visibly, he leaped out from his hiding place and levelled the rifle at the German's chest.

"Stop!" he cried. "I'll shoot!"

The soldiers halted, their eyes riveted on the desperate and half-naked youth, with the empty holster at his belt and gleaming rifle in his hands. But Henry Smith kept advancing, feeling inside his coat for the heavy service revolver.

"I will," screamed Murdo. "I'll shoot!"

But the German leader took no notice.

Terrified and sick, Murdo pulled the trigger.

It was jammed solid. Nothing happened. It would not work! He flung the rifle to the ground.

Henry Smith laughed.

Murdo dug into his trouser pocket, pulled out one of the grenades, and tore out the pin.

Henry Smith stopped abruptly in his tracks, staring at the live bomb in Murdo's hand. Then Murdo flung it, and ripping out the second one, hurled it into the crowd of men gathered near the boxes in the cave mouth. Full length he dived for cover.

There was a moment of silence, then a sudden burst of screaming and shouting as the men scrambled for shelter. Those who had not seen, came running at the noise.

It was cut off abruptly by a loud bang, and a moment later by the stunning roar of an explosion which made the earth heave, and sent great echoes thundering around the sky. Murdo's ears arly burst with the impact of the noise. Huge slabs of rock shivered from the face of the cliff. A massive boulder shattered into fragments on the stack behind him: another embedded itself deeply in the wet sand. Stones were flying all around. A sharp splinter gashed Murdo down the side of the face, and something struck his knee with some force. Then the sand and dust were settling all around him, over his shoulders and trousers and in his eyes. As he stood up he started to cough and spit in the dust and fumes. The cave was no longer to be seen. Huge piles of boulders lay all over the place where the entrance had been, and a cloud of dust hung over it.

The beach seemed deserted, save for himself, and there was absolute silence. Then, as he looked around the rocks, he began to see the bodies of the men, and bits of wood from the gun cases. Murdo's head fell forward, and he sank to his knees, sobbing helplessly.

For a long time he knelt there, staring half blindly at the scene of total destruction. The figures of the men lay twisted and broken on the sand, and there was no sign of movement save in the slowly clearing dust and an occasional boulder that fell from the smoking, shattered cliffs.

Henry Smith, strangely immaculate in his British officer's uniform, lay five yards distant, where he had been tossed by the blast of the explosion. He was quite unmarked and might have been asleep, had it not been for his awful stillness and the unnatural angle of one arm. The outflung hand that had so recently grasped a revolver was empty — trailing and limp. A plain gold ring shone dully on his wedding finger. The sparse hair was blown back, betraying his balding crown. His pale blue eyes, unspectacled, were opened in mild surprise, but the lids did not move. His mouth, for ever, was closed.

At last Murdo's sobs, the catharsis of so much effort and distress, subsided, and he became aware of a voice.

"The rifle, boy! The rifle!"

He looked round, dazed. Hector was stumbling towards him across the sand.

"Murdo!" His voice was urgent. "Give me the rifle! Can you see? He's getting away."

Slowly Murdo turned his head and looked in the other direction. Far across the beach two figures were hurrying towards the dunes. One, silver-haired, leaned heavily on a taller man's shoulder. His leg was trailing. Something tickled Murdo's jaw. Thoughtlessly he brushed it away with his hand and his hand was scarlet. Heavily he pulled himself to his feet and picked up the discarded weapon.

"It's broken," he said flatly, as Hector came past the outcrop where he had hidden and took it from his hand.

His chest heaving with effort, Hector steadied himself against a little crest of rock and checked the muzzle and breech of the rifle. It was loaded and clean save for a few grains of sand which he brushed off with his hand. The safety catch was still on — Murdo had forgotten to check it. He pressed it back with a horny thumb, settled his left elbow comfortably in a rocky niche, and raised the splintered butt to his shoulder. The wind ruffled his white hair. He held his breath. The barrel never wavered as it swung to cover the fleeting figures. Then it was still. His forefinger tightened a fraction on the trigger. A vicious crack split the air, the muzzle jerked up, there was a puff of smoke. Away across the beach the limping figure of Colonel von Kramm spun round as if he had been kicked, and pitched headlong to the sand. But he was not dead, for they saw him raise an arm and wave the other on. It was big Bjorn Larvik. For a moment he paused, but the Colonel waved him on again. There was a faint sound of voices on the wind. Then Bjorn turned and ran straight up a long bank of sand, and the next instant had flitted from sight among the grass of the dunes.

Hector sank against the rock and pushed the rifle towards Murdo. "You get along there and . . . keep an eye on him. I can't move very fast."

Still half dazed, Murdo ran along the sands. The necessity for action helped to clear his mind, and in a minute he was beside the injured Colonel. The man lay on his side and was obviously in great pain. His face was grey and covered with perspiration as he fought to master himself. One leg was twisted oddly in front of him, the other, where Hector had shot him, was dark with blood. An arm was hidden beneath his body, and as Murdo looked along the beach towards Hector, from the corner of his eye he saw the Colonel scrabbling furtively in the sand. He looked round and at once the Colonel was still, gazing frankly back at him from a pair of fine, pain-filled eyes. Anxiously Murdo scanned the line of dunes, wondering how many Germans had remained at the lorries. Momentarily the figure of Bjorn appeared against the skyline, a second man joined him and they dropped from sight. Again from the corner of his eye he saw that secret scrabbling movement of the Colonel's hidden arm.

A minute later Hector hobbled up, gasping for breath. He took the rifle from Murdo and sat on the sand a yard or two above the German officer.

"Are you hurt anywhere," he wheezed at length, "apart from your legs."

The Colonel managed a sardonic smile. "Just my legs," he said. "It is enough."

Hector nodded with relief. "We'll get a doctor to you as soon as we can."

Murdo pointed towards the dunes. "What about up there? There are two of them anyway. There might be more."

As if in answer to his words, there came the roar of a lorry from the graveyard gates.

Again the Colonel smiled. "They are away."

"We'll catch them soon enough now," Hector said.

The Colonel inclined his head slightly. "You might catch one of them, but I would not count on adding Larvik to your collection." He bit back an involuntary cry at a sudden spasm of pain, and eased his body slightly with his arms.

Murdo watched him for a moment, then crouched beside Hector. "I think he's hidden something in the sand," he murmured. "Underneath him."

The Colonel caught their quick glances and understood. "My revolver is stuck," he said too quickly. "It does not fit thi

257

British holster." The words rang false. He laughed ironically and his hand fumbled once more.

"Leave it." Hector's voice was a thick growl. He coughed. "Take it from him, Murdo."

Murdo leaned across the Colonel's body and turned back the skirts of his greatcoat. The revolver, as he had said, was on his hip and half pressed into the sand. Awkwardly he tugged it free.

"Now!" Hector pulled himself up and motioned with the rifle. "Shift over."

"I can't move," the Colonel said.

"I don't believe you."

The Colonel lay where he was and looked down the beach.

"Come on!" Hector sighed patiently. "Look, the boy can drag you away if necessary. That would really hurt. Now shift over."

Slowly Colonel von Kramm eased himself across the sand. His legs, bloody and twisted, dragged after him. He closed his eyes and clenched his teeth to fight back the savage waves of pain.

"Now look in the sand, Murdo," Hector said.

Murdo laid the heavy revolver behind him, then knelt where the Colonel had been lying and scratched his fingers through the damp sand. It was hard below the surface, save in one small area. He dug down, and almost at once his fingertips encountered a solid object, only four or five inches below the surface. He felt around the edge and pulled it out. It was a wallet, a fat leather wallet full of papers.

"Have a look through it," Hector said.

Murdo pulled out a sheaf of the sandy documents and folded them open. They were detailed official papers, but written in German throughout and he could not read a word. They seemed important, however, many with a red stamp across the top. He held the sheaf against the back of the wallet and quickly thumbed through the remainder. They were similarly incomprehensible. He shrugged. Hector held out a hand and he passed them over.

Slowly the old fisherman looked through them. His forehead wrinkled with concentration. Again Murdo saw the small beads of perspiration gathering on his face. Hector coughed quietly, his lungs were completely choked.

At length he looked up and saw the expression on Murdo's face.

"There's no need to look at me like that," he said. "You'll have me thinking I'm for an early grave. I've already told you . . . it takes more than a couple of foreigners and a few nights without my bed to get rid of me." He held up the wallet and shook it slowly and significantly in Murdo's direction. "This is more important. What do you think these papers are?"

Sometimes Murdo was painfully aware of his ignorance. He half looked away. "Plans or something, I suppose," he said.

Hector chuckled thickly. "Aye, that's you. 'Plans or something'! It's more than that, boy. If I'm right — and I think I am — this wallet contains the details of the whole affair. You know, 'Operation — ' what was it he called it?"

" 'Flood-Tide'," Murdo said.

"Aye, that's it. 'Operation Flood-Tide'."

"What? For the whole — ?"

"I think so. Look." Murdo crossed beside him and Hector ran a gnarled forefinger down several of the papers. "I don't know where these places are, but you know the counties. See, in English — Northumberland, Lincolnshire, Cornwall, Cardigan, Wigtown, Argyll. And look — Strathy, Sutherland. It's all the places they're bringing the arms ashore. And those figures underneath, that must be the numbers of men and rifles and explosives and that. Here — " he ruffled over half a dozen pages and pointed six words typed in capitals at the bottom of a sheet. 'Es flutet, es flutet, es flutet'. "Remember that — in Donald's cottage?"

"Es flutet — the tide is flooding!" Murdo cried. "Three times — the code signal!"

"That's it, boy. You've got it. The lot — addresses, arms, all the details of the German invasion — in this little bundle here." He put the papers back in the wallet and tossed it lightly on the sand.

259

For a moment there was silence, Colonel von Kramm look&
away. Though his face was impassive, his proud shoulder&
drooped dejectedly.

"Come on, get yourself up to that village as quickly as you
can," Hector said. "We want the police — or better still the
army — down here. You know what to do." He pointed to the
wallet. "You better take that with you. Just in case. Hide it on
the way up if you see any trouble."

Murdo pushed the wallet with some difficulty into his
pocket and picked up the Colonel's revolver. As he bent, two
thick drops of blood fell from his chin and splashed in red
streaks down his bare shoulder and arm. He put a hand to the
side of his face. It was sticky. Gingerly he touched the gash
down his temple and cheek and winced as his fingertips
encountered the open wound.

"You'll need half a dozen stitches in that," Hector said. "It's
a bit of a mess, but it's almost stopped bleeding."

At the thought of the stitches a faint sickness passed through
Murdo. He tried to put it from his mind.

"I'll be as quick as I can," he said.

As he turned towards the steep sandbank Colonel von
Kramm called softly, "No — one minute."

Murdo paused and looked back.

"I have heard from Bjorn Larvik of your adventures," the
Colonel said. "In the sea and on the moors. You are a brave
boy. I congratulate you." He smiled thinly. "It is a pity you are
not German."

Murdo looked down with embarrassment, then his black eye
caught those of the German officer. "I hope your legs will be all
right," he said.

The Colonel looked from Hector to Murdo and down at his
own bloodied trousers. "We are a strange trio, bleeding and
coughing on this deserted beach. But thank you. I hope so
too." He inclined his head, he had said all he wished.

The Colonel's words revolved in Murdo's mind at he turned
once more and scrambled up the shifting sand to the edge of the
dunes. At the top he paused for a moment and looked down at

e two men: Colonel von Kramm propped on his hands and gazing towards the sea, Hector like a rock on the seashore, the rifle resting easily across his knees.

The occasion lent Murdo strength. Clutching the heavy revolver in his right hand he half ran up the dunes, climbing through the high banks of marram grass. Soon he was at the top. Cautiously he rounded the stone wall of the graveyard. An army truck stood empty at the gate, but there was no sign of any soldiers. Bjorn and his comrade had taken the truck containing the first load of rifles and ammunition. Now they would be armed. From his vantage point above the dunes and river Murdo scanned the land below. It seemed deserted. Then far away on the river bank he saw a group of men from the village hurrying towards the beach.

A few minutes later he staggered into the first house, where only two weeks previously — though it seemed a lifetime before — he and Hector had delivered two bottles of whisky to the old crofter. The windows had been blown in by the force of the explosion. Willie and Meggan stared at him in shocked silence as he gasped out what had happened. They had been down the road when the explosion came, and even as Murdo arrived Willie was on the point of going down to the cliffs to investigate. Now the old man grabbed his twelve-bore and filled a pocket with cartridges. His daughter hurried off to alert the neighbours while Murdo ran on towards the village.

His nervous energy was running out as he descended the steep hill to the crossroads — over which he had skidded in Hector's old Ford — and turned from the stony track. Far down the narrow main road two figures, a man and a boy, were walking towards him from the bridge. Murdo stopped and looked hard. A long shout reached his ears and they began to run. A lump came into Murdo's throat. When he tried to shout in return his voice broke and would not come. Waving his arms he broke into a poor imitation of a run down the road towards them. It was, of all people, his father with his brother Lachlan.

In a minute they were together. Deeply disturbed, Sandy Mackay regarded his son. With a soft oath he took off his jacket and put it around the boy's shoulders. Murdo pushed his arm into the sleeves and pulled it close, still warm from his father's back. Quickly he panted out the main facts of his story, and tugged the wallet from his trouser pocket. His father paid him the compliment of wasting no time on personal details. Briefly he ruffled through the pages and asked a few terse questions. Then he despatched Lachlan to half a dozen houses, with the message that the men were to make their way to the beach with whatever weapons they possessed, keeping their eyes open for strangers or unknown soldiers moving about the dunes. Lachlan nodded briefly, glanced once more at his older brother, then climbed the dyke and raced away towards the first cottage as fast as his legs would carry him. Murdo and his father set off up the road towards the nearest telephone, at the manse.

Sandy Mackay was still young, in his mid thirties, fair as his name and with a disconcertingly straight gaze. Separated from his regiment, he had been one of the last to escape from the Dunkirk beaches: as a sergeant in North Africa, he had seen his full share of desert fighting. He recognised the deep exhaustion and trouble of his son.

"You'll have to get that cut seen to," he said. "You look done in."

He was right. Murdo was nearly finished. His face was haggard and pale with strain. His eyes glittered fiercely beneath the black, shaggy hair. Mud from the river still clung to him. With his exertions the gash had reopened and thick blood oozed down the side of his face. He realised that he was limping. Now the responsibility was being lifted from him, he could hardly make his feet go where he wanted.

"I'm all right," he answered, and forced his legs to keep pace with his father up the road.

"This is a fine homecoming," his father said. "I manage to work two days' leave before we're posted south — travel up with Donald and Lachlan — arrive in the village and nobody has seen you or Hector for ten days." With pride he regarded the stained and bloody figure of his son, and put an arm about

262

shoulders. The boy had grown in the months since he was ~st home. The down was dark on his upper lip. "I want to hear all about it, in your own good time. But likely you'll have to tell the military first."

Warm with relief and homecoming, Murdo ran a hand around his father's waist, then moved away, for they were not demonstrative. Side by side they continued up the road.

In less than five minutes they were at the manse. Murdo's Aunt Winifred stood aside in horror as her brother and his son stepped past her into the gleaming hallway. Sandy laid down the wallet and lifted the telephone from the hook.

While he dialled Murdo looked for a seat upon which he could collapse, but one chair was highly polished rosewood and so flimsy that he dared not rest his weight upon it, and the other covered with striped regency satin. He crossed to the stairs and slumped in a long-familiar position on the second tread.

Briefly his eyes closed, then he sat up and opened them again. His aunt regarded him anxiously, not in the least disapproving, even though he cut such a disreputable, gipsy figure in her beautiful house. He smiled up and nervously she smiled back, putting a hand to the cameo at her throat.

"You sit there," she said. "I'll fetch the medicine chest."

Through the open doorway Murdo could see beyond a clump of stiffly nodding whins to Strathy Water, winding like a silver ribbon from the southern hills where so much had happened. His gaze moved across the hall and down to his trouser legs and feet, filthy toes protruding from his socks. He felt at his wet pocket for the bulge of the knife. In that strange yet so familiar setting his adventure began to take on the elements of a dream.

But his father was speaking to Army Headquarters. "Is that Intelligence?" he said. "Get me the adjutant, please. It's important." He stroked a fair moustache while he waited. "Hello. . . . Yes, good afternoon, sir. This is Sergeant Mackay, Sergeant Sandy Mackay — of the Second Battalion, the Seaforth Highlanders." He looked round at Murdo. "It's rather

a long story. I'm speaking from Strathy." He paused, thoug．
fully considering the face of the youth who regarded him fro·
the foot of the stairs. "Look, you'd better speak to my son. Jus·
a minute." He held the receiver towards Murdo.

For a moment surprised, then appreciating the significance of
his father's gesture, Murdo rose and crossed the hall with as
firm a step as he could manage. He was not accustomed to
using the telephone: by nature not a talkative boy, he did not
handle it well.

"Hello," he said, more gruff than the occasion warranted. "Is
that the army?"

He held the receiver close, his brow wrinkled with concentration. His fierce reflection confronted him from a gilt
mirror above the hall table.

"My name's Murdo Mackay. Can you come to Strathy right
away?"

The captain of Intelligence had been called from a noisy
crowd at the officers' bar. In wry tones, half amused by the
earnest bluffness of the appeal, he wanted to know why and at
first treated the country boy lightly. But his sense of fun faded
as Murdo's story began to unfold, and at last the threat of
'Operation Flood-Tide' was revealed to the British military
authorities. Though he told the tale clumsily and with many
breaks, its truth was transparent in every word.

A few feet across the hall his father lit a cigarette and was
still. Clutching the medicine chest with which she had treated
all their childhood scrapes and bruises, his aunt subsided on to
his abandoned seat at the foot of the stairs.

Beyond the diamond-leaded window at Murdo's back the
waves crawled up the bay, from the foam-edged crags at the
point to a white crescent of shore — where even as he put down
the telephone, the first men from the village drew close to
Hector and Colonel von Kramm. The sun was setting above
the high moors making the bracken glow. Long blue shadows
spread across the heather and broad patches of snow. A gull
whirled past, calling loudly, caught by the wind that blew from
the sea.

ALF'S SECRET WAR
Donald Lightwood

The colourful world of the music hall suddenly falls apart for Alf when his father is arrested during a show for ignoring his call-up papers.

With his father now a reluctant soldier, Alf has to confront his confused emotions. He thinks the world of his dad, but knows there is an enemy to fight. When his mother leaves him to entertain the troops, the hurt he feels can only deepen.

Alf takes charge of his own fate and finds a strange sense of security when he takes a destitute family under his wing. Slowly he comes to realise that his father, too, must be feeling the hurt of rejection.

He sets out on a foolhardy journey through war-torn Britain to find his father. His brave quest provides a thrilling finale to this wonderful story.

Alf's Secret War is Donald Lightfoot's second novel for children. His first, *The Baillie's Daughter,* won the BBC/SLA 'Quest for a Kelpie' award in 1989.

ISBN 0 86241 383 4   £2.95 pbk

THE HILL OF THE RED FOX
Allan Campbell McLean

'Unknown man found shot,' said the newspaper head-line. Alasdair recognised the man he had met on the train to Skye, the man who had slipped him a desperate last message 'Hunt at the Hill of the Red Fox M15'.

Alasdair finds the Hill of the Red Fox on Skye, but the note still makes no sense. Nor at first do most of the strange and dangerous goings on on the island, many of which involve Alasdair's sinister uncle, Murdo Beaton. There is much more than the odd bit of poaching happening—atomic scientists and their secrets are disappearing.

People are not always what they seem. Whom can Alasdair really trust? In finding out he uncovers a web of espionage—and all its perils!

ISBN 0 86241 055 X   £3.50 pbk

SIMON'S CHALLENGE
Theresa Breslin

Simon is really fed up. More than anything in the world he wants his own computer. But with a baby in the house and his dad still away looking for work his chances of ever getting one look pretty slim.

As Simon passes Peterson's shop one evening, gazing at the fabulous display of computers, nothing seems out of the ordinary. But when the police start asking questions Simon realises he was the sole witness of a major burglary. The only problem is he can't remember any of the details!

Theresa Breslin's first novel is a lively, witty and realistic detective story.

Winner of the Kathleen Fidler Award.

ISBN 0 86241 270 6   £2.99 pbk

DOG SONG
Gary Paulsen

'You must leave with the dogs. Run along and find your-self. When you leave me you must head north and take meat and see the country. When you do that you will be-come a man.'

Inspired by the Eskimo shaman Oogruk, Russel Suskitt takes a dog team and sled to escape from the modern ways of his village and to find his own 'song' of himself. He travels across ice floes, tundra, and mountains, haunted along the way by a dream when, to save himself and a pregnant Eskimo girl he has rescued, he must kill a polar bear in the ancient way learned in the dream.

It is a rigorous journey for the boy and his team of dogs, but in a combination of wills, their spirits soar as one to survive in this unforgettable run towards self-discovery.

'There is enough gritty realism to satisfy the most adven-ture-hungry readers. A remarkable book.'

School Library Journal

ISBN 0 86241 323 0   £2.50 pbk

WINNERS
Mary Ellen Collura

'Eleven foster homes in eight years, and moving again. It was enough to make him sick'.

Jordy's past is a blur of white foster homes, courts and social workers. He thinks he knows everything about foster homes but this time it's going to be different. As a young Blackfoot Indian going to live with his estranged grandfather on a reservation, this really *is* home.

But when his grandfather barely notices him and everyone appears to hate him at school nothing seems to have changed much for Jordy. Until one day he is given a wonderful present—a wild prairie horse! As Jordy trains his horse for a gruelling long distance race he learns a new kind of courage and determination—to win!

Winners is an exciting and moving story of a boy's search for the splintered pieces of his past and his struggle to make a new life for himself.

Winner of the Young Adult Canadian Book Award and National Chapter IODE Book Award.

ISBN 0 86241 295 1   £2.25 pbk

CANONGATE SILKIES

The Silkies are human on land, but in water they transform themselves into seals. Canongate Silkies is a new series incorporating folk tales, short stories and poetry that reflect the ancient magic of the Seal People.

THE BROONIE, SILKIES AND FAIRIES
Duncan Williamson

Master storyteller Duncan Williamson vividly retells the timeless travellers' tales of the magical beings of the Otherworld: the testing Broonie; the, elusive Silkies; and the mischievous Fairies of the summer hills.
ISBN 0 86241 456 3   £3.50 pbk

FIRESIDE TALES
Duncan Williamson

On cold winter nights when darkness enclosed the traveller's camp, a father would sit his children down and tell a story. A collection of twelve such folk and fairy tales, entertaining, scary, funny and clever.
ISBN 0 86241 457 1   £3.50 pbk

THE WELL AT THE WORLD'S END
Norah and William Montgomerie

Thirty five folktales, legends and some poems, from almost every corner of Scotland: Celtic legends; animal fables; and fairy tales of mermaids, ogres and princesses. For tellers, readers and listeners of stories everywhere.
ISBN 0 86241 462 8   £3.50 pbk